A real man ~~particulars of his marriage bed.~~

Except this once, Ryder thought. "Have you ever been with a woman..." Ryder said, glancing at Tom. "And she loves you so much you want to crawl right inside her skin until the rest of the world drops off into space?" Ryder thumped his chest. "It's a fire right in here, stoking embers in your blood. Your skin's too small to hold all the feelings in. Anything is possible and everything is right. And the only word in your head is her name...."

Tom slowly shook his head. "I guess, Ryder."

"Well," Ryder continued, "that's how Laura makes me feel, and that's how come I know she's not Laura."

"Then who is she?"

Ryder glanced toward the house, envisioning the beautiful woman still sleeping in his bed. "I don't know," he whispered softly. "I just don't know."

ABOUT THE AUTHOR

Sheryl Lynn lives in a pine forest atop a hill in Colorado. When not writing, she amuses herself by embarrassing her two teenagers, walking her dogs in a nearby park and feeding peanuts to the dozens of Steller's jays, scrub jays, blue jays and squirrels who live in her backyard. Her best ideas come from the newspapers, although she admits that a lot of what she reads is way too weird for fiction.

Books by Sheryl Lynn

HARLEQUIN INTRIGUE

Don't miss any of our special offers. Write to us at the following address for information on our newest releases.

Harlequin Reader Service
U.S.: 3010 Walden Ave., P.O. Box 1325, Buffalo, NY 14269
Canadian: P.O. Box 609, Fort Erie, Ont. L2A 5X3

The Other Laura
Sheryl Lynn

Harlequin Books

TORONTO • NEW YORK • LONDON
AMSTERDAM • PARIS • SYDNEY • HAMBURG
STOCKHOLM • ATHENS • TOKYO • MILAN
MADRID • WARSAW • BUDAPEST • AUCKLAND

If you purchased this book without a cover you should be aware that this book is stolen property. It was reported as "unsold and destroyed" to the publisher, and neither the author nor the publisher has received any payment for this "stripped book."

To Tom, for keeping our young'uns safe and sound.

ISBN 0-373-22367-6

THE OTHER LAURA

Copyright © 1996 by Jaye W. Manus

All rights reserved. Except for use in any review, the reproduction or utilization of this work in whole or in part in any form by any electronic, mechanical or other means, now known or hereafter invented, including xerography, photocopying and recording, or in any information storage or retrieval system, is forbidden without the written permission of the publisher, Harlequin Enterprises Limited, 225 Duncan Mill Road, Don Mills, Ontario, Canada M3B 3K9.

All characters in this book have no existence outside the imagination of the author and have no relation whatsoever to anyone bearing the same name or names. They are not even distantly inspired by any individual known or unknown to the author, and all incidents are pure invention.

This edition published by arrangement with Harlequin Books S.A.

® and TM are trademarks of the publisher. Trademarks indicated with ® are registered in the United States Patent and Trademark Office, the Canadian Trade Marks Office and in other countries.

Printed in U.S.A.

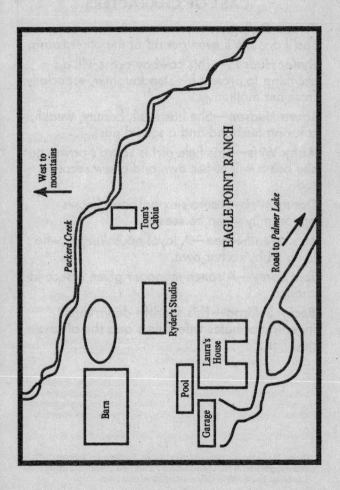

West to mountains →

Packed Creek

Tom's Cabin

Ryder's Studio

Barn

Pool

Laura's House

Garage

Road to *Palmer Lake* →

EAGLE POINT RANCH

CAST OF CHARACTERS

Teresa Gallagher—Whatever Ryder wants, she'll do; she'll even get rid of the other Laura.

Ryder Hudson—This cowboy artist will do anything to protect his stepdaughter, especially from her mother.

Laura Hudson—She has it all, beauty, wealth, a loving husband and a sordid past.

Abby Weis—This little girl is Laura's pawn, but she has a will of her own and a few secrets, too.

Donny Weis—Laura's ex-husband knows opportunity when he sees it.

Mrs. Weatherbee—A loyal housekeeper who loves Abby as her own.

Tom Sorry—A ranch manager given a second chance.

Becky Solerno—This sheriff's department investigator hates wife-killers and she always gets her man.

Chapter One

Struggling with a bulky paint can and bulkier portfolio, Teresa Gallagher shouldered her way into the studio. Spotting her, Ryder dropped a handful of photographs. He rushed between the worktables to her side and snatched the can of primer from her hand.

"You're a lifesaver!" he exclaimed. "I don't know what I'd do without you."

"Slowly starve to death under a twenty-year-old pile of sketchbooks, no doubt," she said dryly. "You'd lie there, buzzard bait, trying to remember how to call for help."

He admired the nondescript can, his dreamy expression saying he was already mentally back at work on his painting. "I'm not that bad."

"You're helpless without me. We both know it."

"Sad, but true. If it weren't for you solving my problems, I'd stay as tangled as a calf in barbed wire." Chuckling softly, he wandered to the corner where he'd set up a stretched and sized canvas in preparation for his next big project.

Teresa deposited receipts in the office before joining Ryder. "When you were a kid, did you ever dream you'd grow up to paint portraits of horses?" She clasped her hands behind her back and peered at the series of photographs Ryder had posted on a corkboard.

Ryder dipped a wide brush into the primer. With sweeping strokes, he applied the white acrylic. "Ma'am, I might remind you, that is Dizzy's Two Times Two, grand national championship quarter horse, so judged at the All American Quarter Horse Congress in Columbus, Ohio. Don't be calling him a mere horse, Tess."

Teresa bit back a smile. Only he called her Tess. At night, when she fantasized about his midnight blue eyes locked with hers and his big hands having their sexy way with her, that's what he whispered in her ear. "Tess, Tess, Tess, my darlin' Tess."

He jerked his thumb at the montage of photographs. "What you're looking at there is the epitome of horsedom. His head is perfect and he's full of pure smart." His eyes gleamed with affection. "Look at the depth in those hindquarters, the muscle in that chest. That's some kind of horse."

"Okay, so did you ever dream you'd grow up to paint epitomes?" Or ever imagine that wealthy horse breeders would be paying him hundreds of thousands of dollars to do so.

He laughed.

Teresa loved his full-throated, and much too rare, laugh. She wished she was in a position to give him cause for laughter every day. Instead, the poor man was stuck with the Dragon Lady, and nobody dared laugh around her. No amount of Teresa's problem solving skills could find solutions for his marital woes—not that he ever asked her advice concerning his wife. Ryder Hudson wasn't a complainer.

"Truth is, as a kid, I didn't see myself as anything other than a cowboy." He flashed her a grin. The broad brim of his hat shaded his eyes. "I figured I'd marry a nice girl and have a passel of kids and live up in the high country. I'd baby-sit cows and draw pictures on the side." He slapped primer onto the canvas with sure, broad strokes. Specks of white dotted his forearms like freckles. "A log cabin, wood-burning stove. Horses in a corral next to the house. Teaching young 'uns how to ride and rope."

The dreamy melancholy of his words made her think he'd trade all his wealth and hard-won prestige for a simple log cabin. Sorry she'd brought it up, she turned to an ash wood drafting table, the only clear work surface in the studio. She dusted the table with a soft cloth, then opened the portfolio and brought out the stack of prints. "I've got the prints of *Eight Seconds*. They came out great."

Wiping his hands on a cloth, he maneuvered through the messy studio. At her side, he looked down at the lithographs of a pen-and-ink drawing of a bull rider holding on to the back of a tornado-twisting Brahma bull.

"Sign, number and date, please," she said, and handed him a mechanical pencil.

"Only one hundred and fifty prints, huh?" he asked, smiling fondly. "I think this is one of my best."

Ryder possessed a sweet naiveté, a truly trusting soul. He'd been born a hundred years too late, and couldn't seem to understand that the sharks outnumbered the guppies ten to one. If left alone, he'd give his art away for the sheer pleasure of it. His limited-edition prints commanded up to fifteen hundred dollars apiece, however, so it was up to her and his agent to keep Ryder's generosity under control. "Supply and demand, boss. But, yeah, it's terrific. I can almost feel the heat coming off that bull."

He gave her an appreciative smile before he started penciling his world-famous signature onto the bottom of the prints. Teresa stepped back to give him room to work.

Unable to help it, she watched his back. Though the premier Western artist in the world, with his paintings highlighted in the finest galleries, museums and private collections, he was a cowboy first.

A red-and-blue plaid cotton shirt strained over his broad shoulders. The shirt was tucked into a pair of jeans that time and hard wearing had molded lovingly around his lean hips and taut backside. A black felt hat was perched at a rakish angle atop his thick brown curls. Her fingers itched to tame those curls.

She made herself turn away. Harboring a wild crush on her boss had never been part of her career plan. She studied the view of boulder-studded forests through the plate-glass windows. She couldn't stop wishing she was Mrs. Ryder Hudson and belonged on Eagle Point Ranch.

A hinge squeaked, and a small dark head eased around the door frame. "Daddy?"

Ryder turned on the stool and his eyes sparkled. "Hey, sugar bear, how was school?" He held his hands open in welcome.

The little girl skipped through the studio. She clutched a sheet of paper. "I drawed a horse, Daddy." She waved the paper at Teresa in passing.

"Hey, Abby," Teresa said. A pang of jealousy cut across her midsection. Ryder's daughter looked like a little angel in her pink velvet and white lace dress and patent-leather Mary Janes. Ryder's childhood dream of a happy family living in a high-country log cabin sounded pretty darn good. Especially the part about lots of kids.

Ryder held Abby's drawing to the light. He oohed and aahed in appreciation. "That's the finest purple horse I ever saw," he stated and sounded as if he meant it. "Let's add it to the gallery."

Abby boasted, "I drawed a finest horse, Teesa."

"I'll be in the office, boss," Teresa said, and left the two of them alone.

The office adjoined the studio, and like the studio smelled strongly of linseed oil and turpentine. Unlike the studio, it was neat and organized with everything in its place. Teresa turned on the computer and typed a letter to Jordan Pallatier informing him that the lithographs of *Eight Seconds* would soon be on their way to Pallatier's gallery.

After she had faxed the letter to New York, she went to the door. Abby had left and Ryder was back at work signing the prints. She waited until he finished before bringing up his least favorite subject.

"September, tax time," she said.

He made a disgruntled sound. He resumed priming the canvas.

Teresa repressed a laugh. She doubted if Ryder had an inkling about how much money he was worth. She doubted if he cared. He loved to paint, he loved his daughter, he loved his horses and the neat little ranch tucked into the foothills north of Colorado Springs—not necessarily in that order. He despised bookkeeping, investments and figuring out his income taxes. Over the past two years, she'd grown from bookkeeper to personal assistant, handling his mail, phone calls, errands, art-show schedules and whatever else he might need. And he needed plenty.

"You know the drill, boss." She gathered the signed lithographs and placed them carefully inside the portfolio. "All receipts and checkbooks on my desk in the morning. I need them before you take off for Fargo."

"Fargo?" His expression twisted in confusion.

She dropped her face onto her hand and groaned. "I'm going to start stapling memos to your forehead."

"Oh . . . McAllister?" he ventured.

"Very good. You promised him you'd deliver his painting personally and attend the reception in your honor. Your flight leaves Colorado Springs at nine."

He grimaced. "I forgot."

"I already asked Tom to take you to the airport." She pointed at the crated painting. "Take that, your tuxedo and your good boots."

"Fargo, tuxedo. Yes, ma'am."

The next morning, Teresa returned to the ranch. While reconciling the books for the ranch, household and business, she discovered five thousand dollars missing from the ranch account. Ryder owned three hundred acres of Colorado high country where he raised quarter horses and longhorn cattle. He treated Eagle Point Ranch like a hobby, but the IRS considered it a business and expected meticulous bookkeeping.

The latest bank statement didn't account for the missing cash. She called the bank and learned two checks had been cashed, one for two thousand, another for three. Unwilling to raise Cain with the bank—yet—she went through the checkbook. Only two signatures were authorized, Ryder's and his ranch manager Tom Sorry's. Ryder never wrote checks on the ranch account, and if Tom had spent five grand in the past week, she'd know about it.

She checked with the bank again and asked for an accounts manager. She explained the problem. The manager gave her the check numbers. They'd been taken from the back of the book.

Teresa frowned at the ledger where a full page, including the register and duplicate sheet, had been removed.

Fearing embezzlement, she asked the accounts manager to fax copies of the canceled checks.

As soon as she received the fax, she knew the checks were forgeries. The thief had done a fair job of forging Tom Sorry's name on the checks, but had tripped herself up writing out the date and amounts in her own handwriting.

Teresa slammed shut the checkbook. The Dragon Lady had gone too far this time.

LAURA HUDSON threw the remote telephone on the couch. It bounced and fell on the floor. Her entire body was rigid, quivering. In her hand she clutched a certificate, so tightly that her fingernails cut into the sepia-toned paper.

Teresa hunched her shoulders and lowered her eyes. Under the best of circumstances, Laura intimidated Teresa, making her feel dowdy and insignificant. At the moment, with the lady of the house openly furious, Teresa felt like a frog trapped by a hawk.

Laura paced, her fingers tightening and grinding against the certificate. A sticky note fluttered to the floor behind her.

Teresa picked up the scrap of yellow paper. She glanced at the handwriting. *This is a bunny trail I bet you don't want the cowboy following,* it said.

Laura turned, gasped and snatched the note from Teresa's hand. She crushed the paper in her fist. "What do you want?" Her voice seethed.

"I'm doing the books, Mrs. Hudson. You wrote two checks off the ranch account. You aren't authorized."

Laura used one finger to draw aside the drapery. Rain pattered against the window, drizzling sullenly from a low, gray sky. Clouds shrouded the mountains. The ponderosa pines and spruce trees looked black; the clusters of aspen trees shimmered like beaten gold. The barn and other outbuildings were softened by fog, as misty as a watercolor painting.

"So what do you want?" She faced Teresa. "To blackmail me?"

Teresa laughed uneasily. She never knew how to take Mrs. Hudson. Sometimes she hated the woman with a passion—surely she was to blame for the sadness in Ryder's eyes. Sometimes she thought the woman had to be playing a joke. No one could be that stupid, shallow and selfish.

Laura kept glaring at her, her eyes glittering. She glided to the fireplace. There, she began tearing the certificate into tiny pieces and tossing them into the hearth.

Teresa cleared her throat and held up the fax transmission from the bank. "I know you forged Tom Sorry's name on these checks. You can't do that. I have to be able to account for every penny."

The amazing thing was, Laura didn't need to steal. She had tons of credit cards. Ryder had explicitly instructed Teresa to never allow his wife's personal checking account to fall below ten thousand dollars. If she needed more, all she had to do was hold out her perfectly manicured hand. Five grand must be a piddly amount to her.

"So? It's my husband's money. His money is my money. I can take it if I want."

"That's not how it works, ma'am." She licked her lips and pushed back her hair. She plucked at the collar of her rayon dress. "You shouldn't forge Tom's name. It isn't right."

Laura tossed the last piece of paper into the hearth. She swiped her hands together as if cleaning off dust. Turning, she rubbed her fist between her breastbone. "Do you honestly think I don't know what this is all about?"

"It's none of my business. My business is making sure the books balance. That's all."

Laura suddenly leaned forward and dropped her hands to the back of a sofa. She tightened her fingers and her knuckles whitened. "You've been lusting after my husband ever since you first walked into this house."

Teresa gasped. Heat rose on her face.

Laura lifted an eyebrow. "Can't deny it, can you? Do you think I don't notice the way you two carry on? His assistant, how sweet. What a joke! I can well imagine what you assist him with over in that filthy studio of his."

"Mrs. Hudson, I—you can't—that's not the—"

"You're fired."

"You can't fire me!"

"Oh, yes, I can. Leave now and I won't tell Ryder how you embezzled all that money and tried to pin it on me."

The heat drained from Teresa's cheeks as quickly as it had arisen. She staggered and caught a chair for support. "You don't understand. All you have to do is properly transfer the money to your household account. We can call it a loan." She held up a sheet of paper. "Either we have to fix it or I have to tell Mr. Hudson."

"I bet if I go upstairs right now, I can discover some valuable jewelry missing. I better call the police and tell them you're a thief."

Angry tears filled Teresa's eyes. Her chin quivered and her throat ached with the effort of not crying.

"Get out of my house. If you ever show your face around here again, I'll make sure you go to jail for stealing." She tossed her hair off her shoulders and smiled in triumph. "And just who do you think Ryder will believe? Me—or an ugly little mouse like you? Hmm?"

"Mrs...." Her voice trailed into a low sob. Teresa turned away and pressed a fist against her mouth. Work-

ing for Ryder Hudson had been a dream come true, and
to lose her job this way was the height of unfairness. "You
can't get away with this."

Laura lifted her left hand and checked her diamond-
encrusted wristwatch. The twelve-carat blue diamond in
her engagement ring flashed fire. "Hmm, Ryder isn't due
home until late tomorrow afternoon. By then I could have
you arrested and put in jail. I think you'll be much better
off if you just leave."

Looking at the tipped corners of Laura's unpleasant
smile and the malevolence glinting in her eyes, Teresa
found a name for what ailed the woman. Laura Hudson
was evil. And yes, she would have Teresa arrested. And
yes, she'd lie without hesitation. And yes, the police
would believe a rich socialite who had absolutely no reason to steal from her own husband rather than a nobody
like Teresa Gallagher who was up to her neck in debt.

Teresa swiped at her hot eyes. "I'm just trying to do my
job, Mrs. Hudson," she whispered through her teeth.

"I want you off this property. If you ever come back,
I'll call the police. If you try to contact my husband for
any reason, I will swear out an arrest warrant. Don't think
I won't."

"Mr. Hudson won't let you—"

"He does anything I tell him." She thrust out her hand.
"Get out!"

"Mrs.—"

"Now!" Laura's face turned purple, ugly and vicious.

Teresa sensed the woman's fear. That frightened Teresa most of all. Trembling, she blindly made her way out
of the house. Laura Hudson wasn't getting away with this.
No way.

RYDER ENTERED the dining room—and stopped short.

Laura posed gracefully next to the sideboard. A white

dress clung to her voluptuous curves like a coating of cream. A slit in the skirt revealed the alluring top of a stocking.

Most eye-catching of all was her hair. When he'd left for Fargo she'd been a blonde with cascades of platinum curls flowing down her back. Today she wore a shining mop of sleek ebony curls in a just-got-out-of-bed style reminiscent of a 1950s sex kitten. Ruby red lips gleamed dark and luxurious against her pale face. A large red pendant hung between her practically naked breasts.

She matched the room, Ryder thought in astonishment. Her hair was as glossy as the lacquered furniture. Her lipstick and jewelry matched the striking touches of red accenting the black-and-white walls and floor.

"Hello, darling," she said.

Ryder figured he was the only man in the universe who hadn't a clue about his wife's natural hair color or what her face looked like without cosmetics. Not that he minded, particularly. No matter what she wore or how she fixed her hair, Laura was an exquisitely beautiful woman. Even looking as starkly weird as an art nouveau statue, she was gorgeous. Still, it was disconcerting at times never knowing how she might appear. It saddened him, too. Laura would be a happier woman if only she could figure out who she was or what she wanted to look like.

He'd be a happier man if she'd stop thinking about her looks long enough to think about him.

"Nice hair," he said and joined her at the sideboard. Her mood seemed good. It generally was after she'd spent bundles of money rearranging herself. He realized the whisper-thin dress was silk, soft as a sigh and about as substantial.

Smiling his approval, he said, "I'd say it's a little nippy for that dress."

She gave him a filthy look and turned away as if he disgusted her.

Desire ebbed along with his smile. He poured himself a whiskey and soda. "I had a good time in Fargo. Mc-Allister barbecued a buffalo. He has a herd of them. I'd like to try my hand at raising buffalo. I can use them for models."

She kept her back to him as she adjusted the hang of an abstract black, white and red painting.

Ryder stared at the smooth, luscious line of her back. How could a creature so deliciously beautiful on the outside be so cold and vacuous on the inside? He also wondered, not for the first time, what it was about himself that kept hoping she'd have a change of heart and love him. Each and every day she reminded him of what a fool he was for loving her. She didn't act as if she even cared he'd been gone two days.

"Where's Abby?"

"I sent her to bed." Laura took her seat.

Ryder clutched his drink, and his fingers squeaked against the glass. "It's only six-thirty."

"She's a brat." Laura lifted her chin in icy challenge.

Caught off guard by the oddness of her expression, it took him a moment to realize she was wearing colored contact lenses again. As with her hair, she couldn't seem to settle on a color for her eyes. Today they were black.

"She was out in the barn again. Getting filthy. She tore her dress. So I sent her to bed."

"Damn it, Laura!" Ryder slammed his drink on the tabletop. Guilt raged through his gut, chopping him up inside. Leaving Abby with her mother was asking for trouble. "How is Abby supposed to play if all you do is fuss at her about her clothes? She's not some Barbie doll."

Laura huffed. "I should let her run around like a little heathen? Or allow her to stink like horse manure the way you do all the time?"

He tightened his lips, holding back the harsh words rising in his throat. He counted to ten, but it wasn't enough. He tried twenty.

"Need I remind you, she's my daughter, not yours," Laura finally said. "You have absolutely no say in how I raise her. If you don't like the way I do things, we can certainly discuss a change."

He suspected nothing would please Laura more than to send her daughter either to boarding school or to live with her biological father.

It took all his will, but he kept his words to himself. If Laura thought for a moment that he cared more about Abby than he did about her, it would be little Abby who bore the brunt of Laura's vengeance. Laura's wrath made *Mommy Dearest* read like a lullaby. He'd do anything, even allow Laura to treat him like a shamed puppy, if it meant protecting the little girl he'd come to think of as his own.

The housekeeper strode into the room. "Are you ready for supper, sir?"

"Dinner," Laura corrected her.

"Dinner," Mrs. Weatherbee said through her teeth.

"Bring it on," he said. "Any idea what's up with Tess? Tom said he hasn't seen her. Did she call in sick?"

"I figured you gave her the day off," Mrs. Weatherbee said. "She wasn't here yesterday when I brought Abby home from school and she wasn't here today."

"She quit," Laura said coolly. "Mrs. Weatherbee, serve dinner. Now."

Ryder trained an incredulous gaze on his wife.

"Don't look at me like that," Laura said. She delicately flipped out her napkin and laid it across her lap.

"Tess wouldn't quit on me. She's as loyal as they come."

"Were you having an affair with her?"

"What?"

Looking bored with the conversation, Laura stared past him. "Honestly, that girl is deranged. I caught her in my bedroom. She was trying on my clothes. I checked my jewelry cases and fortunately nothing was missing. If she wasn't stealing then I can only assume she thought she could somehow replace me. Are you the one who gave her such a silly idea, darling? How long have you been sleeping with her?"

It took several moments of hard thinking to follow this particular flight of fancy. "You fired my assistant. You don't have any right to fire—"

"She *quit.*"

Ryder gulped down the remainder of his drink. Before Tess Gallagher, his life had been chaotic. He didn't have a head for schedules and paperwork. Talking directly to his agent or gallery owners made him crazy. She'd brought order into his life along with a gentle sense of humor and unabashed, unconditional approval.

Laura wasn't getting away with this. He pushed away from the table.

"Where do you think you're going?"

He threw his napkin onto his plate. "Tess didn't quit, you ran her off. I'm—"

"Oh, my God, I'm right! You are having an affair." Her eyebrows raised high, but her eyes revealed no emotion.

"I'm not cheating on you. Never have, never will."

Laura's full lips trembled. "It's because she's younger, isn't it? Thinner. I work so hard every day trying to make myself attractive for you and you want to chase after that little hippie in her ugly dresses and clunky boots!"

Guilt tugged at him. He did like Tess, a lot. And if he had to confess, her companionship was easier on his soul than Laura's ever was. He'd imagined, more than once, what she might look like under her loose, long-skirted dresses. "Now, darlin', I—"

"If you go chasing after that little tramp, don't expect me to be here when you get back."

"You've got no cause for jealousy."

"Don't I? Fine, if you want her, go. Call her. Tell her to come back. Make your choice." She sniffed, and her black eyes glittered like obsidian. "I'll just take Abby and get out of your life."

For a fleeting, bright and beautiful moment, he saw himself leaving the room and calling Tess. He saw Laura carry through on her threat, taking her demands and selfishness and chronic unhappiness with her. He saw a life of peace...

A life without Abby.

He sat down. Humiliation curdled his blood.

Laura daintily patted the base of her throat. "We'll find you another assistant, darling. A professional."

At times like this he wanted to kick Laura out of his life so fast she'd think she'd been shot out of a cannon. If he did, though, Laura would take Abby away from him. Technically, biologically, Abby was the daughter of another man, but in his heart, in his soul, the little girl belonged to him. Losing her would kill him.

Even worse, if he did choose his own self-respect over Abby's well-being, it wouldn't take more than a month, or six weeks at the most, for Laura to tire of being a sin-

gle parent. Ryder didn't doubt for a minute that she'd give
the little girl to her father, and Donny Weis was the human equivalent of a scorpion. Legally, there wasn't a single, blessed thing Ryder could do about it.

Legally....

Somehow he made it through dinner.

He made his escape as soon as politely possible. He
joined the housekeeper in the kitchen, the only room in
the house unaffected by Laura's restlessness, the only
place he felt comfortable.

"I'm sorry about Teresa," Mrs. Weatherbee said.

"What's done is done. Can't undo it." Humiliation
clung to him like a coat of itchy dust. He'd ridden killer
bulls, braved blizzards to rescue calves, faced off a grizzly bear, but he could not stand up to his wife. If it was
only him, he'd walk away from Laura without a single
regret. But Abby needed him, and as long as Laura used
her child as a pawn, Ryder remained determined to play
her game.

Crossing his arms over his chest, he leaned his backside against a counter. "How bad was it today with the
kid?"

"Not as bad as I've seen it. No offense, but I don't
think it proper for the missus to be bringing home those
outfits that make the little one look like she should be
standing on a street corner. I'd pitch a fit, too."

"What am I supposed to do? I can't keep Abby with me
twenty-four hours a day. And I sure can't get it through
Laura's head that Abby wants to wear pants, not froufrou dresses."

The woman's back hitched. She loved Abby as if the
child were blood. "You best do something." She turned
around and held up her hands, wiping them slowly to-

gether to catch soapsuds and water drops. "That baby loves you with all her heart. But the day's coming when she's gonna ask how come you aren't protecting her. When that happens, you're gonna lose her."

Ryder nodded, then grabbed his hat and left the house. He'd wait until Laura's favorite television shows came on, then he'd go see Abby. He rubbed his arms against the biting cold. It was only September, but the weather had been strange with more rain than usual. They'd get their first frost way too early, he thought as he headed for the barn. When he saw lights shining through the garage windows, he changed direction.

He stepped through the side door and spotted Tom Sorry on his hands and knees peering underneath the beat-up Dodge four-by-four Ryder used for driving around the back country.

"Hey, Tom."

The cowboy jumped like a cat stuck with a hot needle. As he scrambled to his feet, he banged his shoulder against the Dodge. Ryder winced. Startling Tom Sorry was never a good idea. The man had lived a rough life, serving two tours in Vietnam, then picking up a drug habit that had landed him a prison stint. But he was a hell of a cowboy, and had a light hand with horses and a sixth sense with cattle. Ryder had been uncertain about him at first, but over the years, Tom Sorry had proven himself. The past no longer mattered. Except for the startling him part.

Rubbing his shoulder, Tom said, "You spooked me."

"Sorry. What are you doing?"

He glanced at the Dodge. "Uh, I was changing the oil."

"At this time of night?"

"Chores gotta be done."

"Something wrong with the wheel? This old pig's about on its last legs, anyway." Ryder sauntered across the concrete. He crouched where Tom had been and peered underneath the chassis. A puddle gleamed. "What's leaking?"

"It ain't a leak." Tom grabbed a flashlight and flicked it on. He shone the light behind the tire. "Somebody cut the brake lines. All of them."

Ryder peered closely where the flashlight beam focused. An unpleasant taste filtered into his mouth, and he worked his tongue against his palate. "How did this happen?"

"It didn't *happen*. Somebody crawled under there with a pair of snips and cut 'em right through."

"Who?"

Tom flicked off the flashlight and stood.

Ryder stood, too. He didn't like what he was thinking, but he saw no other explanations. "Laura fired Tess. I'm thinking it was a right ugly scene."

One side of Tom's mouth pulled into an uneasy smile. He shook his head and cocked his hat with his thumb. "Oh, no, boss, Teresa is a nice girl. She wouldn't have screwed around with your truck."

"I wouldn't think so, but..." He remembered Laura saying she'd caught Tess trying on clothes. Had Tess been obsessed with him, hiding her true feelings, but possessing a dark, twisted side?

He banished the thought. Tess solved problems, she didn't create them. "Forget it. Can you fix the brakes?"

"Yeah, and I'll check around, see what I—"

"I said forget it. No real harm done." If Tess had vandalized his truck in a fit of anger, then he reckoned she had a right to anger. Laura had pushed tougher people than his assistant over the edge. "I wouldn't have gotten out of the driveway before I knew I had no brakes. It's a dumb prank, nothing more. So just forget it. Fix the truck and . . . forget it."

Chapter Two

Shrill ringing cut through the quiet air in the art supply store. Ryder grabbed at the cellular phone holster on his hip. Hope leaped into his heart. No one had answered his knock when he went to Tess's apartment in Monument. Perhaps she was now returning one of the many messages he'd left on her answering machine. He had in his pocket a hefty check and a letter of recommendation as an apology for Laura's meanness.

He fumbled with the flip phone until he remembered how to open it, then punched buttons, hoping for the right combination for activation. He got through. "Hello?"

Tom Sorry said, "Where are you, boss?"

"Downtown at the art store." He gazed at the tubes of oil paint and brushes he'd lined up on the counter for purchase. Buying them gave him something to do until he heard from Tess. "What do you need?" He prayed Tess hadn't called the house. If Laura found out...

"I don't know how to say this—"

Tom Sorry was as laconic as a mountain man, but when he needed to talk, he spoke his mind. His pussyfooting made the short hairs lift on Ryder's nape. The store clerk gazed at him, his eyebrows knitting in concern.

"There's been a car accident."

Ryder looked at his watch. It was almost five. Every day Mrs. Weatherbee picked up Abby from kindergarten at two, then had a long drive along the twisting roads from Palmer Lake to the ranch.

The art store clerk looked alarmed. "Can I get you a drink of water, Mr. Hudson?"

"Ryder?" Tom asked. "Are you still there?"

Ryder cleared his choked throat. "Abby?"

"Abby and Mrs. Weatherbee are fine. It's your missus. She rolled her Mercedes into the quarry."

Uncertain if he'd heard correctly, he whispered, "How bad? Is she okay? Is she hurt?"

"I—I don't know. Mrs. Weatherbee spotted the car while she was coming home. When I got there, the paramedics already took her. They're airlifting her to St. Francis."

Ryder blinked rapidly, unable to focus. Airlift—Flight for Life helicopter. "Meet me at the hospital, Tom. I'm on my way now."

"I KNOW this is a difficult time, Mr. Hudson," the young man said, "but this is necessary." Dressed in a scrub suit, holding a clipboard, the young man stood while Ryder sat on a tweed-upholstered couch in a small conference room.

As soon as the helicopter had landed at the hospital, the trauma team had whisked Laura into surgery. Judging by the hospital worker's expression and the organ donor papers he wanted Ryder to sign, no one expected her to pull through.

For the life of him, Ryder couldn't figure out how he felt about it. If Laura died, he and Abby could live in peace without having to tiptoe around Laura's temper or whims. No more living under a cloud of dread that she'd tear Abby away from him. Her death would free him.

He hated himself for thinking it.

"She's going to die," he said bluntly.

"I didn't say that, Mr. Hudson." The young man held out the clipboard. "But if the worst does happen, her organs can help someone else. In Colorado Springs alone, we have a long waiting list of seriously ill people—"

Ryder jerked the clipboard out of the man's hands. "I'll sign it." As he scribbled his name on the proper line, tears burned, blurring his vision. He blinked hard to keep them at bay. He shoved the clipboard at the man. "I want to talk to somebody right now who can tell me how my wife is doing. Right now, do you hear?"

Right now didn't come any time soon.

Laura remained in surgery until well after midnight.

When the surgeon finally arrived, his weary, guarded expression held no power to frighten Ryder. Hours ago, he had resigned himself to accepting the worst.

"She's in intensive care, Mr. Hudson. Her prognosis is not good."

Tom Sorry dropped a big hand onto Ryder's shoulder. During the hours of waiting, the big grizzled cowboy had seemed to shrink. It occurred to Ryder that he, Laura and Abby were the only family Tom had. Tom hadn't liked Laura, and she'd made no effort to disguise how much she despised him, but she was family nonetheless.

The surgeon catalogued Laura's injuries—multiple skull fractures, brain hemorrhage, shattered facial bones, a broken leg, dislocated shoulder, broken ribs, torn muscles and bruised organs. Her car had rolled off a cliff toward the quarry and Laura had been thrown face first through the windshield.

"The next twenty-four hours will be touch and go."

"And if she's still alive this time tomorrow?"

"I'll be willing to state she has a chance...of survival." The surgeon looked away. "She suffered massive head trauma, Mr. Hudson. Even if she survives, she may remain in a coma. There is no way to judge at this time how functional she will be."

Ryder chewed over the implication of the doctor's words. "She may never wake up?"

"That is a possibility." He glanced at the door as if expecting somebody.

"She's a vegetable." Ryder tasted the words, not liking them.

"I'm sorry, but in all likelihood, she'll be paralyzed and quite possibly nonfunctional. She may very well require institutionalization for the rest of her life."

Ryder steadied himself with a deep breath. A nasty little voice said it was his anger at her that drove her car off the cliff. "I want to see my wife. Where is—"

"You can't." The doctor took a step backward and looked again at the door. "I'm sorry, sir, but no one can see your wife at this time."

Ryder turned a puzzled glance to Tom. Tom's face had lost color under his tan.

Ryder said, "You said she might die. I need to see her."

The doctor crossed his arms and used the toe of his crepe-soled shoe to draw circles on the floor. He frowned at his foot as if it were doing something odd. "Hospital policy is, in these cases, we have to wait for the police. The police haven't arrived yet."

Ryder clamped his hands on his hips against the urge to grab the surgeon by his scrawny neck. "What police? What are you talking about?"

The doctor touched the back of his own neck. "We also extracted a bullet fragment from Mrs. Hudson's third cervical vertebra. We've notified the police. Until they arrive, I can't allow you or anyone in to see your wife.''

AGITATED by sleep deprivation and coffee, Ryder slouched on a chair in the hospital administrator's office. He needed to walk around, clear his head, but if he left the office, he'd be mobbed by reporters. So he stared at a wall, seeing animal shapes in the textured paint. His groggy imagination soon conjured a herd of wild horses cantering across a snowy field.

A knock on the door gave him a start. A woman entered. She wore a blazer and jeans, which meant she wasn't a nurse, doctor or hospital official.

He jumped to his feet and pulled off his hat. He pressed it to his chest.

In her mid-thirties, she was a big, athletic-looking woman with a broad face and glossy black hair. Her smile was attractive, but much too alert for Ryder's mood. ''Ryder Hudson?''

''Yes, ma'am. That's me.''

She pulled back her suit jacket and revealed a gold badge clipped to the waistband of her slacks. ''Becky Solerno. I'm an investigator with the sheriff's department. I know this is a bad time, but there never is a good time for this kind of thing. I need to talk to you about your wife's accident.''

''It took you long enough, ma'am,'' he said, and placed his hat on the administrator's desk. He checked his watch. It was nearly eight o'clock.

''What's the matter? Run out of people to yell at?''

He tightened his jaw. He wasn't proud of how he'd been acting, but he'd been sufficiently provoked by bureaucrats and red tape.

"Threatening doctors and security guards won't win you many brownie points around here," the woman continued. "They're just doing their jobs."

"My wife is dying. I want to see her. The only reason I can't is that I've had to wait for you."

"I apologize deeply for that, but I had to take care of the crime scene. I'll make this as quick and painless as possible. Have a seat."

Her cheerful demeanor made his hackles rise. He sat on a leather armchair. The investigator took a matching chair on the other side of the room. She faced him directly. A notepad rested on her knees. She held a pen ready to write.

"The doctor said she was shot. Is that right?" Ryder asked.

She had dimples in both cheeks. "Please, Mr. Hudson, sir. The procedure is, I ask the questions, you answer them. Okay?"

"Speak your piece, ma'am. I'm not in the mood to dance."

She glanced at the array of paper coffee cups Ryder had left on the administrator's desk. "It's been a long night. You haven't had any sleep. You're worried. I understand. But I need *you* to understand. Your wife's accident was no accident. Somebody tried to kill her."

For hours he'd been trying to believe the doctor's assertion that Laura had been shot. It made no sense at all. Even when this cop said it, it made no sense.

"It looks like whoever shot her was carrying her away from your house. The shooter wrecked the Mercedes on the road above the quarry when the car hit a boulder. It may have been disabled. Or maybe the shooter didn't want to take a chance with a body in a damaged car. So he rolled the car off the road. My guess is, the car was supposed to end up in the water. With your wife inside, of course.''

Ryder's gorge rose. A foul taste like copper pennies filled his mouth. ''You find this funny, officer?''

''That's investigator, please.'' She blinked innocently, her smile never fading. ''And no, it's not funny. This is dead serious. If your wife, God bless her, dies, then it's first-degree murder. So, do you have any ideas about who might have done this to her? No? Fine. Where were you when the accident occurred?'' She glanced at her notebook. ''Around two o'clock yesterday afternoon?''

She'd slipped as easily as a trout through still water moving from the question of who might have done it to the implication that he had. His brain finally caught up to the situation. ''I was here in the Springs.''

''Can you be more specific?''

His discomfort increased. ''Around. I was looking for someone.''

''Who?''

''My assistant. I owe her some money.''

''This is usual?''

Ryder didn't see anything unusual, but the way she looked at him made him feel guilty as hell.

Her smile acquired a twist of skepticism. She turned a page in her notebook. ''You're an interesting man, Mr. Hudson.'' She scanned a page, reading from it. ''Former ranch hand and rodeo rider. Hunting guide. Now a world-famous artist. You did that big painting I've seen over at the courthouse. The longhorn cattle. Up on the second floor?''

He nodded.

''My boss loves your work. I'm pretty sure he has a painting of yours in his office. Or a print. Probably a print. I guess your paintings are expensive. You're a rich man, aren't you?''

"That's no crime."

"You and your wife are photogenic, too. Beautiful people, always turning up in the society pages. Looks like your wife hasn't missed a big function or photo op in the past five years. Do you spend a lot of money on charities and political causes?''

He bristled. "What are you getting at, ma'am?''

"Beautiful wives, tons of money." She held a hand palm up as if weighing her words. "Bullets. They all seem to go together.''

Her smile was getting on his nerves. "If you're fixing to accuse me, say the words.''

"Is there anyone who can verify your whereabouts?''

He thrust out his fists. "If you want to arrest me, then do it.''

"I'm not interested in arresting you, sir. Not yet.''

Ryder grudgingly admired her gumption, but her in-his-face style irritated him. He lowered his hands. "I have attorneys who'd chew you up before spitting you out. So unless you want to deal with them, you best shoot straight with me.''

Her smile lost a bit of sparkle, but she didn't back down. "Shoot straight. Interesting choice of words, Mr. Hudson.'' She wrote something in her notebook. "Let's see if we can get on the right track. How is your relationship with your wife?''

"None of your business.''

"I beg to differ, sir. My entire reason for existence is finding out who tried to murder your wife. Aren't you interested in finding out who did it?''

Anger swirled and churned inside him, and he examined it with numb bemusement. He thought briefly about cutting off this little lady at the knees and calling in an attorney. Curiosity finally won out. "Do you think I did it?"

"I always suspect husbands."

Her matter-of-fact attitude shocked him.

Her smile warmed. "Tell me about your relationship with your wife."

"I didn't shoot her."

"You have a kid, Mr. Hudson." She nodded sympathetically. "I have a son. He's eleven. That's a great age for boys, and sometimes I really resent how much time I have to spend away from him. He's got a football game today. I hate missing it. So trust me, I'm not doing this for fun."

He didn't want to see her as human with a family life. He glowered at his hands.

"How old is your daughter, sir?"

"She's five."

"Does she know about her mother yet?"

Yes and no. Over the telephone he'd told Abby her mother was hurt and in the hospital. The little girl's only reaction had been to ask if her kitten could sleep in the house.

"Your daughter will want to know what happened. Help me. Help her. Talk to me."

"My marriage is rocky," he said, having to squeeze each humiliating word between his teeth. "We've talked about divorce."

"I see. How long have you been married?"

"Almost five years. I didn't shoot Laura. My wife and I have problems, but I love her."

"Then talk to me. You're a loose end I have to tie up before I can go on to the next step in my investigation."

Loose end. He'd been called many things in his thirty-seven years, but that wasn't one of them. A smile reached his face before he could stop it.

Grudgingly, irritably, testy as a mule in fly season, he answered her questions about his whereabouts yesterday and about his relationship with Laura. The only time he turned evasive was when she asked direct questions about Laura's character. Until Laura could defend herself, nobody, him included, was going to bad-mouth her.

Finally she asked him to sign a release form granting permission to search his home.

He scanned the form, trying to clear his foggy head enough to think through all the implications. All he could think about was Abby. Children always suffered the worst in matters like these. Abby didn't need cops snooping through the house, asking her questions and scaring her.

He tossed the paper at the detective. "Get a warrant."

The light was finally extinguished from her smile. Her jaw twitched and her eyes narrowed. "I can do that."

He leaned back on the chair and folded his arms over his chest.

"You're a stubborn man, Mr. Hudson. But that's okay. I'm a stubborn woman." She left him with a parting shot. "I will definitely see you around."

She spoke a few words right outside the door, then Tom Sorry entered the room. He closed the door. For a few seconds he held the doorknob. His craggy face was ashen.

"The cops think I tried to kill her, Tom. What did they say to you?" The full weight of the police interview caught up to him. He gripped his knees to keep his hands from shaking.

Tom's face turned gray. "How can they think you'd do a low-account thing like that?"

"What did you tell them, Tom?"

"Nothing," he mumbled, his eyes downcast. "Only that I didn't see you yesterday."

No one had accompanied Ryder to Monument, where he looked for Tess, or to Colorado Springs. He'd made a trip to Garden of the Gods in search of good background material for the Dizzy's Two Times Two portrait, and then had gone downtown to browse in the art supply store. Except for the art store clerk, he hadn't talked to anybody. He'd left messages on Tess's answering machine, but he could have placed those calls from anywhere. It was logistically possible for him to have shot Laura, taken her to the quarry and pushed her car over the cliff. He could have then run the half mile back to the house, fetched his truck and driven into the Springs.

He hadn't shot his wife, but damned if it didn't look as if he had.

When he reached intensive care, a police officer stood guard outside Laura's room. The cop made Ryder show identification. A nurse archly informed Ryder that he must limit his visit to three minutes.

For all that, he didn't even recognize her. Where she wasn't bandaged up, she was swollen, and her skin was stained yellow by disinfectant. Tubes and wires ran into and out of every part of her body. Monitors flashed and beeped. A respirator schussed in steady rhythm.

He swayed and had to close his eyes a moment. When he opened them, he sought a place on her that wasn't bandaged, intubated, skinned up or bruised. He settled on the tip of her thumb. He stroked it. It felt cold.

"I'm here, darlin'," he whispered. "No matter what happens, I'll always be here."

All the long ride home, he kept trying to understand how the world's most beautiful woman had ended up as that poor pitiful creature laying so broken on a hospital bed.

When he and Tom Sorry reached the ranch, Ryder said, "I won't be staying long. I'll make sure Abby is okay and pick up some fresh duds. Take charge of things."

Tom pulled the Jeep Cherokee into the garage, then glanced at Ryder's old four-by-four. Guessing what he was thinking, Ryder said, "I didn't tell the police about the brake lines. Or about Tess."

"I didn't, either," Tom said. "No one asked." When he turned off the engine, the silence settled over them like a blanket. Neither man made a move to open a door.

"You don't..." Tom cleared his throat. His ears turned red. "Teresa didn't have anything to do with this."

Ryder knew Tom had liked the girl more than just in passing. He'd courted her for a while until finally deciding he was too old for her. "What if she did, Tom? God knows what kind of blowout her and Laura had." He fingered the cellular telephone still strapped to his hip. "I tried to get hold of her all day yesterday. I never heard from her."

"What if... Laura wakes up and tells...?"

"Tells what? We don't know Tess cut the brake lines or had anything to do with the accident."

"Not to say nothing bad about your wife, boss, but she's—" He shrugged and grimaced. "You know."

"She could provoke the Pope into popping his cork." Ryder sighed wearily, so tired he hurt all over. Even thinking hurt. "I still can't see Tess bringing harm to anybody. It's probably just coincidence."

"True," Tom said, giving Ryder a measuring look. "Things like this, they're for the police to figure out. Criminals always leave clues. Cops get paid to find clues."

Ryder nodded in agreement. "Speculations from cow-pokes like us would probably just muddy the water. It's better if we don't say anything." He met Tom's eyes. "Did they ask you anything personal?"

Tom tugged at his hat brim. "Didn't have to. They already know about my past. Guess we just have to wait for your missus to wake up." He sighed heavily. "*If* she wakes up. Damn, I'm sorry, Ryder, I never wanted anything like this to happen."

Ryder patted his friend's ropy forearm. "None of us did."

He left the Jeep and trudged toward the house. As he climbed the two wide steps into the courtyard, Abby's shriek echoed against the walls and a door slammed. The little girl tore across the terrazzo tiles.

Despite the cold morning, Abby wore only a T-shirt. Her bare feet slapped the tiles. He crouched and opened his arms. She leaped against him and locked her arms around his neck.

"Daddy!" She sobbed hoarsely. "You was gone! You scared me. You didn't call this morning. I waited and waited. You were supposed to call."

"Hey, sugar bear, it's okay, I'm home." He stood, bringing her feather weight against his chest.

Mrs. Weatherbee pushed open the French door through which Abby had just run. He entered the house and followed the housekeeper into the kitchen.

"I'm sorry, but she was so upset about everything, I couldn't make her go to school," Mrs. Weatherbee said. "That child is slippery as a blue-tailed lizard. Abby, where are your clothes?"

"Daddy's home," Abby said and tightened her grip on Ryder's neck. Her heels dug into his ribs.

"You best put some britches on." Ryder squeezed her tightly. "Some socks and shoes, too." He tried to put her on a stool, but she clung to him like a little monkey.

"You're stinky, Daddy." She rubbed her cheek against his. "Whiskery, too."

"I can't shower and shave with you holding on to me." He waited for her to ask about her mother.

Instead Abby prattled on about her kitten who'd disappeared somewhere upstairs and how she had hunted for hours before finding the animal in a closet. She told Ryder she'd slept on his bed, "'Cause it smells better than mine." And she informed him that Mrs. Weatherbee had finally read her the latest *Curious George* adventure.

Not a single word about her mother.

Ryder's depression deepened.

Mrs. Weatherbee convinced the child to go finish dressing. After emphatically informing her father that he best stay right here, Abby scampered up the stairs.

"Has she asked about Laura?"

The housekeeper shook her head. "Only about you." She pulled a sliced ham from the refrigerator. "The police came by last night."

"Did you let them in?"

"No, sir. Should I have?"

His mind first registered her cool gaze as challenge. Then he suspected it was triumph.

Ryder slumped on a stool. He told the woman about Laura's condition and how she'd gotten that way. When Mrs. Weatherbee failed to exhibit shock at hearing Laura had been shot, his depression turned black. "Any ideas about what Laura was up to yesterday?"

Shaking her head, Mrs. Weatherbee began making sandwiches. "It was shopping day. I picked up Abby and we went to the grocery store. I left around one-thirty or

thereabouts. Mrs. Hudson was still in bed. Or at least, she
hadn't come downstairs. The police asked all that and
more. I answered as best I could." Her eyes flashed.
"They wanted inside to look around. They even wanted
me to open up your studio. No, sir! I watch television, I
know what a warrant looks like and they didn't have one."
Some of the fire faded. "Did I do right, sir?"

"Yes, ma'am. If I do let the cops in, it won't be when
Abby is around to get upset."

He stayed at home long enough to shower, shave, eat a
hearty meal and convince Abby that he'd be back home
in time to tuck her into bed. He gave Mrs. Weatherbee
explicit orders that if any police officers or detectives arrived, she was not to allow them into the house or anywhere near Abby unless they had a warrant. Even then,
she was to contact him and his attorneys immediately. If
the press bothered her, she was to let Tom Sorry handle
them. If his agent or any gallery owners called, she was to
take messages, but say nothing—he had no wish to see his
personal life splashed across the tabloids.

When he returned to the hospital, Laura was still in intensive care, still critical. The cop was still posted outside
her room. Doctors allowed Ryder into her room for three
minutes. The nurses kept an eye on him as if he was about
to go berserk and attack his helpless wife.

Laura survived the first twenty-four hours.

After forty-eight hours, she remained in a coma, but the
doctors were able to take her off the respirator.

Investigator Becky Solerno obtained her search warrant. She and a squadron of deputies swarmed over and
across Eagle Point—his house, studio, barns, vehicles and
Tom Sorry's cabin. They found blood and signs of a
struggle in the horse barn. A blood trail showed where
Laura had been dragged from the barn to the driveway.

They confiscated all of Ryder's rifles and shotguns for firearms identification tests. Solerno didn't gather enough evidence for an arrest, but she assured Ryder that wife killers always got caught.

After seventy-two hours, Laura's condition was upgraded to serious but stable. When Ryder stroked her thumb, he felt positive her eyes moved behind her swollen eyelids.

Five days after the accident, when Laura had passed out of the acutely dangerous zone, Ryder finally went home and slept. When Mrs. Weatherbee shook his shoulder, he blinked blearily at her, trying to bring her face into focus.

"I'm up," he muttered.

"I'm sorry to wake you."

"S'all right. What time is it?"

The housekeeper checked the old-fashioned brooch watch she wore pinned on her bodice. "Near four o'clock."

Disoriented, he scowled at the light shining around the draperies. "In the morning?"

"Afternoon. You about slept the day away."

He bolted upright on the bed. He'd never in his life spent more than eight hours in bed. "Why didn't you wake me?"

"No need until now. Even Abby knows you need your rest." She thrust a remote telephone at him. "But you have a call. It's urgent."

He eyed the phone. His heart thump-thudded painfully against his chest wall. "Hospital?"

"Bank. It's a Miss Monroe." She placed the phone on the bed beside him and turned away. "I'll bring you some coffee."

He picked up the telephone. "Ryder Hudson here." He raked hair off his face and ears.

"Mr. Hudson? This is Judy Monroe at Colorado First. We have a serious situation."

His life was turning into one big situation. "What is it, ma'am?"

"It concerns the joint checking account you and Mrs. Hudson maintain with our bank." Papers rustled faintly in the background, then she read off an account number.

"Okay." He scrubbed at his aching eyes with a knuckle. His body felt as if he'd gone sixteen rounds with a thousand pounds of angry bull.

"Let me explain in chronological order what happened. On Thursday, the account's automatic teller machine card was used at the Safeway store in Monument. That was at 5:03 p.m. The card was used again an hour later at the north Academy King Sooper's grocery store."

Ryder snapped wide awake. Thursday. Laura's accident had happened on Thursday. He listened in growing horror as Miss Monroe chronicled the ATM card's use throughout Colorado Springs. On Friday, the card had been used in Pueblo, again only at grocery stores. The account had been emptied and overdrawn.

On Saturday, the card had been rejected by an ATM in Albuquerque. The user had tried to force the card, and the machine had confiscated it.

Miss Monroe cleared her throat. "This morning, one of our processors who read the newspaper story about Mrs. Hudson's accident realized that your wife could not have used the ATM card at the times in question."

Anyone could have used it. Despite common sense and warnings, Laura had written her personal identification number on the card sleeve so she wouldn't forget it. "Have you called the police?"

"Not yet, sir. Have you authorized anyone else to use the ATM card?"

Robbery... Laura had been a victim of a robbery. He blinked stupidly. For the past few days, he'd been making inquiries at the hospital about Laura's missing jewelry, including a diamond ring worth almost half a million dollars. He'd already contacted the insurance company so they could figure out if the jewelry had been misplaced or stolen by hospital staff. A robber, or robbers, must have come to the ranch and found Laura alone and helpless.

"Call the police. The ATM card was stolen."

After he hung up, he jumped out of bed. He pawed through his shirts, jeans and jacket looking for Becky Solerno's business card. He couldn't believe how stupid he'd been—he couldn't believe how stupid the police were!

He finally found Solerno's card and called her.

When the investigator came on the line, he told her, "My bank may have a lead on the person who tried to kill my wife."

Chapter Three

She asked them, *Please be quiet.* Her head ached terribly and their voices cut across her skull like dull knives. The man and woman ignored her and continued their argument.

"Why are you always here?" His voice rumbled low and thick with unhappiness.

"I was in the area. Just thought I'd drop in to see how Mrs. Hudson is doing." Her voice was mild, but stubborn.

"Ms. Solerno, we've been having these conversations for more than a month. I'm getting tired of you horning in on my visits to my wife. If you're so hot to solve the case, why aren't you chasing the people who stole Laura's credit cards?"

"I've already explained that to you a hundred times. Those cards were probably sold within an hour of being stolen."

"You've got fingerprints."

"Not off the ATM card. Besides, fingerprints are only useful if they're on file—as your foreman's are. The person who used the card only used ATM machines where there aren't any cameras. But as long as we're talking about useful information, why don't you fill me in about your girlfriend. I'm ready to listen whenever you're ready to talk.''

He made a rumbling noise thick with disgust.

"Come on. The landlady said Teresa packed up on the spur of the moment. If she was so responsible and loyal to you, why is it you don't know where she went? Why doesn't anybody know?''

"She was shy, kept to herself. She wasn't from around here anyway. She probably went back home. How many times do I have to tell you? Aren't you about sick of hearing it?''

"She was also deep in hock,'' Becky Solerno continued, "skipping out on student loans and hospital bills. People don't just drop out of sight, Hudson. At least, not unless they have a good reason. A *very* good reason. From the sounds of it, Miss Gallagher had a good reason to be mad at your wife. She had good reasons for needing the money, too. What I want to know is *your* good reason for covering for her.''

"It's real hard being polite to you sometimes, ma'am.''

"Don't bother with polite. All I care about is the truth. Sometimes I think the truth is, you don't care if I ever catch whoever shot your wife.''

"I care. But you've got it fixed in your head that I did it. Or that Tess did it. Instead of investigating, you're making up conspiracies and affairs. Or maybe you're getting all your information out of the newspapers. I'm telling you, it was a robber. If that's not glamorous enough for you, then I'm plumb sorry.''

"Glamorous?'' The woman laughed. "Do I look like I care about glamour?''

"You sure do like seeing your name in the papers. Do you reckon if you hang me, you'll get yourself a promotion?''

"Ouch! That sweet-talking cowboy act is just that, isn't it, Hudson? An act. You don't fool me. And you know what? I bet it doesn't fool your girlfriend, either. I bet you've got her stashed away somewhere while you wait for your wife to die. But just let me find her. How loyal do you think she'll be when I turn up the heat?"

Heavy footsteps stomped nearby; she felt the vibration in her shoulders. She followed the man with her eyes until he came into focus. He wore a fawn-yellow leather jacket with fringes that swung against his shoulders with every agitated step.

"Her eyes are open. Laura?" he said, his voice gone gentle. "Can you hear me, darlin'?"

I hear you. Where am I?

He leaned over, peering intently at her face. Lovely eyes, she thought, as dark blue as twilight, but melancholy. His sadness touched her and she longed to caress his cheek and soothe him.

"I've heard that patients in a coma open their eyes in reflex. It doesn't mean—"

"Get the doctor, Solerno!" he snapped over his shoulder. He touched the tips of his fingers to her brow. "Laura? You're looking right at me, honey. Talk to me. Are you in there?"

Shh, she told him. *My head hurts very much and I'm so thirsty my throat is filled with sand.*

"I swear to God, she's awake." He fumbled at the side of the bed and caught a cord. He followed it to the end and pressed a call button.

Within moments the room filled with thuds, thumps, footfalls and excited voices. Hurting so badly she wanted to weep, she closed her eyes and wished she could close her ears. The voices melded into soup and drifted into gray.

When she opened her eyes again, the man in yellow leather sat beside her, his head bowed. Unruly brown curls fell over his forehead. He rubbed the bridge of his nose between two fingers. He'd been here all along, talking to her. He'd spoken of Eagle Point Ranch and horses and costume balls and fashion shows.

Other voices had told her she couldn't walk.

A lie. She would walk...soon.

As soon as she figured out what was wrong with her body. She couldn't move—except for her toes. Wiggling them sent cat's claws scrambling from her feet to her hips. Her head hurt terribly. Her entire face felt smashed, squeezed beneath a heavy plate. The smell of antiseptic tickled her nose.

A hospital. The pink-and-lavender walls had fooled her for a while, as had the jacquard striped draperies over the windows and fine art on the walls. The room was much too pretty for a hospital, but the smells gave it away. Sharp antiseptic, flowery air fresheners and the iron-rich scent of medication meant she was definitely in a hospital.

The slight widening of his eyes said he knew she looked back at him. A thousand words jostled in her throat. A thousand questions. Knowing she hadn't the strength to say all she needed to say, she chose her words carefully.

"Water...please?"

The man's expression crumpled and his chin quivered. His beautiful, sad eyes filled with tears.

Her heart went out to this big, rugged cowboy. Oh, but she needed so desperately to drink and soothe her ravaged throat. "Water?" Her voice was as dusty as an August wind.

Her request produced chaos. The room filled with people. Two nurses hustled the man in yellow leather out the door. A short dark man, his name tag reading Dr. Millhouse, lifted her eyelids and flashed a light into her pupils. She tried to pull away, but couldn't move. All she could do was endure as the doctor poked and prodded her.

He leaned over until his face was only inches from hers. "Mrs. Hudson, you're awake. I can see you watching me. Don't bother trying to talk. Blink for me. One blink for no, two for yes. Can you understand me?"

She blinked twice.

All she wanted was a drink, but he continued to question her about how much pain she felt as he manipulated her feet and hands. Gradually she came to understand that she'd been in a coma. Dr. Millhouse appeared highly pleased when she answered his questions.

She still wanted a drink, and finally, painfully, said so.

"Of course, of course," he said, laughing. He ordered a nurse to help her drink.

Thirst slaked, she drifted back to sleep.

When she awakened again, she looked for the man in yellow leather. She wanted to thank him for his concern. He wasn't in the room, and disappointment made her sigh. She recognized Dr. Millhouse. He stood at the foot of her hospital bed, holding a chart and speaking in low, earnest tones to a woman wearing a dark suit. She didn't look like a nurse or a doctor, but her voice was familiar.

"You aren't appreciating the seriousness of the situation, Doctor."

"You're jumping the gun, Investigator. Mrs. Hudson is a fragile woman. That she's awakened at all is a miracle."

"I won't excite her. I won't hurt her. I need to ask her about the shooting." The woman thrust her jaw toward the doctor. "I'm convinced her husband tried to do her in.

He'll try again. Are you going to send this poor woman home with a killer?''

"I'm not impressed by your melodrama." Dr. Millhouse wrote on the chart with a flourish and hung it on the foot of the bed. "Mrs. Hudson will remain in the hospital a minimum of five weeks, but probably closer to twelve. That gives you plenty of time to investigate." He smiled sweetly. "But I think you're wasting your time. Mr. Hudson strikes me as a devoted husband. He's been here every single day—"

"He's hoping to catch her awake before anyone else does."

"Then arrest him."

"I don't have enough evidence. Let me talk...oh. She's awake." The woman lifted her eyebrows. "Good morning, Mrs. Hudson."

She mulled over the way strangers kept calling her Mrs. Hudson. It made her want to look around to see if there was someone else in the room. The man in yellow leather called her Laura. That wasn't right, either, but since she could not muster enough energy to tell him her real name, Laura it was.

"I'm Becky Solerno, sheriff's department. I'd like to talk to you about the accident, ma'am."

Laura looked helplessly at the doctor. He knew fifty times more than she did about how she'd ended up in a hospital bed. She didn't even know what city she was in. Or what state, for that matter. Panic fluttered in her chest.

"All right, all right, you've got five minutes, Investigator. Yes and no questions only. She can blink in reply. Tubes have irritated her throat, so it's painful for her to speak."

"Fine." The woman moved to Laura's side. She smiled gently. "Do you know who did this to you, Mrs. Hudson?"

Did what? From the snatches of conversation she'd been able to follow, she felt certain she'd been in a car accident. She concentrated, trying to recall the date or even the time of year. Snatches of blue sky beyond the draperies told her nothing.

"I'm going to catch the person who hurt you. You can trust me on that. Do you feel up to talking to me?"

Laura liked the woman's broad, sun-browned face, dimpled smile and earnest tone. Laura blinked twice.

"That means yes," Dr. Millhouse said.

"Do you know who shot you, Mrs. Hudson?"

She didn't understand the question. She blinked once.

"Mrs. Hudson, I have reason to believe your husband tried to kill you. Please cooperate. Did he shoot you? There's another woman involved. Her name is Teresa Gallagher. She worked for your husband. Did she do it?"

The woman may as well have been speaking Greek for all the sense her words made. Laura couldn't remember being married, much less having a husband who would shoot her. Perhaps she was asleep and dreaming. That was it. She had a lot of dreams, some pleasant, some horrifying, but all of them seemed at least as real as this pretty hospital room.

"This might be more effective if you'd wait until after I've conducted a neurological study," the doctor said. "She suffered substantial brain trauma. A possibility exists that she'll never remember anything about the accident."

Investigator Solerno pulled out a business card. She made a show of propping it against the bedside telephone. "I'm on your side, ma'am. I'll protect you. You don't have to be afraid of anybody. Do you understand?"

Laura blinked twice.

"Anytime, night or day, if you need to talk, you call me. You're my top priority."

If Laura could have smiled, she would have. She blinked twice again.

"I'll be back to check in on you. So you get strong and we'll catch that creep. Okay?"

After Becky left, the doctor said, "You don't have to talk to anybody you don't want to." He checked her eyes and used his stethoscope to listen to her heart and lungs. "The only thing you have to do is get well. You're a surprising woman. I do believe you'll prove all the doom and gloomers wrong. I have all the faith in the world that you'll do that, Mrs. Hudson."

With tremendous effort, she turned her head. "Doctor," she whispered. "Please…understand…mistake…"

"Don't excite yourself."

"Must understand . . . I am not Laura Hudson."

"CHRONIC AMNESIA," Ryder said wearily. "Why isn't her memory improving? She remembers the president of the United States, so why doesn't she remember me?"

Dr. Millhouse sat behind his desk. Instead of medical charts, his office walls were decorated with Metropolitan Opera posters and framed musical scores. Ryder had spent enough time in this office over the past few months that he'd memorized all the songs. The doctor favored the rousing horns and drums of Tchaikovsky and Ravel.

"On the good side, Laura's brain is healing," the doctor said. "Quite frankly, she has beaten the odds. Her short-term memory is almost normal."

"Meaning?"

"Meaning her brain is functioning and she can retain normal amounts of information. The speed of her recovery gives me hope that her long-term memory will be restored eventually."

"You keep saying that, but she doesn't know who she is. She treats me like a stranger. What about our daughter?"

"Patience, Mr. Hudson. Laura sustained injuries that by all rights should have killed her. I'm not claiming a miracle, but there really isn't any other way to explain how far she's progressed. There's no paralysis. She's intelligent, cognitive. Except for some mild aphasia, her speech is unaffected. Thank heavens, her sight is unaffected, as well. Considering the massive damage to her eye sockets, it's a miracle she can see. As far as I can tell, the most lasting affects will be cosmetic."

He understated. The rolling Mercedes had pitched Laura face first through the windshield. Then she'd struck solid rock, again face first. A scratch was cosmetic; Laura's face had been shattered.

"The best surgeons have effected marvelous repairs, reconstructing her facial bones and managing the nerve damage. But she will never look the way she looked before."

The doc didn't know the half of it, Ryder thought. In the years he'd known Laura, he'd never seen her without her face perfectly made-up and every hair in place. She was as much an artist as he was. Her face and body were her media, a supple, ever-changing display of perfect feminine beauty.

"Maybe she'll never remember how beautiful she was."

The doctor gave him a twisted smile. "What the medical community understands about the human brain is the proverbial single grain of sand on an endless beach. I have noticed a most interesting twist, though."

"A twist?"

Dr. Millhouse chuckled uneasily. "It's a new one on me. She appears to be suffering from a delusion that she is someone else. According to her, she isn't certain who she is, but she is positive that she isn't Laura Hudson." He shrugged. "We've had some lively discussions concerning her beliefs."

It didn't sound twisted to Ryder. Laura had always hated being Laura.

"I am recommending a colleague of mine. Dr. Lopez is a psychiatrist who specializes in trauma patients."

"You think Laura's crazy?"

"Of course not! As I said, our knowledge about how the brain functions is extremely limited. Dr. Lopez can, however, aid your wife in coming to terms with her amnesia. It's a frightening thing, not being able to remember. When you were in school, did you ever come across a question for which you knew the answer, but could not produce it?"

Ryder nodded.

"Apply that moment of panic to an entire lifetime."

When Ryder left the doctor's office, he was deep in thought. In light of her ravaged beauty, which no amount of plastic surgery could ever restore, permanent amnesia would be a kindness.

With her beauty gone, what did Laura have left? She'd probably be grateful if he put her away in a secluded haven where no one she knew could see her looking less than perfect.

He made his way to Laura's private room. Laura sat upright on a wheelchair, her plaster-cast-encased left leg propped on a stool. A pair of orderlies changed the bed sheets.

Sitting up, without bed linens to shield her, she looked tiny. The agonizing stress of numerous surgeries on her face and mangled leg had shrunk her once voluptuous body to frail waifishness. Every bone and tendon showed in her wrists. Her skull, crisscrossed by healing scars, was covered by dark peach-soft fuzz. Pressure bandages covered her face, leaving only her mouth and eyes uncovered.

Looking at her now, it was impossible to imagine her as the woman who once blinded him with her dazzling presence. He barely recognized her at all.

"Hello," she said. She lifted a hand weakly.

He pulled a chair next to her. Knowing she might never remember her past gave him a funny feeling. Without her looks and without her memories, was she even Laura?

"I spoke to Dr. Millhouse. One more week and you can come home. You'll have a full-time nurse and will continue coming back for physical therapy, but at least you'll be an outpatient."

She breathed a wispy, "Oh." She glanced at the tiny Christmas tree in the corner. Though weeks had passed since the holiday, she'd asked him to leave up the tree.

Ryder guessed what she thought. This was home to her. The doctors and nurses were her family. Ryder was the big, bad stranger coming to take her away. "The doc and I talked about your amnesia. He thinks you'll get better."

Tears filled her soft brown eyes. "I hate this... blankness. The confusion. Sometimes I'm sure I know who I am, but I'm usually wrong. I don't know what to be certain about. I can't even tell the difference between dreams and reality." She laughed weakly and brushed at her eyes. "I dreamed Dr. Millhouse broke his arm. The nurses thought I was crazy because I kept asking how he was. It was so real, but it's not real at all."

The orderlies finished the bed. When they moved to help Laura out of the wheelchair, she said, "Please, may I sit up a while?" One of the orderlies promised to ask the nurse. They left the room.

The gentle request had sounded so odd coming from her. Before the accident, Laura would have made a cold demand from the hired help, and if that didn't bring instant compliance, she'd have screamed. *Please* wasn't a word he generally associated with her. He wondered how far the accident-induced personality changes would go.

"Are you absolutely positive I'm your wife?" she asked.

The question startled him. Despite her weak voice, she spoke with a sureness that bordered on bluntness. "Who else could you be?"

"I just don't feel like Laura Hudson. The name doesn't fit. I look at you and you're familiar, but you're not. The idea of going home frightens me. I can't begin to imagine what home is."

"I've told you. Home is Eagle Point Ranch, northwest of the Springs. The house is yours, you designed it from the ground up. Remember, you have a daughter."

She looked away and blinked rapidly. "I can't... remember... a daughter."

Ryder refrained from pointing out that Laura had hated being pregnant, hated having responsibility for a baby and considered children disgusting. At his most cynical, he suspected one of the reasons she'd married him, aside from his bank accounts, was that she'd been a new mother panicked by the thought of having to fend for herself.

Maybe little Abby was something she didn't want to remember.

"Am I crazy?"

"I don't think you're crazy, darlin'. The doc doesn't,
either. It's going to take some time for your thinking to get
back to normal."

"It all feels like a mistake. Every time someone says
Laura, I want to see if anyone else is in the room."

"Nobody expected you to live, much less recover as well
as you have. Give yourself time to heal."

Her eyes flicked at him. "Becky said it was no accident."

So, Laura and the investigator were on first-name ba-
sis. He decided then and there that he was definitely getting a restraining order against the persistent cop. "Is that
why you don't want to be my wife? You think I tried to
kill you?" Deep hurt slithered through him and settled in
a painful knot in his gut. He rose to his feet and glared at
her. "I gave you everything. I laid my heart at your feet,
and I never, ever put a harsh hand on you."

She visibly cringed.

Disgusted with himself and with her, he turned away.
"Looks like there's some things you do remember. Like
how you always have to think the worst about me."

"Ryder, I—"

"I never hurt you."

Yelling at her felt about as good as kicking kittens. He
stomped out of the room.

In the elevator, on the way down to the lobby, his conscience gnawed at him. He didn't deserve the suspicion
Laura and the cops directed his way, but he supposed
getting shot and pushed off a cliff was reason enough for
Laura to be suspicious about somebody. In the hospital
lobby, he found a bank of phones and a telephone book.

He turned to *Beauty*. Laura had spent her happiest moments being pampered head to toe. Seeing the numerous listings for salons and spas made him uneasy. What in the world did he know about beauty parlors? The mere thought of talking about such feminine goings-on made his mouth turn dry. He hadn't the faintest idea what happened in a salon, and he didn't want to know.

He started to close the phone book, but stopped himself. He kept seeing Laura's scrawny arm, so white and frail. He picked the flashiest ad, called and asked for the owner.

A woman with a pleasant, whiskey-warm voice came on the line. "Janelle here, may I help you?"

He rubbed the back of his hand over his brow. He was starting to sweat. "Ah, my wife..."

"Yes?"

"She's in the hospital. She's needing some... lady stuff." He searched his pockets for a kerchief. "I was wondering if you could send someone to her room."

"That's not my usual policy," she said cautiously.

He knew he was fumbling badly. He wished he was at home in his studio, lost in a painting, or on horseback in the mountains. "I can pay, ma'am. Money isn't a problem. See, Laura can't leave the hospital. She's wrecked pretty bad. Some pampering might help her feel better." He licked his dry lips. "A manicure. Cream. Perfume. Stuff."

"Sending someone to the hospital could be expensive."

"Don't worry about that. I can give you my credit card number." He fumbled his wallet out of his jacket and brought out a gold card. He read off his name, number and expiration date.

After a long silence, Janelle said, "I see. Mr. *Ryder* Hudson. When you would like me to see your wife?"

"Today?"

"I'll come myself, sir." Her voice held an odd quaver. "It will be my pleasure. A *total* pleasure."

After he hung up, he used both hands to wipe sweat off his face. No doubt about it, he had to quit procrastinating and hire another assistant.

HEARING THE SOUND of boot heels, Laura recognized Ryder's tread coming down the corridor toward her room. She put down the novel she'd been reading.

Trying to read. She eyed the pretty cover on the romance novel. She longed for light entertainment, something besides watching hour after hour of television, but reading was a chore. Sometimes for no reason at all, the words would jumble on the page and she couldn't remember anything she'd read. At other times a single word would stymie her, and she'd struggle to the point of tears in an attempt to find its meaning. Her doctors thought it fabulous she could read at all, but it was still frustrating.

Ryder entered the room.

Suddenly nervous, she patted her throat and tugged at the neckline of her new nightgown. The fine silk whispered under her fingertips. Her insides tangled. He'd been so angry when she'd last seen him.

"Afternoon," he said gruffly and went to the window. He opened the draperies, allowing in the sunshine.

She splayed her hands atop the bed sheet, showing off her fresh manicure. "Good afternoon, Ryder. Thank you."

"For what?"

"Janelle. She's a nice woman. She brought me this new nightie and gave me a manicure." She wiggled her toes under the covers. "My feet, too. It was so sweet of you to think of me."

His face reddened and he turned away from her. He fussed with a display of get-well cards. His embarrassment touched her.

"One of these days you'll have to tell me who sent the cards. None of the names are familiar." She'd received dozens of cards, plants and flower arrangements. She'd begun to notice, though, that none of the cards contained a personal note. No friends visited her. No one ever called. She supposed Ryder had asked people to stay away out of deference to her easily fatigued state.

He pulled a chair around next to the bed and straddled it. His cotton shirt sleeves were rolled to the elbows, revealing heavily muscled forearms and work-roughened hands. His wristwatch was sturdy with a stainless steel band. The flashiest thing about him was a gold and silver belt buckle with a carved depiction of a cowboy riding a bucking bull.

Yet his unassuming appearance had to be a facade. This room was as comfortable as a fine hotel, and the staff was wonderful. The visit from Janelle must have cost a pretty penny.

She could not imagine being married to him.

Working up her nerve, she smoothed the covers with the flats of her hands. "I have good news. I finally remember something about my past. I remember my mother."

Ryder looked interested.

"Her name is Antoinette and she managed the jewelry counter in a department store. I can't remember exactly which store, but I think it was in a mall. She died a few years ago. I can't remember how she died, but I know her

grave has a brass marker and a little plastic holder for
flowers.''

The interested gleam in Ryder's eyes turned guarded.
He slowly shook his head. "Sorry, darlin'."

"I don't remember being sad. It's okay."

"I mean about the memory. Your mama's name is
Janice. As far as we know, she's alive, but you haven't
heard from her in years. She's an alcoholic."

"No." Tightness invaded her chest. "She's not an alcoholic. I remember her. *I do.* She had curly dark brown
hair. She sang in church every Sunday. She had the voice
of an angel, and I sang with her. She made us dresses, uh,
mother-and-daughter dresses out of flower prints. We
wore them to church."

"When Janice wasn't waling the tar out of you, she
abandoned you to the neighbors so she could go on
drinking binges. She never took you to church."

Genuine pain darkened his eyes to midnight.

That more than anything frightened her. A sob
wrenched painfully from her throat and she covered her
face with both hands. "I remember!"

"You might be remembering somebody's mama," he
said, "but not yours."

Her triumph turned to agony. She wept. Ryder ordered her to stop it. She wept harder. He patted her
shoulder, rubbed her back and stroked her arm. The bed
sagged under his weight and he enfolded her in his big,
solid arms. She turned his plaid shirt front dark with
dampness before she finally mustered control.

"It's all right," he breathed against her forehead. He
pressed a tender kiss against her skin. "It's all right, darlin', don't cry. If you want to remember Antoinette and
call her Mama, that's all right. She sounds a heap nicer
than Janice ever was, anyway."

He didn't understand. She could see her mother's sweet face so clearly, hear the bell tones of her voice and smell flower-scented powder against her skin. If the memory wasn't real, then it could only mean she was going insane.

Chapter Four

"Welcome home, Laura."

She tried to smile at Ryder, but her body ached too much. Even though the pair of attendants were gentle, the transfer from the back of the private ambulance to the wheelchair had left Laura breathless.

Or perhaps it was the altitude, which was at least a thousand feet higher than Colorado Springs. Her view had been limited on the long ride from the hospital, and she'd caught only glimpses of the mountainous landscape. Eagle Point Ranch nestled in a glorious valley, ringed by ponderosa pines and red sandstone formations. Patches of snow glittered under the sun. The air had a crisp taste, like catching snowflakes. The breeze held a bite, and she shivered.

Ryder hovered anxiously over her. He tucked a blanket tighter around her thighs and patted her shoulder. "Are you all right?"

The sky was so blue it seemed formed of layer upon layer of crystalline enamel. A horse whinnied plaintively in the distance. "It's beautiful," she whispered, wondering how she could have possibly forgotten such a magical place.

"You like it?" Ryder sounded surprised. He wheeled her around the back of the ambulance.

The house rivaled the mountains in showiness. Spanish-style, its stuccoed walls rose blinding white, topped by brick-red roof tiles. U-shaped, built around an open courtyard, it was huge. Grates formed of intricate wrought iron covered the windows, and matching ironwork was made into gates for the courtyard.

Laura grasped the wheels. "This is all a mistake. I don't live here."

"You made me build the darned thing," Ryder said. "And Tom Sorry isn't about to give me back my cabin. So you're not skipping out on me."

That couldn't possibly be amusement in his voice. She looked up at him. For the first time, his eyes were neither sad nor grim. Shaded beneath his broad-brimmed cowboy hat, they sparkled with good humor. Glints of light brightened them like sapphires. Her breath caught again in her throat.

"You're fibbing," she said. "I didn't design this."

"You sure did, darlin'." He waggled his eyebrows. "Looks like I could have gotten away with some remodeling. Missed my chance."

He pushed her wheelchair up the two steps into the courtyard, then left her for a moment while he made final arrangements with the ambulance attendants and helped the live-in nurse with her luggage. It gave Laura time to absorb the full impact of the courtyard. Two sides of the courtyard were lined with French doors. Balconies overhead had wrought-iron railings. Chunky terra-cotta pots stood empty, but it was easy to imagine them filled with mums, dahlias, daisies and geraniums. A rainbow flashed in the mist over a triple-tier, verdigris fountain.

A woman emerged from the house. Tall and broad-shouldered, she had a round face and stern demeanor. A light gray uniform fit her with tailored precision.

As the woman approached, her pale eyes boring into Laura, the back of Laura's neck began to prickle. The prickle worked its way downward to join the chronic itch inside the cast on her left leg. Laura felt her helplessness as she'd never felt it before.

"Welcome home, ma'am," the woman said. Her voice was as flat as her expression, yet managed to blare disapproval.

Laura felt this woman's hatred. Her mouth went dry and her heart pounded. Becky Solerno's concerns about the dangers of this household echoed in Laura's mind. Somebody had tried to kill her.

Somebody who hated her enough to want her dead.

"Mrs. Weatherbee," Ryder said as he took hold of the wheelchair handles. "I'll take Laura straight up to her room." He indicated the nurse who had accompanied them from the hospital. "This is Miss Garner. After we get Laura settled, you can show Miss Garner to her room." He looked around. "Where's Tom?"

"Said he had a problem with a water tank."

Ryder flashed an apologetic smile at Laura. "Tom Sorry can welcome you home later."

Mrs. Weatherbee asked, "And where would you care for lunch?"

Laura stared at her hands, but felt the woman's eyes.

"I'll join Laura in her bedroom." Ryder pushed her through the double-wide doorway.

Uneasily, she looked around at the foyer. If Ryder insisted she'd designed this house, she had no choice except to believe him. For the life of her, though, she could not begin to imagine why.

The double staircase seemed to float against a two-story glass wall. The marble steps were open, enhancing the floating effect, and the railing was made of iron pipe, enameled white and fitted with bright brass end caps and joints. Chandeliers made of crystal plates and gold leaves hung at varying heights, suspended by brass rods.

"I think I know why I forgot this," she muttered.

"What was that?" Ryder asked.

She shook her head.

"I thought about quartering you downstairs," he said as he knelt to lock the wheelchair wheels. "But, as determined as you are to walk, you won't be needing this chair much longer. If I'm wrong, we can move you into a guest room easy enough. Ready?"

She wrapped both arms around his neck and braced herself. He lifted her from the chair. She caught a whiff of woodsy after-shave and balsam shampoo in his thick brown hair. His good mood relaxed her. His strong arms were safe. He'd never let anyone hurt her.

As he started up the stairs, she said, "Are you sure I'm not too heavy?" Though he walked lightly, her left leg in its bulky cast bobbed. She winced with each painful twinge. Her back burned as if probed with needles. Pain had become her constant companion, but even her high tolerance had limits.

"You finally got your wish, darlin'. You're skinny as a fresh-whelped coyote. Of course, it's not a weight-loss program I'd recommend to anybody."

She hadn't spoken to anybody about how her appearance had changed since the accident. The plastic surgeons who operated on her face had been concerned about repairing crushed bones and lacerated muscles and nerves, salvaging her teeth and making certain she could see and breathe properly. Pain and the effort of healing had made her appearance seem unimportant by contrast.

But now she was a wife again. From the corner of her eye, she studied Ryder's hard jaw and big, handsome features. She couldn't be ugly. He wouldn't have an ugly wife.

"Was I fat?" she asked.

He laughed.

The sound of it startled her; its richness enchanted her. She tightened her arms around his neck. Suddenly she was glad he was her husband, and she knew with all her heart that Becky was wrong about him trying to kill her. She would remember how and why they fell in love. He'd be easy to love again.

"You weren't fat, darlin', not by a long shot."

At the top of the stairs, he turned left. Mrs. Weatherbee and Miss Garner waited near an open door. Ryder walked quickly through a large sitting room and into a bedroom. He placed Laura atop a bed. Miss Garner was right there, propping Laura with pillows and arranging her broken leg for comfort.

Certain this was another of her more-real-than-reality dreams, Laura looked around the room. The suite was decorated entirely in white and gold. Watered silk covered the walls and windows. Carved carpeting with a vaguely Middle Eastern design spread like velvet over the floor. The furnishings were French classical, polished to a hard shine. Dozens of mirrors in every shape and size covered the walls. There were skirts on the tables, hangings over the bed, glittering crystal lamps and vases filled with yellow roses. The roses perfumed the air with cloying sweetness.

Dominating the overdone decor was a larger-than-life-size reclining nude. The gilt-framed painting hung over a white marble fireplace.

Nonplussed, Laura slowly lifted her gaze to Ryder. She longed to demand to know what kind of man was he that he allowed her to force him to live in this . . . seraglio. All she could do was stare.

"This is fabulous," Miss Garner said. She sounded absolutely delighted. "The furniture is so posh and pretty!"

Laura refrained from grimacing. She couldn't very well comment on the nurse's awful taste.

"Is that you?" the nurse asked, indicating the nude.

"No," Laura said.

"Yes." Ryder lifted his eyebrows. "It's you."

Appalled, Laura took another look at the portrait. The pastel colors gave it a soft, old-fashioned look. Yet the woman was hard-edged and sleek, posed on a swan-shaped recliner. Her golden hair curled in Rapunzel waves over her bare shoulders and breasts. Her face was perfect; her large, dark, sultry eyes seemed to look straight at Laura.

Laura touched her short, brushy hair. "Artistic license?"

"Not much." His expression darkened.

Laura sensed he didn't like the portrait. Perhaps it embarrassed him. It certainly embarrassed her.

The dour housekeeper said, "I'll see to lunch, sir. Miss Garner, I'll show you to your room."

"Oh, please, call me Bertie." Eyes wide, swiveling her head to take in her surroundings, the nurse followed the housekeeper out of the room.

Left alone with her husband, Laura fiddled with the silk sheets and lace-trimmed counterpane. "Well, I'm home."

Ryder nodded. "Do you feel up to seeing Abby?"

Her daughter... she closed her eyes. Of all things to forget, how could she possibly forget a child? Whenever Ryder spoke of the girl, his face softened and his eyes acquired a prideful fondness that was completely endearing. Laura could love him for that look alone.

"Is she terribly angry with me for deserting her?" Laura hated herself for forgetting Abby. A good mother, she felt, would never forget her own child.

Ryder pulled at his jaw and shifted his weight from foot to foot. Laura guessed little Abby was very angry. Ryder had not brought Abby to the hospital, and Laura hadn't spoken to her on the telephone. It had seemed the wisest course at the time, but looking back, Laura decided it was a mistake.

"Truth is," he said reluctantly, "she hasn't said much about you."

Emotion thickened in her throat and spread to her chest, making it ache. During her lengthy hospital stay, Ryder and Becky Solerno had been her only visitors. No friends had come to wish her well; no family seemed concerned for her welfare. The only people who were remotely interested had been reporters who sneaked past the hospital staff.

Now it seemed not even her own child cared about her.

The portrait drew her attention, and this time she saw it wasn't the size or the ostentatious frame that made the piece so ugly. The artist had captured her lush body and perfect face, but he'd also portrayed her eyes in all their sensual malevolence. The woman in that portrait was nobody's friend.

RYDER WATCHED Laura pick at her food. Drawn and quiet, she hadn't said a word all during lunch. Unable to

stand it, he dropped his fork on his plate and exclaimed,
"If you hate it that much, I'll have Mrs. Weatherbee come
up. You can go back to planning the cooking around
here."

"Pardon?"

Her wide-eyed innocence caught him off guard. She
looked so tiny surrounded by the mounds of silk and lace
on the bed. During his countless visits to the hospital he'd
grown used to her appearance. The bandages and fuzzy
hair no longer bothered him.

He couldn't get used to her eyes.

Surgery to repair broken facial bones had changed their
shape. Laura now had the soft, vulnerable eyes of an in-
nocent. Eyes without a trace of guile, greed or calcula-
tion.

Eyes that turned him to mush inside.

He scrubbed at his mouth with a napkin. "I said, if you
don't like the cooking, you can talk to Mrs. Weatherbee." He prayed she never remembered how much she
feared hearty food. He didn't want to go back a diet of
froufrou recipes lacking red meat, fat or sugar.

"The food is delicious." She sighed. "May I ask you a
question? I'd like an honest answer, please."

"Go ahead."

"Now that I'm home, perhaps you can explain to me
why I have no friends." She closed her eyes and caught
her lower lip in her teeth.

His heart sank. While Laura had been in a month-long
coma, Colorado high society had forsaken her as old
news. "You've got plenty of friends." His forced hearti-
ness made him wince.

"Nobody visited me in the hospital. No one called.
None of the cards and gifts I received had a personal note
attached." She breathed hard a few seconds, and her thin

fingers played with the neckline of her nightgown. "My own child is avoiding me."

"She ate before we got home."

Her pained expression said she knew he lied. Up until today, Abby had been having the best time of her life. Knowing Laura was in the house had transformed Abby from Miss Sweetie Pie into Tiny Terror. Mrs. Weatherbee was now trying her best to convince the balky child to bathe and dress appropriately for visiting her mother.

He hadn't the faintest idea how to tell Laura she was a class-A bitch and any friends she had were well paid for.

"I'll go see if she's ready." He made his escape from Laura's suite. An escape from her soft, wounded eyes.

He found the housekeeper in Abby's room. The little girl hid under her bed while Mrs. Weatherbee threatened to get a broom and sweep her out.

"I'll handle this."

"Fine!" Grumbling, the woman marched out of the room.

Ryder crouched next to the bed and lifted the dust ruffle. "All right, sugar bear, enough is enough. Get your butt out from under there, pronto."

"I don't wanna wear that dress! It's icky!"

A green-and-gold taffeta dress lay atop Abby's bed. The puffy skirt looked stiff, and the neckline was lined with scratchy lace.

"You don't have to wear it. Get out from there."

Soft rustling marked Abby's progress under the bed. Her dark head emerged and she lifted reproachful eyes. "I wanna wear my boots."

Ever since he'd bought her a pair of real cowboy boots, she practically lived in them. During Laura's absence, she'd worn only jeans and boots, and acted as horse-happy and rambunctious as any other ranch kid.

He grasped her under the arms and hauled her into the open. She wore a dirty sweatshirt, denim jeans and her boots. Her face was smudged. She smelled of eau de pony. He thought her the most beautiful thing in all of creation.

"You can wear your boots, but you will wash your face."

She scowled ferociously, but he felt her fear. His own fear increased. In the months since Laura's accident, Abby had blossomed. She'd gained at least ten pounds. She no longer complained of tummyaches and headaches, nor did she suffer from night terrors. Her behavior had improved a thousand percent.

Ryder determined that if Laura ever again abused Abby in any way, shape or form, she was gone. He'd find a judge to sign paperwork saying she was nuts, institutionalize her and throw away the key. He took Abby into the bathroom and made her wash her face, hands and neck. He brushed her long brown hair.

"Braid it, Daddy," she said.

She was stalling. Feeling a tad reluctant himself, he carefully divided her hair into three hanks and plaited it into a fat braid that hung to the small of her back. He tied it with a red scrunchy bow.

"You need a clean shirt, sugar bear."

She pooched out her lower lip.

"Wear your wolf shirt. That's your favorite."

Her lively eyes sparkled as she considered it. Without warning she scampered to her dresser and pulled open the bottom drawer. She brought out a cranberry-colored sweatshirt with a picture of a gray wolf on it. She changed shirts then danced an arms-high pirouette.

"Looking good, babe," he said and held out his hand.

She placed her tiny hand against his. "I hate Mama's room," she stated. "It always stinks like those old roses. I hate it."

It occurred to him that Laura had never said a word about the roses. Yellow tea roses were her favorite.

Even though several psychiatrists and psychologists had told him the personality changes were due to her injuries, it still boggled him that she seemed like a completely different woman. He hoped the changes extended to her attitude about children.

"You can stand it for a minute." He and Abby headed for Laura's suite.

As soon as they entered the sitting room, Abby began to balk. Her hand turned hot and sweaty inside his. He kept a firm grip on her. When he finally got her to the side of Laura's bed, Abby hung back, staring at the floor.

"Hello," Laura said.

The child's stubbornness surrounded her like a thorny hedgerow. Ryder nudged her, but Abby refused to speak.

"I'm very glad to see you, Abby." She looked to Ryder.

Her helplessness tore at his heart. But she'd brought this on herself. She was the one who treated her own baby like an unwanted stray cat.

In the awkward silence, Abby twisted and turned in his grasp, refusing to look at her mother. Laura fiddled with her nightgown.

"Ah...that's a very nice shirt, Abby," Laura said.

Abby darted a glance at her, taking in her bandaged face and the bulk of her plaster-encased leg. She ripped her hand away from Ryder's and tore at the sweatshirt. "I hate this shirt! It's ugly! Just like you! You're ugly, ugly, *ugly!*"

Laura cringed. Her eyes turned liquid.

"Abby," Ryder said sharply. "Hush that talk."

Laura caught his arm. "No, she's right. I must be awful to look at. I'm sorry, Abby, but I was in an accident. I've had surgery. Did your father tell you?"

"I wish you were dead!" Abby raced out of the room.

Laura covered her mouth with both hands. Tears soaked the bandages across her cheeks.

"I'll talk to her," Ryder said tightly.

She caught his arm again and held on to him with all her puny strength. "Dear God, what did I do to that baby?"

He could not face her.

Her voice dropped to an anguished whisper. "What did I do to you?"

INCH BY INCH, Laura wheeled the clumsy chair through the doorway onto the balcony. The effort left her sweating and out of breath. The weak spring sunshine was worth it. She lifted her face to the soothing heat and closed her eyes. The bandages were finally off her face, and the healing skin felt as tight as stretched rubber.

Male voices caught her attention. She pushed herself closer to the railing so she could look down into the courtyard.

Ryder and Tom Sorry stood next to the fountain. They spoke too softly for her to make out their exact words. Laura drank in the sight of her husband. His big shoulders strained his light cotton shirt. His well-worn blue jeans fit snugly in all the right places. Lately, instead of his black felt hat, he wore white straw. His skin glowed with vitality.

Ryder clapped the other man on the shoulder and laughed.

Laura closed her eyes. The sound of his laughter washed over her, plucking at her heart...breaking her heart. She saw him only once a day. She had no idea what he did with the rest of his time. If they had been intimate, they no longer were. Of course, she told herself, that was only because her body was still slowly healing. Each evening, he joined her for dinner in her bedroom, but the only thing he ever talked to her about were inanities like the society pages and television. Why he found those subjects so fascinating, she hadn't a clue, but it was better than hearing nothing at all. He'd made some attempts to bring Abby in for visits, but the little girl was so terribly unhappy, Laura couldn't bear to force her to enter the suite.

Ryder suddenly looked up. Even from a distance, his dark blue eyes pierced her, robbing her of her breath and her senses.

She needed to get well as quickly as possible. Instinct said standing up to him, face-to-face, was the only way to win his respect.

He spoke a few more words to Tom. The cowboy tugged his hat down low on his face and strode out of the courtyard. Ryder looked up at her again, waved and headed into the house.

A few seconds later, he appeared in the doorway. He crossed his arms and leaned his shoulder against the jamb. "You're not supposed to be sunbathing."

She fingered the satiny scar tissue along her jawline. "It's not real sun. It's the middle of winter."

"It's spring, but even a little sun will worsen the scars. Even on your hands."

Tucking her hands under her arms, she gazed with longing at the mountains visible over the roof. "I think it'd be worth it. I'm tired of being cooped up. I'm tired of being in bed." She didn't add how terribly lonely she was.

"Where's Bertie?" he asked.

"She went to town with Mrs. Weatherbee."

"Why?" His brow furrowed.

"I don't need anything and she was restless. I saw no harm in letting her enjoy herself a few hours."

The furrows deepened into a scowl.

She fought down the urge to apologize. "She's *my* nurse, Ryder. If I want to give her some time off, I don't see where that's a problem." She caught the right wheel and pushed with all her strength. Her arm muscles quivered like gelatin. The chair turned a few inches. Before she could try again, Ryder stepped in and helped her turn the chair so it faced the doorway. His emphasizing her lack of strength frustrated her.

"I hate being so weak!"

"In all likelihood the doc will take off the cast on your next visit. All your movement's returned. You can start swimming. That should put meat on you."

She glanced toward the courtyard. Other than the fountain, she hadn't seen any sources of water. She imagined swimming in a high-country pond would freeze her to her bones. "Where can I swim?"

"In the pool." He waved lazily toward the back of the house. "There's a pool, sauna and gym out back. You always liked swimming. You used to do forty, fifty laps a day."

"Really?" She thought hard, trying to raise any mental pictures of herself exercising. "What about bicycling and skiing? I love to ski. That's a fact."

He shook his head. "I've never known you to ski. Or ride a bike. You want to be slim, not muscular. That's why you swim."

"I remember skiing!"

"Not since I've known you. You don't own skis. Or a bicycle."

She fought tears of frustration. If what she remembered weren't memories, what were they? "There are dozens of excellent ski areas within a few hours of here. I love to ski."

"Whatever." He stepped behind the chair. "Let's get you inside. If you get sunburned, the doctors will give me the devil." Without waiting to hear her opinion about leaving the balcony, he pushed her through the doorway.

Miserable over her treacherous nonmemories, she suddenly wanted to return to bed. She'd pull the covers over her head and sulk, even though what she really wanted was to scream and shake somebody. Anybody.

He started to lock the wheels, but froze, staring at the fireplace. "Where's the portrait?"

He straightened, his frown darkening, his gaze suspicious. Turning his head slowly, he appeared to notice for the first time the changes in the room.

If she had the strength, she'd have kicked herself. Even though he was sleeping elsewhere temporarily, she should have asked his permission before making changes. Caught, she said, "I'm sorry, but I had to remove it. I'll put it back if you insist, but…it's not very tasteful." She braced herself for his displeasure.

"You took down the mirrors, too."

"I asked Mrs. Weatherbee to store them. Is that all right? She didn't think you would mind."

"Where are the roses?"

"Uh, well, you see—I canceled the deliveries! The expense is much too much, and although I do deeply appreciate the thought, I don't really like all those yellow roses."

Ryder nodded and rubbed the back of his neck, kneading the sun-dark skin with his strong fingers. "Would you like something else? Daisies? Carnations?"

Unable to even guess what he was thinking, she twiddled her fingers. "Actually, I asked Bertie if she'd find me a green plant. A philodendron or ivy. A little bit of color." She made herself look at him. "I know I should have asked, but this room is just so..." She hadn't the words to describe the affect the French whorehouse decor had on her.

"If you don't like it, change it." He lifted her off the chair and onto the bed.

As he arranged her leg cast, she caught a hint of a smile on his supple lips.

"You don't mind? Truly?"

"Do whatever you want. As long as you stay out of the sun." The smile turned thoughtful and he left her.

She wished she could remember how and why she'd married Ryder Hudson. She wished he would talk to her and help her fill in the blanks. He answered most questions she asked, but only the questions she asked. Figuring out the proper questions was the kicker. Figuring out what she actually had the stomach to hear was even more difficult.

Later that day, the telephone rang. She started to lift the handset when she noticed it wasn't the in-house line. It came from outside, on her private line. Bemused by the novelty of someone actually calling to speak to her, she allowed it to ring several times before she answered.

"Hello?" she said cautiously.

"Hey, baby," a man said. His voice was throaty with amusement.

"Hello?"

"This is *Laura* isn't it?"

He recognized her, apparently, but she hadn't a clue as to his identity. "This is *Mrs*. Hudson. May I ask who's calling?"

He laughed. "You don't know who this is? Imagine that. After all we've been through together." He tsked. "Or is it you don't want to remember? Amnesia pays pretty good."

"What—?"

"But old Ryder is taking good care of you, huh? How does he like the new, improved Laura?"

"You must have the wrong number. I'm sorry—"

"Hey!" His hot-honey tone turned rough. "One of us in this little tea party is stupid, but it isn't me. I suggest you do some hard thinking and consider just how much I know."

Frightened by the man's threatening words, she slammed down the handset. Shivering, she hugged herself. She hadn't recognized the voice, but a sinking feeling told her it didn't matter. That man knew her, and hanging up on him wasn't going to deter him in the slightest.

Chapter Five

For several days, Laura worried about the strange phone call. When the man didn't call again and no one in the house mentioned that anything odd had happened, she finally wondered if she'd dreamed the call. Maybe it was another example of the bizarre aftereffects of her injuries.

On the day she had the cast removed from her leg and her physical therapist gave her the go-ahead to use crutches instead of the wheelchair, she also had an appointment with her psychiatrist.

She stated, "I'm going insane, Dr. Lopez. That's all there is to it."

He sorted the pile of paperwork on his desk. "Why do you say that, Laura?"

Of all her many doctors, Dr. Lopez was the only one she actively disliked. Which was funny, because he was the only one who hadn't physically caused her pain. That his demeanor bordered on catatonic calm drove her crazy. He answered questions with questions. Whenever she did manage to pin him down, he tacked on qualifiers.

"I'm still having that dream."

"The book dream. Has anything changed?"

She shook her head. "I hear the animal scream. I'm holding the book. Like this." She mimed clutching a large book against her bosom. "I'm scared. A woman is yelling and there's a bad smell like..." Her nose wrinkled as she tried to conjure the elusive scent. "I don't know what it is. Anyway, somebody is chasing me. He wants the book." She shuddered. She'd first had the dream a few weeks before leaving the hospital. "I dream it almost every night now. It's weird. Some of it seems so real, some of it is obviously a dream."

"Hmm, what else?"

"It's the same old thing. I'm remembering things, but no one else remembers what I remember."

"Such as?" He scribbled on a sheet of paper.

One of these days she'd grab whatever it was he was always doodling on, and see what he wrote about her. "I live in a house Ryder insists I designed and decorated. It's a crazy-quilt mansion in the middle of a beautiful valley. But it looks like a mad French king or a panel of drunks with gold credit cards decorated it. It is truly unforgettable."

"And so you do remember it?"

"No. What I remember is a studio apartment. There are three apartments and wooden stairs in the building, so you can hear everybody going in and out. I have a couch that I bought at a flea market for ten bucks. It was bright orange, but I had it recovered in blue-gray tweed. I have a futon instead of a bed. I have a desk made out of two file cabinets and a door blank." She frowned, wondering what he'd say about her memories concerning computers and the vague worries she harbored about letting somebody down, somebody who depended on her to do something with the computers. Though that sounded nuttiest of all, she finally told him about it.

"Very vivid. What do you make of this?"

She rolled her eyes. "Ryder insists I never lived in an apartment like that. He also says I've never held a job and the idea of me doing anything with a computer is ridiculous. In fact, he laughed at me! It's times like that when I'm just positive as can be that Laura Hudson is someone else and I'm suffering for her crimes."

"Suffering for her crimes? That's a very interesting thing for you to say, Laura. Let's talk about that for a moment."

"I don't mean suffering... I don't know what I mean."

"Do you wish you were someone other than Laura?"

She slipped a finger inside her blouse and tugged up a wayward brassiere strap. Adding insult to injury, all her clothes, including her underwear, were too big for her.

She chewed her upper lip for a moment, and stared blankly at the dusty foliage of a silk ficus tree. "I don't think I was a very nice person before. I don't have any friends. My daughter hates me. The only person who seems to like me is a beautician named Janelle."

She drifted a moment, wondering why Ryder tortured himself by taking her to the beauty salon every two weeks. While she had her hair and nails done, he waited, his expression painfully uncomfortable, an unread magazine on his lap. If a woman spoke to him, he blushed. Janelle's gentle teasing made him sweat.

"Let's go back to your daughter for a moment. Why do you think she hates you?"

Because I'm a bad, horrible person, and you're right, Doc, I wish I was someone else... that other Laura isn't me....

"Talking about your daughter upsets you."

She snatched tissues from a box on the desk. "The only way she'll come into my room is when her father carries

her. If he does make her see me, then she has a tantrum."
She made herself look at him. "I think I've hurt her. But
I don't remember how or when or why."

"Have you asked your husband?"

"Once. He wouldn't tell me." She scrubbed at her eyes
then worried the damp tissue between her fingers. "I'm
scared to ask too much."

"Why do you think he won't tell you?"

She'd asked herself that very question a hundred, no, a
thousand times. The only answer she could find was that
she'd been such a horrible, brutal monster that Ryder
couldn't bear to remind her of what she'd done to an in-
nocent child.

"It's something he wants to forget," she said, more to
herself than to the shrink. Ryder's smile filled her mind's
eye. When he smiled, his eyes shone with wonderful light.
She'd do anything to have him smiling all the time.
"Maybe he hopes I'll never remember. That I won't be
that other Laura anymore."

"Do you want to change?"

"I want a relationship with my child." She closed her
eyes and shook her head. "I can't remember having a
baby, so it really isn't about me. I have a responsibility to
her. She's only six years old. She needs a mother and I'm
the only one she has."

When she finally escaped the psychiatrist's office, Ryder was waiting for her. Setting a magazine aside, he
asked, "How did it go?"

She absorbed his words and his tone of voice. He asked
her that question whenever she finished an appointment
with a doctor or physical therapist. *How did it go?* She'd
always accepted the question as his way of being polite.
Today she heard his concern and remembered the heart-

wrenching vigil he'd kept by her bedside when she'd been critically ill.

Ryder had hope.

He hoped she got well.

Laura wished with all her heart that he hoped they could be husband and wife again.

"It went well," she said.

He hovered anxiously at her back, his hands barely brushing her shoulder. "Are you sure you're strong enough for crutches?"

She didn't feel strong enough to tweak a mouse's tail. Without the cast, her left leg threatened to float away. Her right leg was in only slightly better shape. Her back ached constantly.

She lifted her chin. "I'm getting stronger every day. May I have my hat, please?"

He settled the broad-brimmed felt hat on her head. It served double duty in covering her slow-growing hair and shielding her tender face from the sun.

She prayed Ryder didn't hope she'd ever be beautiful again.

Downstairs in the lobby, while she waited for Ryder to bring the Jeep around, she hobbled into the hospital gift shop for a pack of gum. Rolls of Lifesavers hard candy caught her attention. Butter rum. The memory of the rich butterscotch flavor was too piddly to be anything except real. She purchased two rolls of candy along with the gum.

On the drive home, she watched the scenery. The grass on the hillsides was starting to green up, but the late-blooming scrub oaks hunched prickly and brown around the juts of gray granite and red sandstone formations. As they left the little town of Palmer Lake and turned onto the dirt road leading to the ranch, she chewed gum to ease the pressure on her ears.

Ryder glanced at her. "I can get the road paved, I think."

"What?"

He came to a patch of road that had been washboarded for traction. He slowed the Jeep to a crawl. Even so, they bounced and rattled. "I said, maybe it's about time I thought about paving this road." He swerved to miss a pothole.

She gritted her teeth and clung to the armrest. Her back muscles felt on fire. "Don't bother on my account."

Once they reached the house, Ryder pulled the Jeep around the circular drive. The ride from Colorado Springs always left her feeling as if she'd just run a marathon. She had to lean heavily on Ryder in order to get out.

"I'll carry you upstairs," he said.

"Not on your life, buster." She lowered a glower on the steps leading into the courtyard. "I've been waiting too long for this. Crutches, please."

"Laura . . ."

"It's not like I'm jumping off a mountain, Ryder." She chuckled. "Besides, I survived your driving."

Her gentle spoken dig made him hang his head. A flash of dark hair caught her eye.

Abby peeked at them from around the courtyard wall. Knowing the little girl would probably like nothing better than seeing her mother fall on her butt gave Laura extra incentive to do well with the crutches. Balancing on her good leg, she settled the arm pieces under her arms and made sure she had a good hold on the grips. She concentrated on what her therapist had shown her. Balance, swing the crutches forward, make sure they were firmly in place and lean into them. She made her awkward way across the graveled driveway. She paused to catch her breath.

Eyes wide and astonished, Abby stepped into view. She stared at the crutches. Laura grinned. Already she was sweating and out of breath, but she kept going. Hop up on the step, bring up the crutches, find her balance, hop up the next step.

"I made it!" she announced in triumph.

Ryder loosed a long, relieved-sounding breath. He lifted his hat and mopped his brow with a kerchief.

Even better, Abby crept forward. "You're walking."

Laura raised her left leg. "No more cast." Her leg, so thin her stocking sagged at the ankle, still felt as if it wanted to float away. "So, if you two will excuse me, I think I'll go upstairs." Not caring how long it took her, she made her slow way across the courtyard and into the house.

She stopped at the base of the stairs.

Who in her right mind ever thought this horrible double-curved staircase with open marble steps was a good idea? If she tripped, she'd break her neck.

Sensing a presence behind her, she discovered Abby had slipped through the doors. Why the child was fascinated by the crutches, Laura hadn't a clue. She wasn't going to look this particular gift horse in the mouth, though.

She grasped the white-enameled banister and tucked the crutches under her left arm. It might take all day, but she could do this. Holding tightly on to the banister, she hopped up the first riser.

Up she went, one riser at a time. Hop, rest, catch her breath, adjust her grip on the crutches, hop another step.

Like a dark little shadow, Abby followed her to the second floor.

At the doorway to her suite, Laura leaned against the jamb and grinned at the little girl. She was exhausted, and sweat dripped off her face and soaked her blouse, but she'd made it. She was mobile, a prisoner no more. Triumph as much as exertion left her light-headed.

Looking at Abby's curious little face, Laura remembered Abby was the one who liked butter-rum Lifesavers. She fished in her pocket and brought out a roll. Winking, she tossed it across the hallway and Abby caught it in both hands. Her big eyes got bigger.

"There you go, kiddo, don't tell your mom." Giddy with victory, she entered her room for some much-needed rest.

DAY BY DAY, Laura grew stronger.

Her physical therapist gave her a list of exercises to build her strength and ease the chronic pain in her back and legs. She made good use of the indoor swimming pool and gym.

One day, she finished her sixth lap and was clinging to the pool side, catching her breath, when she noticed Abby. Lately, she'd often see her daughter lurking, peering at her through doorways or shadowing her to the pool. Today the girl stood behind a pool chair.

"Hey," Laura said, gasping. "Did I really do forty or fifty laps a day?"

Abby lifted her shoulders in a quick shrug.

Laboriously, Laura hauled herself out of the water. She slumped on the tiles. "Hand me that towel, would you?"

Wide-eyed, looking poised to run at the slightest threat, Abby sidled to the chaise where Laura had draped a towel. Just as cautiously, she gave the towel to Laura.

"Thanks, honey." She daubed at her dripping hair and wet face. "Do you like to swim?"

"I like riding my pony." Abby clamped her arms around her midsection and thrust her chin forward as if expecting an argument. "He's a nice pony. His name is Buttermilk, just like Dale Evans's horse. Daddy gave him to me."

"I've seen your daddy riding his horse. I bet you two have fun riding around in the mountains." She stretched out her legs and compared them. Her left leg was still thinner than the right, but muscle was beginning to add shape. "Wish I could go riding with you."

"You said horses are icky. You *hate* horses."

"Oh."

"Your swimmy suit is funny."

Laura had to laugh. She'd gained eight pounds since leaving the hospital. It still wasn't enough to fit her clothing. This tank suit was the only swimsuit that fit, and even it took numerous safety pins to keep it from falling off in the water.

"It feels funny, too. I think I need a new one."

"All your clothes look funny."

From the mouths of babes, Laura thought with a sigh. Her suite had three closets, and all of them were jammed with clothes that didn't fit. She hadn't a thing to wear.

She pushed upright. As long as she took it very slow, she didn't need the cane that had replaced her crutches. "I may have to go shopping. What about you? Do you want to go shopping for some new clothes?"

Abby jumped as if touched with an electrified wire. Her face turned bright red and her eyes filled with fury. She screamed, "I hate shopping and I hate you!" Her scream echoed off the tiles as she raced out of the pool house.

Frozen in astonishment, Laura stared at the door where Abby had disappeared. Her throat tightened. Her vision blurred. She drew several deep, cleansing breaths.

"Shopping," she whispered. "All right, baby, I'll cross that one off my list."

RYDER CHECKED his watch. Laura and Abby were both late. He paced the length of the dining room, his boot heels clicking on the marble. He was tired of eating in Laura's room and tired of Abby complaining that he never ate dinner with her anymore.

Laura finally arrived. Using her cane, she made her careful way to the table. Ryder resisted the urge to help her. Ever since the cast had come off her leg, she'd turned fiercely independent. She'd released her nurse. She no longer allowed Mrs. Weatherbee to bring breakfast on a tray. She spent countless hours in the pool house.

All the hard work was paying off, he noticed with a start. Although he'd canceled his appearances on the art-show circuit, he'd been busy lately, catching up on the commissions he'd neglected while Laura had been in the hospital. In a sick sort of way, Laura's accident and the rumors that he'd tried to kill her had been great for business. Notoriety had tripled the value of his limited edition prints, and his agent was even now negotiating a million-dollar commission with a German who was an avid collector of American cowboy art. During all the craziness, he hadn't been paying a lot of attention to Laura's appearance.

Not even the kindest person could claim Laura was the gorgeous creature she once was, but she looked pretty good. Her hair was not quite sable like Abby's, but dark, except for a lightning bolt of pure white following the worst scar on her skull. A soft, simple hairstyle highlighting the white streak gave her a striking appearance.

In her silk lounge pajamas, she reminded him of a yearling doe, all long legs and shyness.

He grabbed the back of a chair and pulled it away from the table. She smiled in gratitude.

Her face wasn't destroyed, he thought. The tender pink scars weren't pretty, but she wasn't Frankenstein's monster, either. He tried to conjure an image of her previous perfection. Her soft brown eyes distracted him.

"You look nice."

Her slim hand fluttered to the base of her throat. She'd used a large brooch to close the plunging neckline. "Thank you." She settled onto the chair and he eased her to the table.

Mrs. Weatherbee brought a tray of canapés.

Laura said, "The table is gorgeous. I just love the centerpiece. You're very clever when it comes to pine cones and ribbon."

To Ryder's utter amazement, the dour woman practically wriggled. The corners of her mouth tipped in a smug smile. "I rather like it myself, Mrs. H. We need some color considering all this darn snow we've been having. Crazy thing, having spring in February and now here it is May and we're having winter. Hmph!"

Laura plucked at her trouser leg. "And thanks so much for taking in the waistband. They fit perfectly."

"Any time." The housekeeper gave Ryder a snooty look before marching back to her kitchen.

He slid a hand over the back of his neck and clutched hair in his fingers. The two women almost seemed like friends. How, why or when that had happened, he hadn't a clue.

"I'm so lucky she's around," Laura said as she selected a bread round topped with smoked salmon and dill. "I had hoped I remembered how to sew, but no amount of hoping helps. If it wasn't for her, I'd have nothing to wear. I'm sorry, Ryder, but I think I'm going to have to break down and buy something."

"No problem."

"You always say that, but honestly, there are tons of clothes up there. It's such a waste."

He scowled, unable to believe those words came out of her mouth. "You never worried about buying clothes before."

"Obviously. Hmm, perhaps a seamstress could alter what I've got." She nodded at the four place settings on the table. "Are we expecting company?"

"Tom Sorry." Tom didn't want to come to dinner, but Ryder had insisted. Tom had been so busy with moving the longhorns from winter to summer pasture; Ryder hadn't had time to talk to him about the ranch.

"Where is Abby?"

"Coming around. Would you like a drink? Wine?"

"No, thank you, I'm fine." She rested her chin on her hand. "I'm curious. That building out back next to the barn. You spend most of your time there. I thought this was a cattle ranch."

He scratched the back of his head. "The only cattle are my longhorns. I use them for models. That's my studio." She had never liked his artwork, except for the money it brought into the house, and he never mentioned it because her dislike hurt his feelings. It hit him that she didn't remember his art and maybe she didn't remember her dislike. All this time, she'd apparently thought he was working cattle. "I'm an artist, darlin'. I paint."

"Oh." She looked to an abstract hanging on the wall. "Did you paint that?"

"You bought that in France. Same place you had the nude portrait done. I paint cowboys and such. You prefer modern art."

Her nose wrinkled. "I have truly horrible taste, don't I?" She sighed. "How in the world do you stand this house?"

Stunned, he laughed. "I figured you liked it. But if you don't, then you won't get any objections from me if you want to change it."

"I can't see wasting your money like that."

He moved to her side and touched her shoulder. The knob of bone underneath satiny fabric emphasized her fragility; a warm welling of protectiveness spread like melted butter through his chest. "I've got lots of money, darlin'. If it makes you feel better spending it, then go right ahead." He wanted to laugh again. The wreck had robbed her of beauty, but had given her some character. To his way of thinking, that was a hell of a deal.

Abby sauntered into the dining room. She was strutting like an underdog contender into a prizefight ring, and the look on her face dared Ryder to say a word.

He was too shocked for speech.

Clumps of reddish mud had dried in her tousled hair. Her blue jeans were suspiciously green, and her shirt looked as if a boar hog had used it for a hankie. Her hands were black to the elbow. Her tight little grimace and glittering eyes challenged her mother to battle.

Holding her glare on Laura, she clambered onto a chair and grabbed a canapé.

Laura's nose twitched.

Seeing Abby was about to knock the platter off the table, Ryder rescued it. "Now, you look here, young lady, I don't know what you think you're pulling but—"

"I hate her!" Abby hollered. She snatched a plate and sent it flying. It crashed onto the marble. "I hate her!"

"That's it! I've put up with about—"

"Ryder," Laura said. She grasped his upper arm, and her slim fingers squeezed his biceps. "Please."

He shook her off. "Young lady, you've stepped way out of line this time."

Abby faced him squarely. In the months of Laura's convalescence, she'd acquired reckless courage and she wasn't about to back down now.

"This isn't your fight, Ryder," Laura said. "She's angry with me, not you. So please, sit down. It's about time I start acting like her mother."

Fear tied a slipknot in his guts and jerked tight. That he had no parental rights was one thing he hoped Laura never remembered. Even Abby heard the implied threat. The skin paled around her eyes and mouth.

"Now, Abby," Laura said, her voice calm and assured. "If you are angry with me, you can tell me you are angry with me. Are you?"

The girl fidgeted her way off the chair. She eyed Ryder uncertainly.

"Well, fine. If you don't wish to speak to me, you don't have to. But, just because you're mad, you are not to break plates. We don't do that in this house."

"You break plates," Abby said. Her sullen glare dared Laura to contradict her.

Laura looked to Ryder for confirmation. He'd stopped counting long ago the number of plates and lamps she'd busted. He nodded.

"Oh. Well, I was wrong, then. I apologize, deeply and truly. I will never break a plate again as long as I live. But I know I don't come to dinner filthy. So you go wash your hands and brush that gunk out of your hair." She held up an admonishing finger. "But first, you will tell your daddy you're sorry for being rude."

"Daddy?"

"Yes, your daddy. He's very proud of you and it hurts his feelings when you act naughty. You're mad at me, not him. I think you should apologize."

Her big eyes turned liquid and her lower lip trembled. "I'm sorry, Daddy."

Certain he must be dreaming, he murmured, "All right, sugar bear, I accept. Go wash up."

Abby scuffled to the door. She glanced at Laura then picked up the bigger pieces of broken china. Casting her mother a last mournful look, she slunk out of the room.

Laura turned a gentle, reproachful gaze on him. "Honestly, Ryder, you spoil that child rotten. You've no call to lose your temper when she acts up."

His temper.

"I appreciate so much the way you've taken up the slack, but I don't know if that's the best thing for her. I have no right to criticize because I've been so passive, but you're much too indulgent. We have to set limits and stick to them. It's for Abby's own good. She'll be much happier if we do. I'm sure of it."

His cheek muscles twitched.

"Ryder? Are we agreed?"

"Ah, depends on the limits you're talking about."

"The usual. Regular bedtime, meals with the family, not so much television. I understand she's quite responsible with her pony, so perhaps a chore or two around the house—"

He sat down hard. One of the first things he'd done after Laura's accident was finally give Abby a pony. "You know about the pony?"

She raised an eyebrow. "If you mean to keep it a secret, then Abby needs to bathe more often."

"You hate horses. You always forbade Abby to have anything to do with them."

She shook her head in firm denial. "Oh, for goodness sake. In any case, it will be good for her to have a chore. She is in kindergarten, after all. No longer a baby."

Tom Sorry walked into the dining room. Head down, he looked as uncomfortable as a hound dog at a wedding. He swept off his hat and held it to his chest. "Ma'am, boss. Evening."

"Have a seat, Tom. Can I get you a drink?"

"Whatever you're having is just fine." He eased onto a chair and set his hat beneath it. He gave Laura a shy smile. "Looking mighty fine this evening, ma'am. I take it you're doing good?"

Laura smiled. "I'm doing..." Her words faltered and so did the smile. A crease appeared between her eyebrows.

"Laura?" Ryder watched in alarm as color drained from her face. "What's the matter?"

She gave a start. "Oh! I'm sorry, I, uh, excuse me." Hot pink bloomed on her cheeks.

Ryder looked between her and Tom. The man's expression was frozen in mortification. Ryder guessed Laura finally remembered how much she despised his best friend and how shabbily she'd treated him in the past.

Laura dabbed at her lips with a napkin. Looking at the tall, craggy-faced cowboy, she remembered vividly the way he'd once kissed her. She could almost feel her hand clasped firmly inside his and the way his calluses rasped her skin. He had swung her hand in rhythm to their walk.

"Take a ride with me in the moonlight, honey," he'd teased.

He'd kissed her. She'd kissed him back and tasted pink bubble gum on his breath and smelled horse on his collar. She'd kissed him!

God only knew what else they'd done.

Chapter Six

If you remember...

Laura spent a restless, tormented night hearing those words over and over again.

In the early morning, she stood before the antique secretary in her bedroom and stared down at Becky Solerno's business card. The investigator had penciled her personal home telephone number under her office number.

"Anytime," Becky had said, "day or night. If you remember anything about the accident, call me."

A wave of nausea left Laura shuddering. She clearly remembered walking hand in hand with Tom and listening to the self-effacing way he talked. She remembered kissing him. Whatever else had happened between them was blotted from her memory, but how dare the man, anyway! Enduring dinner with that aw-shucks hypocrite while he pretended to be Ryder's friend had been more painful than plastic surgery, more agonizing than physical therapy.

Tom must have been the man who called her. The more she thought about it, the more she realized he had tried to take advantage of her injuries and amnesia. What a thoroughly disgusting creature.

Disgusting enough to have attempted murder?

She picked up the card, but immediately set it down.

Ryder must suspect she'd taken lovers. Which would explain why he never kissed her and had yet to return to their bedroom. Thinking about her with another man—or several men—must repulse him. She stared at a wall, envisioning her closets, which were full of sexy, clingy, trampy clothing; spike-heeled shoes, peekaboo underwear and skirts slit up to never land.

She'd been an adulteress! A cheater, a liar and a woman on the prowl.

Self-loathing curled around her like a python, squeezing her ribs and choking her throat. Her child hated her, she cheated on her husband, she had no friends—she wished she had died in the accident.

She picked up the investigator's card again. *Day or night . . .*

Their probable conversation played through her head. She heard herself say, "I think Tom Sorry is the man who tried to kill me. You see, Becky, I remember he kissed me. I must have been loose and easy, a cheater. And I think he's the man who threatened me on the telephone."

Then Becky would reply, "So how many men do you think you slept with while married to Ryder? Is Tom Sorry the only one?"

Becky would interrogate Tom Sorry. Ryder would find out about the affair. It might be the excuse he needed to get rid of her. At the very least it would destroy his and Tom's relationship. And all based upon what? She didn't have a shred of real proof anywhere that the cowboy had harmed her.

For all she knew, kissing the cowboy could be another trick played by her flaky memory. Or it could be part of a dream, like the book dream, which was still making regular appearances in her sleeping consciousness.

She swept the investigator's card into a drawer and shut it. Uneasy about whether she'd done the right thing, she limped through the doorway to the sitting room. She pulled the gold silk draperies aside. Yesterday it had snowed like crazy. Today the sun shone, burning away any trace of winter. Misty steam curled off the pastures. Moisture on the aspen trees made them glitter as if made of glass.

Lights were on inside Ryder's studio. So, he was an artist. At least that explained why she occasionally smelled turpentine when he was around. It didn't explain why he bored her with vacuous talk. It didn't explain his quiet caution around her, or why he was always in a hurry to get away from her. More and more she was beginning to think he didn't want her to remember her past.

Or maybe *he* wanted to forget her past. Forget her. Leave her locked inside this ugly house—isolated, ignorant, friendless and unloved.

She wanted to talk to him about her accident and their life together. She'd even risk confessing her affair with Tom Sorry if it meant bringing her and Ryder closer.

"Mrs. H.? Are you all right?"

Laura turned from the window. Dashing surreptitiously at her teary eyes, she flashed a weak smile at the housekeeper, who carried a large brown box.

"The UPS man stopped by." She placed the box on a table. "Would you like me to open it?"

"Sure." She'd ordered some clothing from a catalog. The prospect of wearing something that fit gave her a flutter of excitement. The housekeeper ripped off tape and opened the flaps.

"There you go, ma'am. I'll be pleased to press the packing wrinkles out of your new things."

"Thank you." Laura pulled out the top item, a simple linen and silk dress with three-quarter sleeves and buttons up the front. She searched through the box for the flower-printed petticoat to wear under it.

"That's very nice," Mrs. Weatherbee said.

Laura glanced toward her closets. "Everything I have is so …" *Flashy and trampy.* "Fancy." She smoothed a hand over the soft dress. The order included several dresses, underwear and a pair of pink ballerina flats.

"I just can't get over how much you've changed," Mrs. Weatherbee said as she shook out the dress. She eyed the wrinkles critically.

"Am I really that different?"

"As long as you're asking, then I'll tell you. No offense, but it's all for the better. Used to be, you were all outside and no inside. I wouldn't wish what you've been through on anybody, but it knocked loose what good there was inside and brought it to the light."

"I'm not certain I follow."

"Hmm." The housekeeper held up the dress by the shoulders. "Before, the only thing that mattered was the way you looked. I don't think you even liked that. Shoot, I never knew what you'd look like from one day to the next. Sometimes you were a blonde and sometimes a carrot top. You spent more time in beauty parlors than most women spend in the kitchen. I must have seen fifty different hair colors on your head."

Laura touched her hair. The white streak that followed the surgical scar had at first bothered her, but now she rather liked it. It drew attention away from the shiny scar tissue ringing her face.

"What color looked best?"

Mrs. Weatherbee sniffed. "I think that pretty chestnut you're wearing is just fine. If you're asking." She laughed suddenly and her big shoulders lifted. "You couldn't even decide what color your eyes were! One day blue, another green. You were a regular chameleon."

"Oh." That solved a minor mystery Laura had been pondering. Though her eyesight was fine, she'd found dozens of contact lens cases in her bathroom.

"To tell you the truth, I like this dress a hundred times better than anything in your closets."

Laura silently agreed. "I take it I was quite fashion conscious."

"Oh, my good Lord, yes. You couldn't miss a fashion show or pass up one of those magazines. I don't think you ever wore an outfit twice. You reminded me of that actress, what's her name, who always looks like a different person in every show. She even puts on a different voice..." Her mouth twisted in a disapproving grimace. "No offense, but shop and show off was about all you ever did."

Another mystery solved. Ryder spoke to her of fashion not for him, but because of her. He must think that's all she cared about. She could have cried.

"I appreciate your candor, Mrs. Weatherbee. Far more than you can know. And yes, I'd appreciate it very much if you'd press this dress for me. I'd like to wear it today."

Time for a chat with Mr. Ryder Hudson, Laura thought.

It took the housekeeper about as much time to press the new clothes as it did for Laura to brush her hair and use a curling iron. In her bathroom, she lightly pushed around bottles and cases of cosmetics. No memories filtered to the surface. Nothing felt familiar.

She didn't have the same tastes as she did before.

She no longer felt any urges to cheat or lie.

Maybe Dr. Lopez was right after all and at least some of her amnesia was psychological. The accident gave her an opportunity to shed her unhappy past like an outgrown skin.

She applied a bit of mascara to her lashes and a dusting of blush to her pale cheeks. A light coat of lipstick made her crooked mouth look more natural.

Her new dress was loose and airy, pretty in its soft blue color over the bright petticoat.

She smiled at her reflection, mustering courage. Her husband was a good man. He was generous and kind and he went out of his way to take good care of her. He stinted on nothing—except his time. If she wanted more of his time, then it was up to her to earn it.

Using her cane because Ryder grew anxious when she didn't, she braved the cool air outside on the way to the studio. She let herself in.

The studio astonished her. The high ceiling with exposed beams was cut with skylights that enhanced the light streaming through the banks of plate glass. A country-and-western singer crooned mournfully through wall-mounted speakers. Tables held stacks of wood, rolls of canvas and boxes and jars full of paints and brushes. The smells of pine-sharp turpentine and linseed oil mingled with the flat chemical smells of paint.

The studio fairly breathed with vitality, crackled with creative energy. After the overblown sterility of the house, it was an oasis of color and texture and scent.

Hearing Ryder speaking to someone, she wandered slowly between the tables. One held dozens of tiny wax figures of cowboys, horses and cattle. Another was covered with watercolor paintings. Every inch of wall space and every thick column post was covered with sketches and photographs. Framing materials hung in one corner over a table laid with an elaborate framing machine and mat cutter.

She reached a doorway and peered in at an office. It was little more than a closet big enough for a desk and file cabinets, and it was as messy and overstuffed as the studio. Ryder perched a hip on the desk while he talked on the telephone.

He didn't look happy. "I don't care about the deadline. The colors aren't right and the prints look muddy. I'm destroying the whole run. I can't be putting my John Hancock on something I hate." He rubbed his eyes with the flats of his fingers. "All right! One week, I promise. I'll find another printer." He smiled, nodding. "And same to you, buddy. Say hello to Penny and the kids for me." He hung up and sighed.

He looked at Laura and jumped. A cup overturned and pencils clattered to the floor.

"I'm sorry," she said. "I didn't mean to startle you."

"What are you doing here?"

His suspiciousness disheartened her. "Is this forbidden territory?"

"Uh, no." He cleared magazines and file folders off the desk chair and offered it to her. He crouched to pick up pencils.

She eased onto the chair. "I wanted to talk to you. But it's a bad time, I suppose. You seem busy."

"Discombobulated, more like," he said with a wry grin. "The faster I move, the more behind I get."

"Who were you talking to?"

"My agent. I was supposed to send him some lithos, but they didn't come back right from the printers. So I'm behind schedule and the galleries are chewing on his leg. I don't like the printer, so that means shopping for another." He dropped the pencils in the cup. "Never mind, it's nothing that would interest you."

"Don't say that."

"What?"

"That it won't interest me. I think you're a very interesting man. This studio and your art, it's like wonderland. It's a side of you I hadn't expected, but I think it's marvelous."

He pulled at his jaw and lowered his face so she could see only the suspicious gleam in his eyes beneath his hat.

"The entire world has disappeared for me," she said softly, "and I need to start living again."

His eyes darted around the room. Leaning his backside against the desk, he rubbed his hands on his thighs. "Do you want to go shopping or throw a party?" He thrust his face forward and his gaze swept her head to toe. "That's a new outfit. Nice."

She choked down her impatience. "Thank you, but what I want to do is have a serious talk with you." She held up a hand. "Please, no fashion, no sales, no who's doing what for what foundation and wearing what to what party. Not a word about television shows. I hate TV. Maybe I wanted to talk about those things before, but I'm not in the least bit interested now."

The broad brim of his hat cast a shadow over his face, but still his skepticism came through loud and clear. "So what do you want to talk about?"

"Us."

He crossed his legs and slid a hand over the back of his neck. His cheek twitched. "There's not much to say."

"We're married. We must have a history."

His voice dropped to a mumble. "We never were much of an us."

Her chest began to ache. "Surely we have some common interests."

He frowned and idly adjusted the angle of his hat. "You never liked the ranch. You refused to live in my cabin, so that's why I built the big house for you. You think my friends are hicks and stump-jumpers, and you won't go to a rodeo or stock show on a bet. You can't stand animals. You don't have much use for my painting. You never went to art shows with me." He lifted his shoulders. "I went with you to those fancy shindigs, but I'm not much for formal parties. You always had a taste for folks who like your bank account better than they like you."

Not feeling tremendously sorry for herself took almost physical effort. She forced her hands to remain still in her lap. She focused on keeping her breathing slow and steady. That he preferred to be doing anything other than having this talk came through loud and clear. All her questions and logical thoughts shriveled and dried into dust.

"I guess you want to go back to work."

He nodded and pushed away from the desk. "We can talk more at supper."

His relief broke her heart. She knew if she accepted defeat now, she'd never work up the nerve to try again. "If I promise not to bother you, may I stay here?"

He recoiled, eyes wide. "It's dirty."

"I can neaten it up. Please, Ryder? I need something to do. I'm so bored, I'm dying. I can't live like this anymore. I feel like a turtle in a glass bowl. I promise, cross my heart, I will not disturb you or throw anything away." Though ashamed of her begging, desperation made her try a winning smile. "Please?"

Looking more confused than anything, he said she could stay. He left the office and went to a large canvas mounted on an easel. From the doorway she watched him. He picked up a brush, but looked at her instead of the canvas.

She slipped back inside the office and slumped on the chair. Holding the cane in both hands, she ground the rubber tip against the floor and tried to remember what Mrs. Weatherbee had said. The good inside her had been knocked free so it showed outside—or words to that effect. She *had* changed. Her life meant more than empty society shindigs and spending Ryder's hard-earned money.

From the floor she picked up an envelope. It had a return address from an art gallery in Atlanta, Georgia. The postmark told her it had been mailed more than a month ago. She noticed a lot of unopened mail. Some was stacked willy-nilly on the desk and file cabinets, some had fallen onto the floor. Gathering the mail, she noted some of it was months old.

She stepped to the doorway. "Ryder? There's a lot of mail to tend. Would you like me to sort it?"

He gave her a wave that told her to do whatever she wanted. She doubted he'd paid any attention to what she'd said.

She cleared a spot on the desk top. For a moment the computer distracted her. She fingered the monitor screen lightly, mindful not to rub dust so it scratched the glass. The white casing plucked a faint chord deep inside her.

Shaking the strange feeling away, she began opening Ryder's mail. Several envelopes, from a man she guessed was Ryder's agent, contained checks. One check, two months old, was for one hundred and twenty thousand dollars. Incredulous, she counted the zeros several times until she convinced herself the amount was for real.

She wanted to march up to Ryder and demand to know why he was so careless. Except, if he cared, then he wouldn't have let his correspondence get so far behind in the first place. So she squashed down her irritation and kept sorting the mail, eventually ending up with several piles stacked in order of perceived importance.

A quick check of the desk drawers produced a bank ledger and deposit slips. The ledger hadn't been reconciled in months. How the man survived, she hadn't a clue.

She took the checks to Ryder.

She glanced at the painting he worked on, then did a double take. It showed a dilapidated log building with crooked windows and plank doors. A pair of saddled horses was tied to a hitching rail. In the foreground, using a wooden fruit basket tacked to the building, two cowboys played basketball.

Placing a hand over her mouth to keep from laughing at the whimsical charm of the scene, she watched him paint. With a firm hand, he daubed color onto the canvas. There was something incongruous about the sight of him, tall and lean and hard-bodied, in his tight jeans and boots, his hat cocked at a rakish angle, looking as if he should be riding the range chasing cows, yet wielding the paintbrush with the sure confidence of a master. Even as she watched, the cowboy holding the ball developed a mischievous glint in his eyes as he laid up for a shot. It was ten—no, fifty times better than any of the ugly, abstract paintings hanging in the house.

She waited until he lowered his brush before speaking. "It's wonderful."

He actually blushed. "It's different, anyway." He looked between her and the painting. "Do you really like it?"

"They look so real, I can see the dust on them and how their boots are worn from rubbing against the stirrups. The horses are beautiful. So alive." She met his eyes and the warmth in them melted her insides, making her knees feel weak and her stomach all funny. She thrust a pen and the checks at him. "I don't want to disturb you. So if you'll just take a moment and sign these, I'll put them in the mail to the bank."

He caught his lower lip in his strong white teeth. He endorsed the checks.

For the first time she could remember, Laura felt like Mrs. Ryder Hudson, wife and member of the family.

LAURA PAUSED in the doorway of Abby's bedroom. The room represented every cliché possible for sugar and spice and everything nice—white-painted French provincial furniture with hand-painted roses and ribbons on the bed headboard and on drawer fronts; pink gingham ruffles on the canopy bed and windows; wallpaper patterned with pink and white roses among pale green ivy vines; floor-to-ceiling shelves stocked with fluffy stuffed animals; children's classic storybooks perched on bookshelves; heart-shaped throw rugs atop the velvety carpet.

It was as neat as a museum display. None of the toys looked played with.

Hearing footsteps on the back stairs, Laura recognized Abby's skipping tread. Her baby, so tiny and perfect, home from kindergarten. Every day, Mrs. Weatherbee picked her up from school. No doubt, on the long ride home Abby had regaled the woman with the doings of her class and what she'd learned from the teacher.

Laura wanted that place in her daughter's heart. She wanted to read her stories and help her learn her numbers and letters. Abby turned the corner and stopped short. Rebellion tightened her features.

"There's a lot of pink in your room," Laura said, taking care with each word. "Do you like pink?"

Abby eyed her suspiciously and edged a step closer to the stairs. "No."

"Why did I put so much pink in your room, then? I don't particularly like this cotton-candy color, either."

Abby shrugged.

"It was rather silly of me to put all your dolls up so high, too. How do you reach them?"

"They're leckables," Abby said.

Laura had to think about it a moment before realizing the child meant collectibles. "Oh. So where are the toys you play with?"

Abby fingered the wall and twisted her boot toe on the floor. "I let my pony keep 'em."

An image formed in Laura's mind. The lonely little girl sneaking into the barn, far away from her mother's critical eye, and stashing her precious toys under the straw or inside a wooden box full of dusty grain. Emotion rose in Laura's throat. She struggled to maintain her calm. "What would you think about redoing your room? Only this time you pick the colors and we'll put those collectibles somewhere else so there's room for your toys."

"I can pick the colors?" Abby asked suspiciously. "Even green?"

"If you want. It's your room."

Abby sidled toward Laura. "And purple. I like purple."

"Green and purple, very cheerful. Some catalogs came in the mail this week. While you have your snack in the kitchen, we can look at them and see if there's anything in there you like."

"Okay."

"And maybe you can help me pick some nice colors for the living room."

"I'm not 'lowed in the living room."

Laura bit back an exclamation of disbelief. She forced a smile. "That's the old rule. The new rule is, this is your house and you can go anywhere you want to."

Abby glanced at the French doors. "Even on the balcony?"

"Sure. You're a big girl, you won't fall off. You do promise to not fall off, right?"

Abby narrowed her eyes. "Even your bedroom?"

"If you knock first. It's only polite."

"I'm polite, Mama."

Laura's heart filled and overflowed. *Mama.* Pushing her luck, she offered a hand. "Let's go on down to the kitchen and look at the catalogs. I think Mrs. Weatherbee made some apple crisp. I bet she'll let us snitch a little piece."

Abby eased her tiny hand into Laura's.

"You know what? You're the best little girl in the world. I sure am glad you're mine."

Abby squeezed Laura's finger and held on tight all the way down the stairs to the kitchen.

PREOCCUPIED with thinking about bison, Ryder strode from the garage to the house. His rocky forest land wouldn't support many animals, but after spending a day at Shook's Hollow Ranch photographing its domesticated herd, the idea tickled him more than ever.

His daughter stood on the very top of a six-foot ladder, stretching precariously toward a spruce tree branch.

His heart dropped into his belly. His camera bag dropped to the ground. He raced across the driveway.

"Whoa there, short stuff!" He caught her around the waist and brought her down to the ground. "Just what do you think you're doing?"

She held up a seed-encrusted suet ball. "I'm gonna feed the pee-pees!" She all but shoved the ball into his face. "Mama said I can."

"Mama did, did she? Did she tell you could break your silly little neck falling off a ladder?"

"I didn't fall."

"Where did you get this ball of seeds, anyway?"

"Mrs. Weatherbee got it at the grocery store."

"What in the world are pee-pees?"

"Oh, Daddy!" She rolled her eyes. "You *know,* the little bitty birds. Chickadees and juncos and creepers. They stay all winter and needs lots and lots of seeds and sewer."

"Suet."

"Suet. Mama says if we hang the balls, they'll be like living Christmas lights. And since it's spring, they need extra."

"Uh-huh. And you asked Mama if you could hang it up? Where is she?" Apparently Laura had forgotten how maddeningly literal and independent Abby could be. Tell the child to take a hike, and before you knew it, she'd be fifty miles away.

"I dunno."

"You stay off the ladder. I'll hang it for you." He set her on the ground and took the seed ball. He asked her where she wanted it. She changed her mind several times before settling on a suitable branch. He gave the wire hanger a securing twist.

He closed the lightweight aluminum ladder. "Now you dragged it out here, you drag it back where you found it."

"Okay, Daddy, thanks!"

He retrieved his camera bag and checked his equipment for damage. No harm done, so he stomped through the house, leaving the bag on a table, and went in search of his wife. She wasn't in the house. He checked his studio.

For a moment, the clean desk and neat stacks of paperwork in his office distracted him. Laura appeared to enjoy puttering around in the office. More amazing, she had a knack for organization. The place was cleaner than it had been in months.

He went to the pool house. Laura wasn't in the water.

He looked through the small window in the sauna door and spotted her inside.

Laura lay on her back, stretched out on a redwood bench. A white towel was draped over her breasts and belly. Eyes closed, pearled with sweat, her body outline softened by clouds of steam, she looked as if she belonged in a sylvan forest.

Heat flooded his groin. He hadn't had sex in what felt like years. Not that he hadn't had ample opportunities. Society columnists had followed Laura's progress from the hospital to her recovery at home, and part of the readership apparently saw the accident as an indication that he was eligible to play the field.

He didn't want a mistress, or even a fling. He wanted his wife.

He turned the handle on the door. Drawn by the stillness of her, he silently slipped into the sauna cell. Hot, wet air made his shirt cling to his back. Laura breathed slow and steady.

He looked down at her, his artist's eye critically studying the changes. The scars on her face were mostly around her hairline and jaw. Her nose and cheekbones were flattened, giving her features an exotic cast. Her lips were thickened, the skin on them smooth and pink. No longer perfect and gorgeous, she looked genuine and real, a natural woman with character. He touched her crooked chin then traced his finger down the long, slim length of her throat. Her collarbones were too prominent, and her breastbone formed a ridge under thin skin.

Her eyelids fluttered and she looked at him.

She gasped and caught the lower edge of the towel, pulling it down on her thighs. "Ryder," she whispered.

The husky note drove straight to his heart.

She bolted upright, clutching at the towel. It slipped, revealing the sensuous curve of a breast and the cool expanse of her hip.

"What do you want?" she asked breathlessly.

He couldn't remember. All he knew was that he was aroused and he wanted her.

"You shouldn't fall asleep in the sauna," he said, more gruffly than he intended. His tongue felt too big.

She scooted down the bench and rose, tucking the towel around her nakedness. "I know. Thanks for waking me. What are you doing here?"

She was escaping, edging toward the door. He sidestepped and slipped an arm around her, pulling her to him. The sharp nip of her waist reminded him of her fragility.

She pressed a hand against his shoulder. Her lips parted and her pupils swelled, darkening her soft eyes. Staring into those soft, curious eyes, he was lost, he drowned. Unable to resist, he kissed her. She was wooden, unresponsive. He kissed her anyway, tasting the salt on her lips and the sweetness of her breath. Underneath the chlorine, she smelled warm, faintly musky.

Her lips softened, and hesitantly, experimentally, she kissed him back. She stopped pushing with her hand and caressed his shoulder. Trying to kiss her easy, he made himself slow down. Effort made him tremble. He wanted her too much, but he felt her wariness the way he could sense when a horse was about to spook.

Her mouth turned hungry, meeting his with hot desire. Her tongue flicked tentatively against his. She slid one hand from his shoulder to the back of his neck, and her fingers were hot underneath his hair. In the small of his back, her other hand clutched convulsively above his belt, fanning his desire.

He held her tighter, kissed her deeper, absorbing her sweetness and the heady scent of womanly musk. His teeth touched hers. Her tongue slithered silkily, wet and soft against his, parrying his thrusts.

She made a small, strangled sound. Alarmed, he lifted his head.

She wept.

He cursed and pulled away. He'd hurt her.

"I'm sorry," she whispered. Tears quivered on the brink, making her eyes shine hotly. "I want to remember you. I want it more than anything. Please, believe me, Ryder. *Please.* I don't know what to do. I don't know how to hold you. How to kiss you or love you. *I don't remember!*"

He pressed the back of his hand to his mouth. The lingering taste of her inflamed him, colored his vision and muddied his thoughts. Her tears shamed him.

"I want to be your wife again, but we're such strangers." Her voice was rough and anguished. "Did you ever love me, Ryder?"

The sauna heat filled his head with wool, and his clothing clung wetly to his body. The ache of his arousal throbbed low in his belly, but her meaning finally penetrated.

Shaking his head to clear it, he held out a hand. "Come on, darlin', it's too hot in here."

Ignoring his hand, she clutched the towel over her bosom. "Do you love me, Ryder? Did you love me once?"

He did—and he didn't. He pushed through the redwood plank door. The chlorine-heavy air hit him like ice water. He gulped in cool breaths.

He'd loved his wife because she was his wife, and husbands loved their wives.

But love *Laura?*

He'd lusted for her. The first time he'd ever seen her it had been as if lightning struck. Her fabulous beauty had blinded him, inflamed him. Nothing had mattered except owning her, and she'd been a hard-won prize.

But love her?

Not the way his father had loved his mother, honestly and simply, sharing a mutual concern and affection for each other that had carried them through nearly thirty years of marriage. Loving Laura had never been comfortable, or honest, for that matter. They'd danced through their relationship like a pair of hungry wolves, respecting each other's teeth, but craving the same piece of meat.

Sensing her behind him, hearing her soft, raw breathing, he acknowledged the sickness of what he'd once felt. Laura had satisfied his pride. He was a simple cowboy who never had expected much more from life than hard work. Fame and fortune had caught him flat-footed and swelled his head. For a man who'd scrabbled from the bottom of a dung heap to the top of the world, she'd been the ultimate status symbol.

The pleasure in having a trophy wife—and that's exactly how he'd felt—had lasted about as long as it had taken to get from that rinky-dink chapel in Las Vegas back to the ranch. As soon as his ring was on her finger, she'd turned off the sweetness like turning off a light. Pride carried an expensive price tag.

"Ryder?" She placed a hand against his back. "I'm sorry. I know you don't like me crying. I'm so sorry. But you—you scared me. I scared myself. I want to be your wife. I do! But..."

He looked over his shoulder. She'd put on a white terry-cloth robe and cinched the belt tightly around her narrow waist. She blushed bright red. Astonished, he turned around.

"But what, darlin'?" Laura's blush intrigued him. Before the accident, nothing had ever embarrassed her.

Her chin quivered. The blush spread down her throat. "I've forgotten how."

Her vulnerability shoved all rational thought from his head. Pulling her against his chest, he embraced her and rubbed his cheek against her seal-sleek damp hair. "It's all right, Laura, it's all right. Don't cry."

Holding her brought back the heat. Helping her remember about lovemaking was a chore to look forward to.

Chapter Seven

Laura balked on the third step. She grasped the rail in her left hand and tugged Ryder with her right.

Her husband. The man she loved.

She wanted him so much her skin tingled and her joints had turned to syrup. But kissing him had touched nothing inside her head.

Confusion drove her crazy. One good close-up look at Tom Sorry had made her remember kissing him. Although Ryder's searing passion had dropped the world from beneath her feet and filled her veins with molten silver, he failed to trigger even the tiniest memory. It made no sense.

"Come on, darlin'," he coaxed. His midnight eyes sparkled with compelling light. His eagerness had a taut, teasing quality that formed responsive tension low in her belly. "You can shower in my room. I'll wash your back."

Her knees threatened to buckle.

The doorbell chime echoed in the two-story, open foyer. Ryder's face turned thunderous. He hopped down a step, caught Laura around the waist and stared fiercely into her eyes. Her fears evaporated like ice cubes under the sun.

"I'll see who it is."

"Are you expecting someone?"

"Nope." He rubbed the tip of his nose against hers. His eyes were hot, liquid, searing her soul. "Go on up and shower. Change into something...not too comfortable."

She practically floated up the stairs.

Once in the shower, she faced the pulsing water and closed her eyes. She rubbed her soapy hands slowly over her breasts, and for the first time in her memory felt truly alive. Ryder hadn't said he loved her, but he hadn't said he hated her, either. He certainly didn't act as if he hated her.

He gave her hope the past could be forgotten, perhaps forgiven, as well. She finished in the shower and stepped onto the marble tile. She selected a bottle of perfumed body lotion and smoothed it over every inch of skin. Her reflection in the mirror made her frown. Her ribs jutted ladderlike against her sides and her pelvic bones were as prominent as her collarbones. Her legs were acquiring some shapeliness, but not nearly enough.

Standing straight, she pulled back her shoulders and turned this way and that. Her breasts kept her from looking like a preadolescent, but only barely. She made a mental note to speak to her physical therapist about how to put on some weight.

Have a baby.

The thought startled her. She splayed her fingers over her flat belly. With a hunger so richly turgid it made her limbs heavy and her mouth water, she wanted a baby. A little sister or brother for Abby, another child for Ryder to indulge and adore. A baby to fill her belly and swell her breasts.

She pressed her fingers against her tummy. In the accident, she'd suffered internal injuries. Her back ached almost all the time, and probably always would. Yet not a single doctor had given her any reason to believe she couldn't have another child. For another baby, she'd willingly go through any kind of physical pain or inconvenience.

Surely Ryder wanted more children. He was a wealthy man, and this house was huge. He had infinite patience with Abby. With the neighbors so far away, Abby must want siblings to play with. Closing her eyes, Laura could almost hear the sound of children laughing and running in the wide halls and smell the sweet-sour milk scent of babies.

She practically floated to the closet containing her lounge wear. She trailed her fingers over yards of silk, satin and chiffon. Unable to recall what Ryder preferred, she closed her eyes and turned a slow circle. She stopped and thrust out a hand. She grasped the first article of lingerie she touched.

Her choice made her laugh. The gown was a collection of electric blue satin and peekaboo lace with a long skirt slit up both sides. The matching robe was trimmed in lace and frothy marabou.

Sticking to her choice, she worked the slithery gown over her head. Fortunately, the bodice wasn't fitted, so it being too big didn't matter much.

The telephone rang and her heart sank. Ryder must be calling to tell her that he was busy and would be tied up for a while. Jamming her arms into the robe sleeves, she hurried to answer.

Ryder said, "You need to come downstairs, Laura." He sounded as if he'd been kicked in the belly.

"What's wrong?"

"Living room." He hung up.

For a few paralyzing seconds, she stood with the dead telephone in her hand, wondering what could possibly make him sound so miserably flat. Dry-mouthed, heart pounding, she returned to the closet. She selected a simple rayon dress she'd ordered from a catalog. It had a long floating skirt and enough fabric to disguise her scrawniness. With trembling fingers, she fastened the long row of tiny wooden buttons. She slipped on a pair of pale pink slippers.

When she finally made her way down to the living room, she found Ryder standing by the fireplace. He held a glass of whiskey. Her alarm shifted into dread.

"Laura?"

The stranger startled her. She turned about in time to see a man rise from the sofa. Lean and dark-haired, he had bright green eyes too large for his face and a wispy mustache that perched under his nose like a fuzzy caterpillar.

Laura's scalp prickled. Ryder hunched his shoulders, and his face was dark, rigid with anger. He looked as if someone had invited a grizzly bear into his home and forbidden him to chase it away.

The stranger walked toward Laura. Instinctively, she hurried to her husband's side. She hooked her arm with Ryder's. The stranger stopped next to an étagère holding a display of crystal sculptures. He studied them as if they were the reason he crossed the room.

Knowing she was being terribly rude, Laura cleared her throat. She felt as if every hair on her body stood on end and anxiety cramped her belly. "I'm very sorry, sir. My memory . . ." She shook her head and forced a smile.

"Donny Weis," Ryder said through his teeth. He shot the other man a malevolent glare.

The name meant nothing.

"You sure you have the right wife, Hudson?" Donny chuckled. "Man, oh, man, you don't look nothing like yourself, Laura."

Laura gasped. Ryder moved with startling swiftness. Donny's eyes widened and he backed furiously until his knees struck the sofa and he sat down hard.

Cringing, Donny held both hands open in placation. "Hey, I didn't mean nothing, Hudson. But you have to admit...you know."

Holding one clenched fist against his side, Ryder said, "Laura, Weis here wants to see Abby."

"I don't understand."

Donny whistled long and low. "You really do have amnesia. I guess you do, too, Hudson." He waggled his eyebrows, and his eyes glittered like a cat's. "He forgot to tell you I'm Abby's dear old dad."

Laura had to sit down.

Head down, brow thunderous, Ryder said, "Donny's your ex-husband and Abby's father. He has visitation rights." He snapped up his head and focused the full force of his glare on the man. "Even though he's about as reliable as a one-legged dog in a horse race."

Donny shrugged lazily. "Hey, I'm a traveling man. Business here, there. You know how it is, Laura."

She didn't. She was still trying to figure out the ex-husband-and-Abby's-father part.

"I'm hurt you forgot about me," Donny said. "But I guess you don't look too bad. From what I hear it's a miracle you even lived. So what really happened?"

His glittering green eyes reminded Laura of the tails of greenbottle flies. Metallic, somehow dirty.

Evil.

She'd had this man's baby? Her stomach churned.

"Laura?" Ryder had set down the whiskey glass—empty. He looked ready to explode. "Visitation is up to you. You have sole custody. And Weis here is way behind on his child-support payments."

"Hey." Donny waggled his fingers. "What's forty bucks a week to a rich dude like you? A guy like me has to hustle for his pennies. It's a big, bad world out there. But don't think I don't appreciate you taking such good care of my little baby."

Laura breathed deeply to clear her head. Ryder probably hadn't told her about Donny Weis because Donny's demands to visit with Abby were nearly nonexistent.

Still, he was Abby's father.

And she had no right to keep them apart.

Ryder had absolutely no right whatsoever to keep this information from her.

She forced a smile and rose. She nodded graciously to Donny. "Please, Donny, help yourself at the bar. Ryder, may I speak to you for a moment, please?" She nodded toward the doorway.

She left the room and kept walking until she was outside in the courtyard. A stiff breeze ruffled the hem of her skirt. Silently, Ryder followed. Once the doors were closed, she whirled on her husband. "Why didn't you tell me I was married before?"

His face darkened. "It never came up."

"This is my past we're talking about. My daughter!"

"*My daughter.* I raised Abby, fed her, walked her and helped her through teething. It was me sitting with her through chicken pox and earaches. I put clothes on her back and food on her table. I kissed her knees after she wrecked bicycles and read her stories at night. I'm her daddy, not that sidewinder in there." He jerked his hat so low on his forehead his eyes were hidden. "And I'm ten times the mother you ever were, too."

She forced down her anger, swallowed it. She'd discuss this properly with Ryder later. "So what are the legal details? What are his rights?"

"You have sole custody. He's supposed to pay child support, but he never has. He's only been around to see Abby six or seven times in the past six years. You always let him see her, but not alone, and it's not smart to let him take her any place, either."

"Has he hurt her? Threatened her?"

Looking as if he'd rather swallow razor blades than answer, Ryder whispered, "No."

"So other than him being delinquent in child support, there's no reason to deny him visitation."

"No."

That one word looked as if it was breaking Ryder's heart. Laura fought down tears. She touched his arm. "What should I do?"

He turned away. "It's up to you, darlin'."

"You're her father."

"*Stepfather.* If you want to shoot Abby to the moon, there isn't a damn thing I can do to stop you." He did an about-face and stalked away.

"Ryder!"

He slammed through the door on the opposite side of the courtyard.

Torn, not knowing what to do or even what was the right thing to do, she wavered. The door where Ryder had disappeared eased open. Abby peered around the frame.

Laura urged the girl to join her at the fountain. Hugging herself against the wind, Laura sat on the wide pool rim. Thunder boomed from storm clouds far over the mountains.

"Did your father tell you Donny Weis is here to visit?"

Eyes narrowed with mutiny, Abby nodded. She clenched and unclenched her hands and shuffled her feet like a racehorse in the chute.

"Do you want to see him?"

"He's not my daddy, Mama! Daddy is Daddy!"

"Has Donny Weis ever...hurt you? Does he hit you?"

Abby shook her head. She looked ready to cry.

There were other ways to harm a child. "If you want to see him, then we'll see him. If not, then you don't have to."

"I don't like him. I don't wanna see him."

Torn between wanting to do the right thing and needing to protect her child, Laura dangled her fingers in the cold water.

"I don't want to see him, Mama." Abby wriggled against Laura's leg. "He's mean and he don't like me. All he wants to do is talk to you. He tells me to shut up." Her chin and lower lip quivered. Her big eyes turned liquid. "He makes you act mean."

Laura caught the little girl to her and buried her nose against Abby's hair. "I won't act mean to you, honey, never, ever. Cross my heart and hope to die. You're my baby and I love you and I'll never hurt you."

Abby wrapped her arms around Laura's neck and squeezed with all her wiry strength. "I love you, Mama," she whispered.

Laura straightened and smoothed messy hair off Abby's face. "So you go on in the kitchen with Mrs. Weatherbee. I'll tell Donny Weis he has to go home. Okay?" She'd make up for whatever wrong she might be doing later...after she knew the full story, and after Abby was old enough to make rational decisions about her biological father.

She joined Donny in the living room. The man had helped himself to a snifter of brandy.

He swirled the brandy, reminding Laura of an old black-and-white movie where all the women were dolls and all the men were dramatically debonair. "Where's the kid?"

"She's not feeling very well. You should have called beforehand so we could plan for your visit. This is a most inconvenient time."

"You've changed," he said. "You don't look the same. You don't sound the same. You don't even act the same. What does Ryder think about this?"

His intimate tone rankled. His failure to argue about her allowing him to see Abby rankled even more. How could Ryder conceal this part of her past from her? Had he honestly thought she'd never find out? "I'm very sorry, but you need to leave. Like I said, this is a bad time."

"Laura, Laura, Laura, after all we've been through. You don't remember me at all?" He raised the snifter to his lips. The tip of his tongue darted out, lapping at the liquor. "We had some great times, baby."

Not only couldn't she remember him, she couldn't imagine why she'd have had anything to do with him. He gave her the creeps.

But he was Abby's father.

She sat on the edge of a chair and folded her trembling hands on her lap. "I'm very sorry...Donny. I have changed. I'd like to remember you, but I don't."

Donny sat, too. He peered intently at her face. "If I didn't know you were Laura, I'd swear you weren't. Nothing about you is the same. What happened?"

"It was a car accident."

"Way I heard it, it was no accident."

She lifted her shoulders. "I don't remember. I don't remember anything before I awakened in the hospital. Ryder said it was probably a robbery." She waggled her left hand. "They stole my wedding rings."

"That's low. Do the police know who did it?"

She shook her head. "The robber used my ATM card, but other than that there aren't any clues. No witnesses. None of the jewelry reported stolen has turned up." She balked about telling Donny that Becky Solerno still considered Ryder the prime suspect. That was none of her ex-husband's business.

Donny whistled. "Leave town for a few months and everything goes to hell. I'm real sorry to hear about this, Laura. I really am."

Maybe he wasn't so terrible after all. She smiled weakly. "I'm much better now, thank you."

"I just can't get over the way you look."

Self-conscious, she lowered her face. She knew he meant she looked ugly.

"If I passed you on the street, I'd never recognize you. You could be anybody. So, uh, how are you and Ryder getting along?"

His question had an undertone that made her hackles rise again. The vague good feelings wisped away. Her thigh muscles tensed. She wanted to escape. "I don't think that's any of your concern. You must excuse me, I have to help Mrs. Weatherbee." She waited a beat for him to move, but he remained still. She stood. "Please call before you visit again."

"All right. I can do that." He stood.

They were the same height, and his sweetish cologne reached her nose. After he finally left, Laura wanted to take another shower to wash his sliminess away. Thoughtful, wondering how much more about her past

Ryder had deemed fit to conceal from her, she approached the bar. Not being a drinker, she fingered decanters and bottles before selecting a bottle of Kahlua. It smelled comforting, like coffee. She poured a healthy dollop into a glass and filled the glass the rest of the way with soda.

The drink tasted awful, matching her mood. Nose wrinkled, holding her breath, she sipped the fizzy, coffee-flavored drink and gagged on its not-quite-sweetness.

"Laura?" Ryder said from behind her. "I saw Weis leave. Abby told me you said she didn't have to visit with him."

Anger tumbled willy-nilly through her, tightening her ribs and tensing her belly. Her forehead ached. The low, chronic throb in her back pulsed sharply.

"We're going to talk, Ryder." She tried another sip of the drink, but it was too nasty even for her mood. She set down the glass. "Right now."

"I never expected Weis to show up."

"You mean, you hoped he never would." She made herself turn around. The sight of him worsened the pain in her heart. She did love him, with all her heart and soul, but love based upon what? His kindness, his generosity... it certainly wasn't because of his openness and honesty.

He shuffled his feet and jammed his hands in his back pockets. He looked rather young at the moment. Young and caught. "You're mad at me," he said.

"Mad doesn't begin to cover it. Why didn't you tell me you're my second husband?"

He caught his lower face in his hand and pulled his jaw. He muttered something she didn't catch.

"What was that?"

He lifted his unhappy gaze. "Fourth husband." He cleared his throat. "Only I'm not supposed to know about husbands one and two."

Her vision swam and she felt certain that at any moment the top of her head would fly off. She caught the back of a chair for support. Like a creaky elderly woman unsure of her balance, she held fast to the chair back and arms as she made her way around to the seat. Her legs wobbled so badly, her hips hurt. "I want you to explain what that means."

Ryder sat as if fearing the chair might collapse under his weight. Hunched over, he dangled his clasped hands between his knees.

"Well?" She urged him to speak. "I want the truth, Ryder Hudson. I want it right now."

"The only husband you ever admitted to was Weis. I found out about the others after we got hitched. My agent thought you were a gold digger out to rip me off, so he hired a private investigator to check up on your past."

"And?" She didn't want to hear this, but she had to.

"You married the first time when you were sixteen. He was a garage mechanic ten years older than you. He drank and beat you. I reckoned you hopped out of one fire into another."

"Because my mother... drank."

"And beat you, too. The marriage broke up when you were twenty. You went to Vegas and got a job in a casino. You hooked up with a wise guy named Jimmy Langella. He beat hell out of you, too."

Shocked, she raised a hand to her throat and toyed with the soft lace on her collar.

"He died. Officially, his death was ruled accidental, but gossip said he was murdered."

"What happened to me?"

"You got a lot of money and a taste for the good life."

"Then I married Donny." The only thing that kept her from collapsing was her inability to remember any of her sordid past.

"He lasted a lot longer than the other two. He liked spending your money and I reckon you were happy to let him do it. I met you at an art-show reception in Las Vegas." He chuckled weakly. "I'll never forget the first time I saw you. You wore red. I'd never seen anything so beautiful in my whole life. I still remember what you said to me."

She feared it wasn't anything romantic.

"You looked me up and down and said, 'You sure are tall enough, cowboy, but only time will tell if you're good enough.' You roped me, but good. After that, nothing mattered except having you for my own." His face darkened. The rims of his ears turned red. "I didn't care you were still married to Donny Weis."

She clapped both hands to her mouth.

"It was my doing, darlin'. I wouldn't let you be. I think I'd have killed Weis if he hadn't turned you loose. Then you disappeared on me."

"I went back to Donny?"

"I'm thinking he's the only man you ever loved all out. You broke my heart. I couldn't eat, couldn't sleep. I was miserable. You got pregnant to try keeping your marriage together, but Weis dumped you and the kid. When you turned up on my doorstep, I was happy to have you back. We went to Vegas and you divorced Weis and married me."

"I see."

"Marriage never suited you much. You made it clear the only reason you married me was because of my money, but not even money was ever enough. I tried to make you happy. Gave you everything you wanted. Built this house for you. Raised Abby as my own." His head quivered in mournful negation. "Nothing was ever enough."

"Did I ever love you?" She couldn't muster more than a whisper.

"No."

A fat tear plopped on her dress. She swiped the back of a hand across her eyes. "You loved me and I...hurt you." She didn't want to know any more, but she had to know. "So I cheated on Donny. Did I cheat on you?"

A long pause preceded his soft answer. "I dunno."

She heard the lie he wanted to believe. She pressed her forearm against her aching belly. "Is there anything else?"

He shook his head. "You've changed. You aren't the same woman."

Not the woman he knew, not the woman he'd once loved.

"Do you...want me to go away? I'm strong enough now to live on my own."

"No!" He jumped to his feet and crossed the distance between them in two long strides. His eyes glittered with blue heat. "The past is past, Laura. You're different. We've got a chance. We can start over."

"What happens if I start remembering? What happens if my brain heals and I return to being what I was before? I don't want to hurt you. Or Abby. Or anybody, ever again!"

"You're not leaving me," he said fiercely. "You can't."

"We don't have a marriage. From the sounds of it, I don't know if we ever will." She closed her eyes and sagged against the chair back. "Oh, Ryder, I don't know if you can ever forgive me."

"You aren't taking Abby away from me."

She looked up at him. "Abby? I..."

"I don't know what Weis said to you and I sure don't know what kind of schemes you two are concocting, but I'll fight both of you tooth and nail. I'll fight you to the death."

"This doesn't have to do with Abby—"

"It has everything to do with her, damn it! I let you put me through hell, treat me like a dog, gave up my home to build you this blasted house. I did it for Abby. She's mine, Laura. *Mine.* You aren't taking her away from me, and Weis isn't getting his claws on her, either."

Realization hit with such clarity, it felt physical. He'd do anything, suffer any pain, tolerate any humiliation, give her anything, say anything if it meant keeping his daughter.

He'd even stay married to a woman he despised.

"I'd never take her away from you."

"You've got that straight." He stepped back, his head raised and nostrils flared. "If you try, I'll stick you in a nuthouse. I'll lock you away forever."

Hearing his fear, seeing his dark blue eyes snapping with pain and panic, depressed her. No wonder she'd been miserable before. A loveless marriage, knowing her husband cared more about his stepchild than he did his own wife, knowing he'd wanted her only for her looks.

Sweeping past him, pushing away his attempts to take her arm, she blindly made her way to her room. She closed the door and sagged against it.

He'd never love her. Never.

Chapter Eight

"Mama?"

The mouse-soft whisper wrenched Laura's heart. She rolled over on the bed. Fumbling at the bedside, she found the lamp and turned it on. Her daughter hung back at the edge of the pale gold-tinged light. "Hello, Abby. How was summer camp today?"

"I knocked, Mama." Abby teeny-tiny baby-stepped toward the bed. She clutched her hands together over her tummy. Her big eyes were scared and worried. "I knocked lots and lots, but you didn't answer."

"I didn't hear you, honey. I was sleeping. I'm sorry." Sighing, feeling as if her limbs weighed a thousand pounds apiece, she dragged herself upright and fluffed a pillow. Sitting up made her a little dizzy, and she glanced guiltily at her untouched lunch tray. She patted the mattress beside her. "Come on up."

Abby climbed onto the bed. Laura wrapped an arm around the child's shoulders. Abby said, "You didn't go swimming today."

"I didn't feel like swimming."

"You didn't swim yesterday and yesterday afore that. You won't come for supper. Mrs. Weatherbee says you got vapors. What are vapors? Are you sick, Mama?"

She wished she was vapor and could disappear. She wanted to go away. Dig a hole in a desert and bury herself. "I'm not sick. Don't you worry about me, honey. I'm fine."

Huge tears rolled down Abby's cheeks.

Laura hugged her tighter. "I swear, I'm not sick! I'm okay, really."

"You gonna go back in the hospital?"

Deep and horrifying shame washed through Laura. Wallowing in misery was stupid and self-pitying, but harmed no one. Playing the not-so-noble martyr, staying out of Ryder's way, harmed nothing and accomplished nothing except to give her more fuel for the embers of self-pity. But frightening a little girl was inexcusable. Even if Ryder didn't want a wife, Abby desperately needed a mother.

"Here, snuggle with me." She scooted down and hugged Abby to her belly. She pulled the coverlet over both of them. Abby smelled of sweet baby-sweat and crayons and fabric softener. "Mama's a little sad right now, that's all, honey."

"Why are you sad, Mama?"

"It's...it's a grown-up thing."

"Daddy's sad, too. Are you sad like him?"

"What do you mean?"

Abby shrugged. She fiddled restlessly with the appliquéd trim on the coverlet. "I dunno. He just looks sad. And he didn't laugh at my riddle. He always laughs at my riddles."

Laura's chest tightened. Her eyes burned. She rocked them both, seeking comfort from her baby's warm, solid little body. Abby deserved so much. A good home, a good education, parents who loved her, cherished her, kept her safe and taught her right from wrong.

Sad parents who avoided each other, hurt each other, threatened each other and refused to laugh at a little girl's jokes—that she didn't deserve.

"You make me feel better," she whispered against Abby's ear.

Abby giggled and squirmed.

"You're the best reason for living in the whole wide world."

"That tickles, Mama!" She scratched at her ear. Wriggling, she turned in Laura's arms and pulled the covers to her nose.

Speaking soft and low, Laura asked Abby again about her day. The little girl happily told her all about the camp counselors and a nature hike and learning a song about a little clay pot. She even shared her riddle. What's red, blue, green and flies? Answer, Superfrog!

Hiding in bed wouldn't cut it anymore. Forcing Abby to tiptoe around one parent or the other and worry that she'd done something bad was the depth of cruelty. Laura and Ryder had a responsibility as grown-ups to work out their problems. For better or worse.

Abby's chatter faded to a mumble and then stopped. Laura lifted her head enough to see Abby's face. Eyes closed, cupid-lips parted, she slept. Laura stroked her tender cheek with a fingertip, marveling at the silky texture and angelic curve.

The past was a horror show. All the wishful thinking and false memories in the world couldn't do a thing to change what she had done. But the future was a clean slate.

Her choice was clear. Spend the rest of her life hiding from her husband and hoping it did no harm to her daughter. Or she had to figure out a way to make amends, to make this house a real home—even if it meant accepting that Ryder would never love her.

"WHAT DO YOU THINK, boss?" Tom Sorry crouched, resting on his heels. He had cocked back his hat as far as it would go.

Ryder touched the faint mark of a shoe heel in the damp, sandy dirt. They'd had several good rains in the past few days, which meant this track was fresh. Shoe prints crisscrossed the dirt between the boulders. A candy-bar wrapper was wedged in a crack.

"I think we found ourselves a hunting blind, Tom." He'd spotted the tracks while taking his afternoon horse-back ride. He'd noticed them first on the dirt track that cut across a pasture from the road.

He put himself in the mystery man's shoes—city shoes, with a broad heel and rounded toe. He could look straight between the barn and his studio for a clear view of the back of the house. He imagined with a pair of binoculars a watcher could see whomever walked up or down the main staircase, see into Laura's sitting room if the drap-eries were open, and watch anyone who went in or out of the pool house.

Tom pointed northeast. "You say they go all the way to Packerd Creek? So what do you reckon, boss? A bur-glar? Art thief? Rustler?"

Ryder wished he could think in such mundane terms. But the discovery of these tracks followed too close on the heels of Donny Weis's visit. He'd always figured Weis as a lowlife con man who'd do anything for a buck. Includ-ing making veiled and not-so-veiled threats about start-ing a battle for Abby's custody. Ryder had been tempted on many occasions to buy the man off. But that wouldn't work. Once he gave Weis a taste for easy money, the man would bleed him dry.

"Might have been Donny Weis."

Tom shifted a suspicious glare between the tracks and Ryder's face. "You really think so?"

Ryder shrugged. Weis had probably never done more than an hour's worth of manual labor in his life. He was more inclined to live off women, and didn't have the decency to see anything wrong with it. He didn't appear to be the type of man who had the patience or the physical stamina to watch Laura and Abby.

A sickening thought drew Ryder's gaze to the house. Suppose Donny Weis's visit had knocked loose Laura's memory for good? She'd been hiding from Ryder for days now, refusing to leave her room or speak to him. She might have gotten around to remembering how much she hated him. Worse, remembering how much power she held over him.

What if she allowed Donny Weis to snatch Abby? With Abby held hostage, she could figure out how to handle Ryder.

"So what do we do?" Tom asked.

Ryder rose and stretched, kicking the stiffness from his knees. "Keep an eye out."

"Are you going to report this to the sheriff?"

Ryder picked up the candy-bar wrapper. This had been no casual look-see at the house. "Report what? Sneaking a peek at the house isn't much of a crime."

"Trespassing."

Ryder thought of Becky Solerno, who still saw him as a suspect in the shooting of Laura. "Who's going to bother investigating a trespassing? We'll take care of this ourselves."

"WHERE'S ABBY?" Ryder asked. He hung his hat on the peg inside the kitchen door.

Mrs. Weatherbee glanced at the kitchen staircase. "Up in her room, I believe." She lifted her brooch watch and scowled. "Lord, where'd the time go? I haven't heard a peep out of her since she got home from camp."

Alarmed, Ryder took the stairs two at a time. A quick search of Abby's bedroom produced only her backpack. He checked his bedroom where she sometimes watched television. His bedroom was empty, as well. Trying to not feel the insistent fear clawing at his diaphragm, he hurried to the main staircase.

He noticed Laura's open bedroom door. The door to her sitting room was closed, as usual, so it was odd that her bedroom door would be open. He walked quickly but quietly to the door and peeked inside the room.

A television played with the volume on low. Laura and Abby sat on the bed, with the covers over their legs. Laura had an arm around the girl. Abby held a book open on her lap.

In her bright, high voice, Abby laboriously sounded out, "Buh-buh-buh."

"Very good. Buh for *B*," Laura said. "What's this letter?"

"*A! A* for Abby."

"Excellent. Now what does *A* sound like with the *B?*"

Ryder's heart caught in his throat. The two of them, their dark heads bent together, snuggled like a pair of kittens on the big bed, were so beautiful that his mouth went dry and his eyes ached. All the yearning for Laura, which he'd been bottling like shook-up soda, burst free.

That silk-covered bed contained everything he'd ever wanted from life. A lovely wife with a sweet smile and gentle hands. A beautiful kid full of sugar and spunk.

Laura glanced his way. Her eyes widened and her smile faded.

Abby noticed him, too. She flashed him a milewide smile and hoisted the book in triumph. "I can read, Daddy! Listen." She scrambled off the bed. Her cowboy boots hit the floor with a thud.

Well, if Laura remembered how much she hated him, she hadn't remembered that little girls were supposed to wear prissy dresses and Mary Janes, or that one never, ever for any reason put shoes on a bed. Laura had a fear of dirt and disorder that bordered on a phobia—used to have. The head injuries appeared to have knocked that quirk out of her, too.

"Listen, Daddy," Abby said insistently. She wrapped one arm around his leg. The cardboard pages of her book flopped like wings. "Buh a—"

"Ah," Laura prompted. She drew up her knees and hugged them to her chest. She glowered at the television. "*A* in that word sounds like ah."

"Buh-ah...uhl." Abby frowned in concentration. She suddenly gasped. "Ball! It spells ball, Daddy. Look! I can read, Daddy. *Ball.*"

"That's brilliant, sugar bear." He couldn't help a little puff of pride. "I always knew you were a wizard."

"What's a wizard?"

"Somebody who's very smart, like you," Laura said. "You need to go wash up for supper, baby. I imagine that's why your father's here."

"Guess what, Daddy?" Abby twisted around on his leg, grinning up at him like a little monkey. "Mama likes 'Sesame Street.' We watched. She knows all the songs."

Since when... "Good for you. Now go get washed up."

"I'm eating supper here with Mama. She needs company. She's sad."

Laura blushed. "I'll come downstairs, Abby."

Leaning far to the side, Abby eyed the television with longing. "Can we watch TV while we eat? Downstairs?"

"Don't press your luck, kiddo."

After Abby skipped away, Ryder stepped into the bedroom. Laura rested her chin on her knees and stubbornly watched the television set.

"So you decided to join the living," he said. As soon as he spoke, he was sorry. He was wrong, Laura didn't remember hating him. If she did, she'd remember hating Abby, too, and it was clear as day to him that she loved the girl. Which meant if Donny Weis was lurking around, then he was troublemaking on his own.

"I don't see what difference it makes to you," she said coolly. "You made it perfectly clear that you don't care whether I'm a part of your life or not."

"I never said that."

"Oh? Then I must have misunderstood your threat to institutionalize me." She flung back the covers and swung her legs off the bed. Her knee-length nightie rode up her thighs. She immediately tugged down the hem.

He moved in to help her rise, but she jerked her arm from his touch. His temper rose. "You can sulk all you want, darlin', but don't be putting words in my mouth."

"You are quite right, *darling*. I believe the word you used was *nuthouse*."

She stood for a moment, the cords standing out on her neck and her eyes closed. When the spell passed, she limped away. Without so much as a how do you do, she entered the bathroom and closed the door. The lock clicked loudly.

His daddy had always told him to be careful what he said—some words sure tasted nasty the second time around.

SUPPER WITH RYDER and Abby had been like some kind of twisted art film with swirling undercurrents and subtitles. Abby had been chirpy, chatting away like a little bird. Ryder had been so stiff-backed he'd looked sculpted from stone; his gaze had never once left his plate. Fearing the slightest verbal error, Laura hadn't spoken beyond necessity.

Now Abby was tucked into bed, and Laura was in her room alone. Again.

Anger was one thing—acting stupid was entirely another. She pulled on a fleecy robe, stalked out of her room and across the hall to Ryder's door. She drew several long, deep, steadying breaths and knocked.

Ryder opened the door. He wore pajama bottoms and held a loaded toothbrush. He looked her up and down. "Yes, ma'am?"

Shaken by his near nakedness, she struggled to remember her mission. His bare chest was hard-cut and deep with muscle. A line of dark hair bisected his flat belly, pointing like an arrow below his navel. He made an impatient noise. She focused on a spot near his left ear. "We have to talk," she said firmly.

"I'm tired."

It had taken her hours to work up the nerve to confront him; a little grumpiness wasn't going to dissuade her. "This shouldn't take long."

He stepped out of the doorway. "Come in."

His back was almost as interesting as his front. It amazed her that he seemed somehow bigger without clothing. His sun-browned, tough-looking skin begged for a touch. Aching for what might never be, she made herself look elsewhere.

His bedroom walls were dark, and the furniture was large and weighty. Just as Abby's room had been a girl's room, this looked like a lord of the manor's room. A sneaking little suspicion made her think that this room wasn't a temporary measure for Ryder.

Water rushed. She edged closer to the bathroom door and saw him bent over the sink, brushing his teeth. The vulnerability of his posture filled her with longing, and she absorbed the sight of brown curls brushing his neck. His arm muscles flexed and relaxed in an intriguing display.

"How long have we had separate bedrooms?"

He glanced at her, but said nothing until he finished and rinsed his mouth. He wiped his face with a towel. "Always," he said. "My getting up at four every morning disturbs your beauty rest."

She wasn't going to cry, she thought fiercely. She focused on a framed photograph of a horse. He strode past her to the bed and slid under the covers. Propped on pillows, he hooked his arms behind his neck. His posture emanated cold resistance. He wasn't going to throw her out, but he wasn't going to make her welcome, either.

She sat delicately on the end of the bed. The mattress was so high, her feet barely touched the floor. "What are we going to do, Ryder?"

"About what?"

"About us. I can't live like this. I don't see how you can, either." What she wanted to do was throw herself on him, beg his forgiveness and plead for his love. Tatters of remaining pride held her in place.

"What do you want to do?"

His harsh tone failed to conceal a plaintive note. Did he dare feel hope? She guessed he might wish for a solution to their problems, too, perhaps as much as she did.

Clasping her trembling hands, she said, "Do you mean what you said about locking me away?"

He lowered his arms and his face.

"I'll never take Abby away from you. You're a wonderful father. She needs you. Please believe me." Hesitantly, fearful of him drawing away, but craving the feel of him, she placed a hand over his leg. He twitched under the covers. "And it isn't because you threatened me. Abby needs me, too. She needs both of us. It's not right for a little girl to have to worry so much about her parents."

"I protect her. She's my whole world."

"You can't protect her from watching and noticing. Or feeling. She's worried because both of us are sad. It's true. At least, it is for me. I'm miserable."

Melancholy filled his eyes.

"I want us to make our marriage work," she continued. "To make our family work. I've hurt you badly in the past. I know that now and I am so sorry. If I could change any of it, I would. I don't know if you can get beyond that. If you can trust me." She bit back the urge to ask if he could love her. That much she didn't, couldn't dare.

The mattress shifted and he touched her arm. "Look at me."

Willing herself to not blow this by crying, she lifted her head.

"Do you mean it?"

"I'm not beautiful anymore. I'm not certain what I did before to make myself useful, and I don't know if I can do it again. I don't know what I have to offer, Ryder... except my solemn promise that I will never, ever hurt you again."

He raised a hand slowly and touched her cheek with his knuckle. His eyes held the most peculiar expression.

"But you have to be honest with me." His touch turned into a caress, and she leaned into the pleasure of his warm, rough-textured palm against her cheek. "I can't keep discovering all these horrid things about myself. A part of me dies every time I learn something new and terrible."

"Ah, darlin', I wanted to protect you."

"It's impossible." She placed her hand over his and folded her fingers. "Is it too late?"

"I don't know."

She closed her eyes. "We have to do something. I can't take this anymore." Determined not to distress him with her tears, she coughed away the growing lump in her throat. "I want to be good to you. I really do." She made herself look at him. "I don't know why I didn't love you before. You're a wonderful man. You deserve the best. I'll do anything for you, anything to make this work."

The corner of his mouth lifted as if he wanted to smile but didn't quite trust himself to do it.

She'd started it, and if she demanded honesty from him then she had to be honest with him. "I love you. I want our marriage to work. I want our family to work."

His eyes darted to hers, then searched her face. "You mean it."

"I've been dying inside, trying to figure out what to do. I can't even properly apologize for what I've done because I don't remember. All I can do is go forward. All I can do is beg you to show me how to love you."

He cupped her chin, gently tugging her toward him. "You mean it."

"I do." He was so close to her now she could smell the toothpaste on his breath. She could read the aching hope in his eyes. Out of words, she pressed a gentle kiss to his lips.

"You love me," he whispered.

"I must have been crazy before if I didn't love you. I want to be your wife. I want our family to be a real family." She kissed him again.

He responded by wrapping a powerful arm around her waist and falling in slow motion against the pillows, pulling her on top of him. He kissed her, hard and eager and delicious. She caught the sides of his face, reveling in the light stubble on his cheeks and the sun-toughened texture of his skin. She worked her fingers through his thick hair, parting the curls. His busy tongue teased and tantalized, erotically slick. She wanted to kiss and kiss and kiss forever, lost in the warmth of arms.

When she lifted her head to catch her breath, she whispered, "How could I forget making love to you?"

He tugged at the belt holding her robe. After loosening the knot, he pulled the belt from around her waist and dropped it on the floor. He pushed the heavy robe off her shoulder and lifted his head to press a hot kiss to her bare flesh.

"You're still beautiful, Laura. Different, but...I think you're more beautiful than before."

"Oh." She laid a finger against his lips. "Don't say nice things to me. You'll make me cry."

He laughed and rolled her toward the middle of the bed. "You are beautiful." With achingly slow tenderness, he spread her robe open over her shoulders. Underneath she wore a light cotton gown. He rubbed the flat of his palm in a slow circle over a sensitive nipple.

A shudder gripped her and worked its way from her knees, up her spine and back down, settling deep in her belly. A fluttery groan escaped her lips.

He breathed through parted lips, his expression one of eager anxiety. "I want you, darlin'. I want you with me."

Clumsily, her hands feeling as if they belonged to someone else, she pushed and pulled at the robe until she worked it off her arms. As she sat up and gazed down upon him, she recognized the glowing approval in his eyes and the desire in the heat of his skin, and she felt beautiful.

He slid a hand under the hem of her gown and inched it up her thigh. She traced the hard lines of his face, examining up close the crinkly crow's-feet at the corners of his eyes and the strong jut of his nose.

He reached the top of her leg, and her breath turned liquid and heavy in her chest. Working on instinct, she shifted and tugged the gown from beneath her. Watching him watching her, she pulled it over her head.

He made a fluttery noise of his own.

"I'm not...too..."

"You're just right," he assured her, nodding.

Bolting upright, he caught her naked body to him and kissed her fiercely, deeply. She clung to him, hungry for the feel of him. Together they fell onto the mattress, sinking into the mound of silky coverings. Never pausing in his kiss, Ryder kicked off the covers, sending them billowing off the end of the bed.

He rolled her onto her back and covered her with the long, hard length of his body. He quivered with the effort it took to keep from crushing her with his weight.

He searched her eyes. She greedily absorbed the dark sapphire blue and the heated depth of his pupils. She drowned.

"I want you too much, darlin', I can't go slow."

Burning with need, she caressed his hard shoulders and sides, marveling at the thick bands of muscle and controlled strength. His wild eyes and flushed face enchanted her.

"You can go fast if you want," she whispered in a voice gone husky. She licked his chin, her tongue rasping on whiskers. A spasm shook him head to toe. She took it as a sign he liked that. When she worked her hands under the waistband of his pajamas, he shuddered again and made a strangled noise deep in his throat.

"You have a beautiful face," she said. She worked her fingers up his back, lovingly savoring the sensation of supple skin and taut muscle.

Hunger to have another child filled her, heightening her desire. She wriggled against him, working her way up his chest. Fate had pulled her from the brink of death for a purpose. Fate gave her a second chance. If fate meant for her and Ryder to make a baby, then she wasn't about to stand in the way of fate. She captured his mouth with hers and boldly shoved her hand beneath the waist of his pajamas.

She claimed, she conquered . . . and he was hers.

FEELING HIS WAY in the darkness, Ryder sneaked through the kitchen. He used both hands to open the back door without a sound. Cool night wind slapped him. A half-moon offered enough light for him to make his way along the familiar path to his old house. Wind captured the sound of his boots and wisped it away. On the porch, the wooden planks, dried to kindling stage by recent winds, creaked and groaned.

He pounded on the door. "Tom! Wake up!" He kept knocking until a light was turned on inside.

Tom Sorry opened the door and blinked blearily at him. "What is it? What's wrong?"

Ryder strode inside. "I'm in trouble, Tom. Big trouble."

The cowboy shut the door. He wore only blue jeans, and his belt flopped. Though nearing fifty, he had a lean, spare body taut with hard-used muscle. He caught the big brass buckle and fastened it. Then he turned his attention to a small cabinet. He brought out the good Kentucky bourbon and hoisted the bottle for Ryder's approval.

"Make it a double." Ryder paced the wooden floor, back and forth in front of the big stone fireplace dominating the room. This had been his house once, and he'd lived a happy bachelor's existence here. He was starting to think he'd never be happy again.

Tom handed him the drink. Ryder drained it in one long fiery gulp. It hit his belly with a bang. The back burn made his eyes water. He shook his head. "Thanks."

"Now what's going on?"

He rested his forearm against the mantelpiece. "Laura. Or whoever she is. She isn't Laura."

Looking as confused as a calf stuck in mud, Tom pushed hanks of hair off his sleep-ruddy face. "What the hell are you talking about?"

"It's Laura. I don't think she's my wife." He clutched a handful of hair and tugged his scalp. "I've been working my tail off convincing her she is Laura, but she's not."

Tom backed up a step. He glowered from beneath shaggy brows. "You're crazy."

Frustrated, Ryder grabbed Tom's broad shoulders and shook him. "Listen to me! The woman asleep in my bed is not my wife. She is not Laura Hudson."

"Did she . . . say she's not your wife?"

"No, damn it!" He threw his hands in the air. "She's Laura, but she's not Laura. You're going to make me say it. Okay, fine, I'll speak it right out. I made love to her." His entire body shivered in remembered pleasure. Mak-

ing love to her had been heaven and moonshine. No one
in all his days had ever touched him with such passion and
loving and hungry urgency. Even thinking about her now
made him hot and cold.

She loved him.

And he hadn't the faintest idea who she was.

He choked out the words. "I just had sex with a virgin."

Chapter Nine

"She's out there somewhere," Ryder said. Another stiff drink and a hefty dose of Tom Sorry's stolid companionship had gone a considerable way toward calming Ryder's agitation. This particular problem, however, wasn't getting better with thinking. The more he thought about it, the worse the situation seemed. If the woman he loved wasn't Laura, then he was a low-down cheating dog—and where the hell was Laura?

And who was the woman in his bed...who had shot her and why?

He rubbed his shoulder where Laura had bit him. He deserved the bite since he'd hurt her, but by the time he realized she'd never made love before, it had been too late to stop.

Tom emerged from the kitchen. The smell of brewing coffee followed him. "I still say you're crazy, boss. Your missus has been through a lot. It's been a long time since you..." His ears and cheeks reddened. "You know."

Ryder couldn't believe they were having this conversation. A real man just plain didn't go around discussing the particulars of his marriage bed. "I don't think I'm wrong."

Tom gave him a dry look. "You know a lot about the subject?" His face turned crimson. "About... heifers?"

Ryder pulled fiercely at his jaw and mouth. "Not much."

"Me, neither. But you can't go putting a lady out of your house because you're thinking she lacks experience."

He clenched his jaw. "You're making me feel like a damned fool, Tom."

"You sound like one. She's your wife. Now, I've never held it secret, I think you made yourself a bum choice. But you married her and you have to stick with it."

Ryder began to catch on that Tom thought he was trying to get out of the marriage because he didn't like the way Laura made love. A laugh rumbled from him before he could stop it. Tom drew his shoulders back, looking offended.

"Laura never liked fooling around," Ryder said. "Might say, if you stuck her in a snowbank, she'd have warmed up."

Tom's cheeks flushed.

"When she did warm up," Ryder continued, "it was only because she wanted something. Even a jackass like me could figure out she was fooling." Remembering her habit of immediately leaping out of bed after lovemaking so she could rush into the shower made his jaw muscles tighten.

Laura had never desired him.

Looking toward the house, envisioning the warm and beautiful woman sleeping like an angel in his bed, he said, "I don't care about amnesia and whatever else the doctors might want to call it, some things just don't change. That's not Laura. Nothing is the same. Not the feel of her or the taste of her. Not the way she..." A tremble of lingering passion rippled through his muscles. His voice dropped to a whisper. "The way she says my name."

Managing to look both skeptical and fascinated, Tom leaned forward, resting his elbows on his knees.

"Ever been with a woman and she loves you so much you want to crawl inside her skin and her into yours and the rest of the world drops off into space? Your heart gets six times too big for your chest. Like it's going to explode." Ryder thumped himself on the breastbone. "It's a fire right here, stoking embers into your blood. Your skin's too small to hold all the feeling in. Anything is possible and everything is right. The only word in your head is her name, and man, you can fly."

Eyes wide, mouth slack, Tom slowly shook his head.

"That's how Laura makes me feel, and that's how come I know she isn't Laura."

"You've been sniffing paint too long." Tom crossed his arms over his chest and lifted his chin. "It's not like you to spit at good fortune."

"I'm not doing it now."

"Then who is she?"

"I don't know."

"I'm not saying I'm the smartest fellow on this patch of ground, but sense tells me you're turned around. If what you're saying is true, then where did your missus go? Who is the lady in your house?"

"She could be anybody."

Tom shook his head in firm negation. "Her people would be missing her. And she has to have a reason for being in your missus's car. How'd she get on the property in the first place? Who shot her? And the biggest question of all, where's the real Laura? That's too many questions common sense can't answer." Tom went to the kitchen for coffee. His bare feet rustled against the wooden floor.

As Ryder mulled over the questions, he began to see Tom's point. Except... He jerked his head. "Teresa Gallagher."

Tom nearly dropped the coffee mugs. He set them down quickly enough for Ryder to know he'd burned himself. He stuck his thumb in his mouth.

"How did I miss it? She's Tess." The more Ryder thought about it, the more obvious it seemed. "Look at the way she dresses. Just like Tess. The way she talks. The way she's been puttering around in my office."

"Ain't no way in hell. The police took fingerprints." He no longer sounded so sure of himself.

"They took Laura's fingerprints off her hand, but they aren't on file anywhere, so there's nothing to compare them to. They assumed she was Laura. Shoot, everything else was anybody's guess. All this time she's been telling me she's not Laura. I've been telling her she's crazy. The doctors were telling her she's crazy."

"I'm saying you're crazy. You don't have any proof."

Ryder rubbed the bite mark on his shoulder. If the woman in his bed truly had been a virgin, then he supposed a doctor could tell that she'd never borne a child. Or a simple blood test could prove she wasn't Abby's mother.

What if he was wrong? *Well, shoot, darlin', we had such a fine romp in bed I thought it a swell idea to find out if you really are my wife.* That would go over like a box of rocks.

"I'll have a blood test done."

Tom laughed uneasily. "What will you tell her?"

"I won't."

"Can't do it on the sneak," Tom said. "It's her blood, you can't go taking it behind her back."

Ryder began to see how dangerous demanding a blood test or doctor's examination might be. If Laura was Laura, which he truly doubted, his suspicions could destroy their fragile relationship.

"It's more like she had one of those near-death experiences," Tom said. "You know, she got so close to dying that she saw the error of her ways. She finally got it in her head that she loves you. That lady is your wife."

The idea of her being Tess Gallagher swelled in his mind, gaining weight and substance with every passing moment. "You went around with Tess. Took her to the fair and a movie. You knew her."

"Not much. Shoot, I might have kissed her once, but it was like taking out my kid sister. But I'm telling you, if she is Teresa, I'd know it. Mrs. Weatherbee would know it."

"She doesn't look like Tess anymore, but she dresses like her and talks like her and—and she calls Abby kiddo. Laura never did that." He thought hard, seeking other proof. "She likes my paintings. Laura hates cowboy art. Hell, she hates cowboys."

Tom leaned back and clamped his arms over his chest. An implacable wall of skepticism. "So where is your missus?"

Good question.

"What I'm about to say might offend you, so don't be taking a swing at me."

Ryder drew back warily. He picked up a coffee mug to occupy his hands.

"If there was one word that would've described Laura Hudson before the accident, it was grubber. She'd have sold her soul for a buck. *Before* the accident."

Ryder wasn't offended, but he didn't like Tom's tone. "She wouldn't run out on your money."

A sickening truth. Ryder held not the slightest doubt that Laura would desert him and Abby, but only after grabbing as much of his money as she could.

Tom leaned forward. "Now let me ask you something else here, boss. What if that lady isn't Laura? You go sticking your nose in that hornet's nest, what's gonna come swarming out? Donny Weis? And what about that lady cop? She'll be dancing the jitterbug trying to figure out how you switched wives. I can just hear what sort of noises she'll be making. What'll happen to the kid when the newspapers find out?"

Abby...for once in her little life she had a real mother. Laura—whoever she was—loved and cherished the child. Abby was blossoming under the healthy attention. He didn't want to think about the damage it would do her to lose her mother—the woman she loved as a mother. But Tom was right. If Ryder's suspicions became known, they could lose Abby forever.

"Use your head, boss," Tom said slowly, "there ain't no way in hell that lady could be Teresa Gallagher. Take your good fortune and be happy with it."

LAURA STRETCHED luxuriously. She liked Ryder's bed. The firm mattress felt good, and the silk-cotton blend sheets held his masculine scent. Even better was knowing that soon it would be her bed, too. This separate-bedrooms nonsense was ending today.

A movement caught her attention. Ryder eased through the doorway. Sighing happily, Laura rolled onto her belly. How amazing and admirable that a man of Ryder's wealth and talent still rose before the crack of dawn to do chores.

Chores. That's what she needed. She was strong enough now to be a real wife. Surely, Mrs. Weatherbee could use all the help she could get around the house. There was a full-time job waiting in Ryder's office. Abby needed constant care and attention, too. It was ridiculous to pass off her responsibilities.

Starting today, she determined, she was lady of the house.

Ryder used both hands to close the door. He tiptoed into the bathroom. Tingles of remembered pleasure tickled her nerves. She pushed off the covers and slid off the bed.

Her back twinged, her legs ached and she was sore in places she'd never thought about before. She supposed lovemaking was like any other exercise; she needed to get in shape. Super shape, if she was going to keep up with an energetic, enthusiastic lover like Ryder. Even thinking about him stripped the strength from her knees, and she had to sit down until the quivering stopped.

She heard the shower running. Grinning, eagerly anticipating the sight of his nakedness in full light, she slipped into the bathroom. Ryder's silhouette was dark behind pebbled glass.

"Good morning," she sang.

A loud thump was followed by Ryder's cursing.

Laura flinched and clapped a hand to her mouth.

"Laura?"

"I'm sorry, honey. I didn't mean to startle you." She pulled open the shower stall door and joined him under the spray. "Hi." She pulled the door shut with a click.

He pressed his back into the corner and stared wide-eyed at her. Water dribbled off his face. "What are you doing?"

She drank in the sight of his incredible, chiseled-from-stone shoulders, and the patterns water rivulets formed through the patch of dark curls on his chest. "Showering?" She fluttered her eyelashes, thinking his bashful act was cute. She plucked the bar of soap from his hand. "Want me to wash your back?"

"You—you shouldn't be here."

"I thought you liked to share," she murmured huskily. Slowly lathering the bar, she inched closer to him. "Last night was so special, Ryder. I can't believe I ever forgot. It was like the very first time." She rubbed the soap back and forth across his chest.

He slid down the wall, and his eyes rolled up in the sockets. "Darlin'...you..."

"I don't have to stop at your back," she whispered, a scant inch from his face. She kissed him. His mouth was hot and wet, fresh as rainwater. She continued lathering his chest and his belly and his sides. The effect on him was pleasurably obvious. She pressed her body against his slick arousal. "Have we ever made love in the shower before?"

"No," he said, his voice raw and choked. He grabbed her suddenly, and kissed her.

Making love in the shower was something Laura vowed to do often. It was slightly uncomfortable, a little bit dangerous and thoroughly exquisite. Afterward she lazily toweled off in front of the steamed-up mirror, watching Ryder's sexy, shadow shape behind her.

"How old are you?" she asked.

"Thirty-seven." He tossed his towel at the hamper and all but ran out of the bathroom.

Wrapping the towel around her body, she followed him. "What's wrong?"

He jerked a pair of briefs over his hips and grabbed for his jeans. "Nothing."

"There is too something wrong. You're acting very strange. Did I say something to upset you?" She tried to recall what she'd said, but other than *I love you* and *oh, yes* and *don't stop,* she couldn't recall saying much at all.

He refused to look at her. She finally marched across the room and grabbed his arm. His hand turned white-knuckled where he held a shirt.

"Don't do this to me," she said. "We're going to make our marriage work, remember? We're going to be honest and work out our problems."

"I've got stuff to do."

She glanced down at herself. Her breastbone protruded like the neck of a turkey. The hand holding the towel was bony. Why, oh, why had she risked the harsh glare of the bathroom lights and approached him naked? She dropped her hold on him. "Oh, God, you think I'm ugly."

He jerked up his head. "No!"

She stroked her wet hair. "I'm not beautiful anymore. I don't know how to make love to you anymore. I disgust you, don't I? I offend you."

"You're talking nonsense, darlin'."

"You're an artist, you love beauty. You don't love me. You can't love me." She whirled toward the bed and found her robe. Fighting the tears turned her body rigid and her limbs uncooperative. A sleeve that was turned inside out stymied her best efforts to dress.

"Don't." He caught her shoulders from behind.

"I thought... I thought last night... the shower... I didn't know—"

"It's not you." He snatched the robe from her hands, shook it out and helped her into it. She dropped the damp towel before tying the belt around her waist.

The muscles in his jaw flared. She studied his stricken gaze, and the way his eyes darted around the room, looking everywhere and anywhere except at her. Her chest hurt and so did her belly, a deep, aching hurt that made each breath agony.

"I understand," she whispered. The tears were rising, gaining power in a low, slow-burning pressure building in her throat and behind her eyes. If she cried, he would comfort her because he was good and kind. He'd show her the same kindness he'd show any wounded creature.

But that wasn't love.

"I understand," she repeated and trudged toward the door.

"Ah, darlin'—"

She thrust out a hand. "I don't want to discuss this! I made a mistake. I understand that now."

"It's not your mistake, it's mine."

His? she wondered. How could... The implication struck her like a blow, and she gasped. "There's someone else. Oh, my Lord, you're in love with another woman."

"No!" His entire expression skewed. "I mean, not exactly—"

The door opened and Abby walked in. She held a hairbrush and a scrunchy hair tie. "Daddy, braid my— Hi, Mama." Bright-eyed, she skipped to Laura's side. Her smile faded. "You been crying, Mama." She shot her father a filthy look. "How come you're crying? Are you sad again?"

Laura stroked Abby's shining hair. "I'm fine, baby. I'm not crying."

"You look sad. Daddy looks sad, too. You said you wasn't gonna be sad no more. How come everybody's sad?"

Laura knew at any second she was going to burst into a monster crying jag. She forced a smile. "I am perfectly fine. Now let's get you ready for camp, young lady. Then we'll all have breakfast together. Okay?" She refused to look at Ryder. If she did, her heart would finish breaking.

"'Kay," Abby murmured,

Laura hustled Abby out the door and across the staircase landing to her suite. Through sheer force of will she maintained a mild, pleasant air while brushing and braiding Abby's hair. Then she sent the child downstairs to the kitchen.

While she selected a dress, Ryder rapped on the wall next to the closet doorway. Her back muscles tensed. She wore only panties and a bra.

She glanced over her shoulder. He'd dressed in a checked shirt tucked into his jeans. Damp curls clung to his forehead. He was so handsome it hurt to look at him. She refused to look at him. He was a healthy man, virile and sexy, and she'd been an invalid. She couldn't blame him for taking a lover.

She'd been a cheater, too. He stayed with her only to keep from losing Abby. He didn't love her, he'd never love her, and last night she'd been fooling herself.

"You did good with the kid. Thank you."

"I can't do this." She clutched a gray-and-rose print rayon dress to her bosom. "I can't live like a stranger in my own home. I can't share you with another woman."

"There's no other woman—"

"You said so yourself! You said you love another woman!"

He winced, and a guilty flush spread across his cheeks.

She closed her eyes and concentrated on her breathing. "I don't blame you. I'm not condemning you. I know more than anyone that you deserve better than me."

He took her in his arms. At first she resisted, but his big hands were gentle and firm against her back. His breathing was cool across her damp hair. She pressed her ear against his chest and listened to the comforting thud of his heart.

"I've got a bit of a problem right now," he said, his tone uncertain. "Give me time to work it out."

"Whatever you want," she said. "Excuse me, I need to get dressed. I won't be but a minute." She squirmed out of his embrace and turned her back on him, tense with unhappiness. She held her breath until he was gone.

She dressed and went downstairs. Somehow, she managed to make it through breakfast. She managed to keep her patience with Abby, who despite Ryder's and Laura's assurances, anxiously acted up. She dumped catsup on her eggs, then refused to eat them. She spilled her milk and soaked her sleeves in it. When Mrs. Weatherbee announced it was time to leave, Abby pitched a tantrum.

"I don't wanna go! I hate summer camp!" She threw herself onto the floor and wailed.

"Now, sugar bear, you love camp and playing with all your friends. Besides, it's your last day." Ryder picked her up and she went rigid, shivering and keening. "Abby!"

She knows, Laura thought in horrified dismay. Somehow Abby knows something is terribly wrong. "Put her down, Ryder."

He scowled.

"She's pitching a fit for your benefit. Put her down and leave the kitchen. She'll be all right."

Abby cut off her screaming in midnote. Wide-eyed, mouth agape, she stared at Laura. Laura arched her eyebrows and checked the wall clock. "You need to leave in ten minutes, Mrs. Weatherbee. Why don't you get ready? Put her down, Ryder."

Slowly, reluctantly, he set his daughter on the floor. She started screaming again and pawing at his arms.

"Please leave, Ryder, I'll handle this."

"No, Daddy!" Abby caught Ryder's knees in a bear hug. "She'll hit me, Daddy! Don't go away! She's mean!"

"Ryder, she's playing to her favorite audience."

His expression twisted in a mixture of anger, confusion and resignation. He forcibly peeled the child off his legs and swung her onto a stool. Without another word, he stomped out of the kitchen. The door swung back and forth on its hinges.

Abby turned off the screaming and crying.

"Boy, are you mad." Laura made a soft sound of amazement. "I bet I know why you're mad."

Abby sank into herself. Her little fingers twisted restlessly on her lap.

"You're scared. It scares you when Mama and Daddy are sad. Why does that scare you so much, baby?"

"You're gonna 'vorce him. You're gonna take me away and never see my daddy again."

"I'm not going to do that. I'd never do that to you or your daddy. I love you both too much."

"You was in his room. Every time you go in his room, you says you're gonna 'vorce him. You cry and break things and call the other daddy to take you away."

Imagining what had gone on in this house before her accident sickened Laura. "I'm not going to divorce him, baby."

"You was crying. Every time you go in his room, you cry and say you're gonna 'vorce him."

"Not this time." She sat on the stool next to Abby's. "You know your daddy loves you. And you're the most important thing in the whole wide world to him. You know this?"

Abby nodded.

"Your daddy would fight dragons to keep you safe. He'd never let anybody hurt you. Nobody is going to take you away from him. I won't let anyone take you away." She plucked a paper towel off a roll and daubed at Abby's tear-streaked face. "When you get scared, you can say, 'I'm scared.' You don't have to yell and scream."

Abby snuffled loudly.

"So you hurry upstairs and brush your teeth. Grab your backpack. Mrs. Weatherbee is waiting."

Abby snuffled loudly. "Okay, Mama."

Promises made that might be broken tasted like bile in Laura's mouth. Laura caught Abby in a hug. The little girl hugged her back as if she never wanted to let her go.

Chapter Ten

Another woman.

Laura's suspicions drove her crazy. Ugly images and thoughts whirled and swirled, leaving her sick and dizzily off-balance. She could not stop seeing another woman in his arms, another's lips upon his, another's hot voice murmuring love talk in his ear—it was enough to drive her insane.

After seeing Abby off to camp, Laura went directly to the studio. Ryder was already at work, using a palette knife to lay paint onto a canvas as if burying a demon. His misery hung over the studio like a coating of dull grime. Even the music filling the air was a wailing dirge of broken hearts, straying feet and dying love.

Her self-loathing deepened. They needed to talk; she didn't trust herself to talk. Her jealousy was too fresh, too ripe with dangerous passions. If she spoke, she might scream or accuse or cry or wail, or something equally horrible.

Ryder glanced at her.

"At least tell me her name." She'd blurted out the words without thinking. Now they hung in the air, taunting her—jealous shrew! She covered her mouth with her hand.

Ryder dropped his palette on the table behind him. He cocked his hat to a challenging angle. "I'm not having an affair. Damn it, Laura, I'm not a cheater."

She bit back the urge to argue.

Ryder stalked out of the studio. He slammed the door behind him. Through the big window, she watched him head for the barn.

She entered the office. Miserable, wondering why she couldn't have lost her voice along with her looks, she glowered at the desk and computer. She trailed her fingers over the items on the desk. Images of her recurring dream rose in her mind.

Running, panting... a ledger. Not a book, a ledger.

Stiff-legged, she approached the desk and placed her hand atop a ledger she'd so laboriously balanced. A ledger...

She picked up the book and clutched it to her chest, exactly the way she held it in her dream.

"Dead!" A woman's voice echoed in her brain, high and strident and furious. "I want him dead, dead, dead! Right now, do you hear me? I want him dead!"

She held the book tighter, felt ghost pains in her legs as she ran faster and faster—

Knowledge clapped shut around her like a trap. She was seeing herself. She, Laura Hudson, was the screaming woman, and she'd clutched the ledger and screamed her rage.

Mouth dry, heart pounding, palms sweating, Laura rubbed a hand over the heavy smoothness of the faux leather ledger cover. What had so enraged her? Why had she run away with the checkbook ledger... away from whom?

Had she discovered evidence of Ryder's infidelity? She didn't want to think in this direction, but the thoughts acquired a life of their own, tripping faster and faster, gaining strength. She'd discovered the identity of his mistress. They'd argued. She'd threatened to leave him. She'd wept and raged and screamed about how much she hated Ryder for being a bounder.

And he'd stopped her from taking Abby away.

She gasped and touched herself, feeling the scar of the gunshot wound. *No!*

Ryder was gentle, caring, principled and honest. He'd never hurt her.

He'd do anything to protect his daughter.

All her efforts to not think about what exactly *anything* meant produced only a headache. She sank to a chair, bent over until her face nearly touched her thighs and moaned her misery.

She glanced at the office doorway. Theirs had been a loveless marriage from the very beginning. He'd all but admitted there was another woman. God only knew for how many years the affair had been going on.

Proof. She must have stumbled onto irrefutable proof and then threatened him with divorce. She snatched open a drawer. Ryder maintained several checking accounts. Two used identical ledgers, his business account and the ranch account. She opened both ledgers on the desk top.

If she did find proof he'd been seeing another woman, was it proof Ryder had tried to kill her?

She'd figure out that part when she got to it. After another furtive glance at the doorway, she reached under the desk and hit the power switch for the computer.

"JUST GET ON OVER HERE, Tom," Ryder said, dragging the cowboy along with him toward the studio. He ignored Tom's protests about needing to finish shoeing a horse. The horse would wait.

"Gone off your fool head," Tom grumbled, holding on to his hat as he trotted after his boss. "I've got thirty-six hours worth of work to do today and you're acting like a crazy man."

"Shh." Ryder eased open the studio door then put a finger against his lips. "Just look. You don't have to say anything, just look." He tiptoed between the worktables and sidled up to the office doorway. He pressed a finger to his lips again as an additional warning, then pointed inside the office at Laura.

She sat on the chair at an angle in front of the computer. Slouching down on the seat, she had her legs stretched out and crossed at the ankles. Her long skirt draped gracefully, covering her legs to below the calf. The keyboard rested on her lap. In her right hand, she held a pencil and she used it to keep time to the music playing over the speakers.

Abruptly, she shoved the pencil between her teeth and typed rapidly without looking at the keyboard. Images flashed on the screen.

A glance at Tom's bug-eyed, slack-jawed face filled Ryder with triumph. Who was the loco cayuse with his head full of clouds and nutty notions now? With hand and eye gestures, he urged the man away from the door. The pair sneaked out the way they'd come.

Outside, Ryder exclaimed, "Who did that remind you of?"

Tom lifted his hat and ran a hand through his hair. He settled his hat, then fiddled with his shirt collar. He eyed the clouds building to the south over the mountains. Finally, he said, "I don't know."

Ryder strode toward the barn. "You're being a knot head, Tom Sorry. That's Teresa."

Tom swung his head from side to side. "Can't be."

Inside the barn, Ryder stopped and looked toward the studio. Behind him, horses whickered in curious greeting and shuffled in their stalls. Soothed by the rich, green smells of horses and hay, Ryder leaned his shoulder against a post.

"Do you remember the cut brake lines?" Ryder asked.

Tom faced him squarely. "You pay my wages, so if you want to tell me the moon's made of green cheese and I'm supposed to believe it, then I'll speak the words to make you happy. But that don't mean I believe it."

Ryder had always admired Tom's staunch sensibility. At the moment, though, it irritated him. "I never told you what Laura told me. Laura said she caught Tess upstairs trying on clothes."

Tom snorted in derision.

"Hear me out, now. It sounds foolish in my head. I've got to test the words, though." He cleared his throat. "What if Laura told the truth and Tess had one of those fatal attractions for me or something." Seeing Tom was about to protest, Ryder held up a hand. "Stranger things have happened. Anyhow, Laura pitches a fit and fires her. Hell, she thought Tess and I were having an affair, anyway. Catching Tess in her closet would have about cinched it."

"So you think . . . Teresa came back here to get even?"

Pleased the man was finally getting it, Ryder nodded. "Tess cuts the brake lines. Only that's not good enough. So she comes back, finds Laura alone, and . . ."

"Tries to shoot her?"

That part made everything inside him protest. For nearly two years Tess Gallagher had been his angel, his trusted assistant and problem solver. No matter how complicated or screwy a task seemed, she'd handled it with gracious aplomb. He'd never heard a harsh word cross her lips. Her patience had been deep and unrelenting no matter who she'd dealt with, be it his agent or advertisers, flaky gallery owners or temperamental printers.

He'd always been more comfortable around animals than around people. His agent had accused him of being naive as a country bumpkin. He supposed in many ways that was true, but he still couldn't believe he missed knowing she was murderously crazy.

Ryder heaved a deep breath and stroked his jaw. "Laura wouldn't give up my money or that house without a good reason."

"Like she thought she killed Teresa."

"The ATM card. Laura was the one pulling out cash."

Tom dropped a big hand on Ryder's shoulder. "We're just playing a game of what if, right? So I'm not saying it's true or anything, just what if. What if Laura did try to kill Teresa. So she panics and takes off in Teresa's car. By the time she calms down, she must have read in the paper that Teresa was alive."

Ryder chewed over the possibility. "I don't know. She could claim self-defense."

"After pushing the Mercedes into the quarry?" He huffed a dry laugh. "Newspaper stories said the car got wrecked, then pushed over the cliff." Tom shrugged. "Only reason she'd have to run would be 'cause she can't claim no self-defense. So she took Teresa's car and skedaddled."

Ryder grew light-headed.

"Maybe you ought to let it drop, boss. Laura, Teresa, whoever she is, she thinks she's your wife. She's treating you good, treating the kid good. Why stir up trouble?"

Why, indeed. "Maybe you're right," he muttered.

"Some things are best left alone."

Ryder nodded, but he didn't believe it. As much as he wanted an uncomplicated life with a loving wife, he couldn't bear the questions or the possible lies. "I'll think on it."

He headed to the tack room. A ride through the forest should clear his thinking. It always did.

As Ryder turned away, Tom said, "Damn it, boss, you're sure stubborn. You go charging around like a blind bull, and you could end up hurting lots of folks."

Ryder hunched his shoulders and kept walking. If the woman in his office was Teresa Gallagher, it could demolish his entire world. In one clean stroke he could lose Abby.

His breath caught in his throat. He could lose Tess, too.

WHAT A MESS.

Laura maneuvered through the pages of the spreadsheet program. Up until the time of her accident, the books had been kept properly, most likely by a professional. It appeared that no one had touched them since. Considering the mess she'd been slowly organizing, it looked as if the only thing Ryder had done since her accident had been pay bills. He hadn't sorted important papers from the junk, or filed anything, or balanced the books. It explained the big box of bills and receipts she'd found one day. Ryder must have dumped everything in a box for an accountant to sort out in order to figure his taxes. Poor accountant.

After searching through the spreadsheets, bank statements and a filing box full of old ledgers, she'd determined that an entire checkbook ledger for the ranch account had disappeared. She could tally up about a third of the checks from the book, including two taken out of sequence, but the book itself was gone.

That was important, somehow. It had to do with her dream and running with the book clutched to her chest. Her efforts to remember why it was important gave her a headache. Giving up on the puzzle of missing checks, she turned her attention to a credit card account. Maybe that's where she'd find proof of a mistress.

She pulled a manila folder from the file cabinet. It was fat with receipts and statements for a single credit card. The majority of purchases were for clothing, lingerie, jewelry and perfume, but all the receipts bore her signature. It sickened her to see how wildly, almost vengefully she'd spent Ryder's money. She returned to the file cabinet and pulled the folders for all the credit cards.

Laura's disgust grew as she totaled the thousands of dollars she'd spent on beauty parlors alone. Her clothing bills had been through the roof. She stared at one receipt that listed simply, *Blouse,* the cost six hundred and fifty-nine dollars. She'd also had a propensity to spend cash, four and five hundred dollars at a time taken as an advance against her credit cards or drawn via ATM from her checking account.

Ryder's lone credit card showed a far different life-style. He used the card for gasoline purchases, airline tickets, art supplies, books and miscellaneous items from feed and tack stores. He'd spent approximately one dollar for every hundred Laura had spent.

She found a few receipts from jewelry stores. There he showed a lavish streak. One receipt was for a very expensive bracelet. Before accepting it as proof of infidelity, she returned to the file cabinet for a household inventory sheet filed under insurance. She found a listing for a diamond tennis bracelet. The date of purchase matched the credit card receipt.

Painstaking research of the household inventory accounted for every piece of expensive jewelry Ryder had purchased with a credit card. She also followed a hunch about hotel charges, but all of them matched up to trips he'd taken to attend art shows. It didn't prove he'd been accompanied by a girlfriend, but it didn't disprove it, either.

A listing on a monthly statement made her heart race. For months and months he had a regular charge running with a florist. Then she remembered the yellow roses with which he'd once filled her bedroom.

Frustrated in her search, she turned her attention to telephone bills. The ranch had five telephone lines—hers, Ryder's, the house, the office and Tom Sorry's cabin. The office bills showed hundreds of long distance phone calls. Guessing they were legitimate business calls, she set those aside. She checked six months worth of bills for Ryder's private line. She copied down every long-distance call recorded, and then did the same for the house line.

His girlfriend probably didn't live so far away that calling her was long distance, but it was a lead.

"Daddy!"

Abby's yell startled Laura and she jumped, knocking her elbow against the file cabinet. White-hot pain shot up her arm to her shoulder. For a long moment she stood perfectly still, not breathing, eyes shut, teeth clenched.

"Mama?"

"Yes, baby?" She opened her eyes. Her stinging funny bone throbbed. She rubbed it briskly.

Abby peered with interest at the open file drawers, stacks of folders, piles of receipts and the slow-motion geometric shapes of the screen saver floating across the computer monitor. "What you doing?" She clutched a large construction-paper folder in both hands.

Good question. Ryder had all but admitted to having an affair, so she didn't need hard evidence. No matter what logic said, she knew in her heart Ryder would never, under any circumstances, have tried to kill her.

Abby thrust forward the folder. Its chalky red surface had been drawn on with markers and crayons. "I got my pictures."

"Oh, that's right. Last day of camp. My goodness, where is the summer going? You'll be starting first grade pretty soon." Her heart climbed into her throat and lodged there. If Laura did find proof of the girlfriend and she did inform Becky Solerno that she believed Ryder might have a motive to hurt her, then what would happen to Abby?

Inviting Abby to sit on the desk chair, Laura took the folder. It was filled with drawings, nature-hike worksheets and shapes cut out of construction paper then carefully pasted onto card stock.

Laura fixated on Abby's name. For the first time she saw it in print, not Abigail Hudson, but Abigail Weis. How that must distress Ryder. It caused her almost physical pain.

"You did very well, baby. Your counselors must be sad to see you go."

Abby cocked her head. "I'm not going nowhere." She suddenly pushed off the stool and hopped excitedly. "There's Daddy!" She raced out of the office.

Through the big windows in the studio, Laura saw Ryder riding his big buckskin quarter horse. Moving gracefully with the horse, he was so handsome, so big and sure, it hurt her heart to look at him. Looking around the now messy office, she was torn. If Ryder had been the one who tried to kill her, it must have been because she meant to take Abby away.

Did that excuse him?

She moved to the window and put her hands behind her back.

Abby ran up to her father and grabbed his stirrup. His horse stopped dead in his tracks and stood patiently while the little girl twisted, wiggled and danced dangerously close to his hooves. Ryder leaned over and caught Abby by the back of her britches, hauling her up behind him. Holding on to the back of his saddle, she was talking a mile a minute. Even under the shade of his broad-brimmed hat, Laura could see the smile on her husband's face.

She turned her head enough to see through the office doorway. That was the past, dusty and disordered and mostly forgotten.

If Ryder had hurt her, it must have been in a moment of panic. How he must suffer for it every day. He'd suffered enough.

She loved him.

She didn't think of herself as one of what Becky Solerno called love-thick women who'd suffer horrible abuse and even the threat of death at the hands of men they hoped would change. If there had been any type of physical or emotional abuse in her marriage, she didn't remember any of it.

She remembered his voice encouraging her to awaken from a coma. She remembered his tears when he realized she would live. He'd been there every single day while she'd been in the hospital. During her long months of convalescence and countless surgeries to repair her damaged face and mangled leg, he'd been there, holding her hand, enduring her pain with her. It had been him seeing to her comfort, making sure she had everything she needed. He accompanied her to the hospital for physical and emotional therapy.

She remembered the heat of his soulful kisses and the sparkling, hungry joy in his eyes when they made love. His tenderness when he held her. The gentleness of his strong, callused hands. The husky way he whispered endearments in her ear. She remembered all that.

She didn't remember jealousy and hatred and threats to rip away Abby from his side.

She walked steadily, head high, to the office. She turned off the computer, shut off the lights and closed the door.

If Ryder had a girlfriend, Laura determined right then and there, he wouldn't have one for long. She'd been through too much, survived too much, fought back for too long to give up now. A piddly little creature like a mistress didn't stand a chance against her.

STRANGE DAY, Ryder thought as he opened his bedroom door. He now stood firm in his conviction that Laura was actually Teresa Gallagher. He also felt certain that until he had proof, it would be hurtful, if not downright cruel, to inform Laura that she wasn't his wife.

Finding proof would be the hard part.

He suspected figuring out what had happened would be even more difficult.

He'd ridden to the quarry in the hopes of getting an idea. The quarry was about half a mile from the house, off to the side of the county road. Ryder had always considered it a death trap. Around the turn of the century, red sandstone had been a popular building material. Back then, the quarry owners hadn't figured leaving a hole in the ground would hurt anything. Over the years it had filled with twenty or thirty feet of water, an irresistible lure for reckless kids and a danger for drivers who didn't know the road.

If Laura had shot Teresa, it was easy to see how in her panic she could have smacked into a boulder, disabling her car. If it had been him, though, he'd have gone to the other side where the drop-off was steep, straight into the water. So why push the Mercedes over the side where chance said it would catch on the rocks rather than hit the water?

Because Laura wasn't smart. She was clever and she was sly. She had a gift for finding a person's weakness and exploiting it. In her cruelty, she could be as cunning as a rat. But she was mostly arrogant, shortsighted and pretty damned stupid.

Imagining she was out there somewhere, figuring out a way to cover her blunder so she could come back, gave him chills. And she would be back. Of that he felt not the slightest doubt. If not for the money, then because she couldn't bear the thought of another woman taking her place.

In the meantime, he didn't know what to do about Tess. If he said, "Honey, let's go to the doctor and find out if you're Laura or Tess," she would freak. After all the hell she'd been through, it seemed downright mean to tell her it was all for nothing.

It seemed mean, too, to leave things as they stood.

He guessed she'd spent the day looking for proof of his infidelity. She hadn't been any too subtle about pawing through receipts and old ledger books in the office. Next, he supposed, would be her going through his clothes in search of lipstick stains, alien perfume or phone numbers in his pockets.

He entered the dining room with every intention of broaching the subject. Her mood made him suspicious, though. She and Abby were giggly and silly, celebrating Abby's last day of summer camp. Laura set the table with the finest china and silver. They had cake for dessert and drank grape juice out of crystal champagne flutes. Laura didn't exhibit a single sign of jealousy.

Ryder couldn't get a whiff of the storm he knew had to be brewing. Unable to bear his thoughts, he retreated to his room. He found a baseball game on television and a Western novel to read.

Abby skipped into his room and climbed up on the bed beside him. She made faces at the ball game and pronounced it icky. She demanded the remote control.

"Beat it, sugar bear." He tucked the remote under his body. "I'm watching the game. You're going to bed."

"I wanna watch cartoons," she said, pouting.

"Listen to your father, young lady."

Ryder looked up as Laura entered the room. Her peignoir grabbed his attention. Made of shiny peach-colored silk, trimmed in ecru lace, the gown flowed like liquid over her slender figure and puddled luxuriously around her feet.

"Ah, Mama." Abby hugged Ryder around the neck. "I wanna stay up with Daddy."

Laura held out her arms. The thin fabric over her breasts outlined erect nipples that beckoned for his touch. His fingers tingled with the urge to fondle her.

"Come on. Kiss your daddy. I'll tuck you in." She gave Ryder a faint smile. "Say good-night to your child, father dear."

"Good night, child," he said obediently, and peeled her arms from around his neck. He looped his arm around her and pulled her over his shoulder. She giggled and squirmed, resisting his efforts to kiss her good-night. He finally planted a big one on her forehead.

Playing baby, she squealed for her mother to pick her up. Laura held out a hand, tapping a foot in mock impatience until Abby hopped off the bed and took her hand. "I want you to read Winnie the Pooh, Mama."

Mama... the word slashed Ryder's heart. The pair of them fit as if matched in heaven. When Laura closed the door, he groaned and buried his face against his arm. Please be Laura, he prayed, let this all be crazy thinking and she's my wife and everything is okay.

Twenty minutes later, his door opened and Laura walked in. "What are you doing?" he asked.

"I'm getting ready for bed, dear." The corners of her mouth tipped in a smile. She shrugged out of her dressing robe.

The loose-fitting gown gaped, revealing the rounded swell of her breast. When she turned to drape the robe over a chair, the fabric clung to her backside as smooth as still water. The back of the gown was cut so low he could see twin dimples at the base of her spine. Heat flooded his groin.

"Bed?" he said.

She used both hands to fluff her hair through her fingers. Her breasts bounced gently, fixating him. "That's right. Bed. Sleep." She plucked the paperback Western off the bed and set it on the nightstand. "Whatever."

Paralyzed by desire, he watched her swish around the end of the bed and climb onto the other side.

She wasn't his wife. He couldn't cheat on his wife.

She reached around his chest and felt under his ribs. His breath lodged in his throat. Liquid heat melted his joints. She found the remote control and muted the sound on the baseball game still in progress.

Maybe she was his wife. She could be Laura. Chances were she was Laura and he was loco and looking for trouble.

Nearly nose to nose with him, she said, "I don't mind getting up at four o'clock in the morning. I'm sure I can find plenty to do."

Desire burned in her soft brown eyes . . . desire for him. Delicate perfume tickled his nose.

Slowly, luxuriously as a sinuous cat, she lowered her head and placed her soft lips to his throat. His Adam's apple constricted. "I love you," she breathed against his skin. "I'm sorry I ever doubted you."

He couldn't resist her to save his life.

Or hers.

Chapter Eleven

Ryder stood tall and waved both arms in wide arcs, trying to catch Abby's attention. Whooping and hollering, the girl raced her palomino pony across the meadow. The pony splashed through a puddle and water rooster-tailed behind his flying hooves.

Ryder glanced at Laura. Seated upon an Indian blanket spread over the ground, she pressed both hands over her mouth. Wide-eyed, she stared in fascinated horror at Abby's daredevilry.

Abby ripped loose with a war whoop and hauled in the reins. Buttermilk obediently tucked his hindquarters, giving his best scrub-pony imitation of a champion quarter horse slide stop.

"She's so little," Laura breathed, her complexion slightly green.

Abby did look like a monkey perched on the saddle. The stirrups were raised so high that the leathers looked like balls beneath the housing. Ryder stuck two fingers in his mouth and whistled sharply. When Abby looked his way, he gestured for her to come back. Abby reined her pony in a wide, lazy circle and urged him into a lope.

Laura lowered her head so her wide hat brim shielded her face. "She rides too fast. I don't know if my poor heart can take this."

"She rides like a buffalo hunter," he said with a prideful grin. "Shoot, my daddy had me riding before I was walking. Owned my first horse when I was three. She's just being a kid."

He sat beside Laura. She handed him a glass of lemonade, along with a look that said she thought *he* was just being a kid, as well.

Ryder loved that look. He loved all the ways she looked at him. The hot, smoky looks that turned him to molten butter inside. The gentle, humorous glint in her eyes when he or Abby did something she found funny. A look of serious concentration putting faint lines in her forehead when she was working in the office.

Abby reached them. She jumped off the saddle and let Buttermilk's reins trail. The pony blew a wet snort and lowered his muzzle to graze the grass. "I'm gonna ride rodeo, Mama! Daddy's gonna get me a barrel racing horse and I'm gonna ride broncos, too."

"Is that so?" She lifted an eyebrow. "What about steer roping? Mrs. Weatherbee said she caught you trying to rope the barn cats."

Abby pulled a face. "I'm just practicing the hula-hula."

Ryder pressed knuckles to his smile. "Hoolihan, sugar bear."

"What's a hoolihan?" Laura asked.

"It's a way to rope horses," Ryder explained. "Kind of quiet and slow so as not to spook them." He turned his attention to his daughter. "All right, you've showed off enough. Walk Buttermilk to cool him off and head him back to the barn. After you rub him down, ask Mr. Tom to put some fly spray on his face and ears."

"Okay, Daddy."

Side by side on the blanket, Ryder and Laura watched Abby walk her pony around the meadow. The picnic in the meadow above the house had been Laura's idea. "It's a perfect day," she'd declared, and he had to agree.

The temperature was not quite eighty degrees; a touch of cooling wind rustled the tops of the ponderosa pines and made the aspens sing. A prairie falcon soared overhead, and a cheeky gray jay teased them for handouts from the safety of the scrub oak. All around them the meadow was abloom with red Indian paintbrush, bright yellow cinquefoil, blue lupine and pink fireweed. Far to the south, mountain peaks above twelve thousand feet still wore tattered mantles of snow in defiance of the summer sun.

Laura had packed cold steak sandwiches, noodle salad and chocolate cupcakes. Ryder couldn't imagine a nicer way to spend the day.

Unless... A straw hat with a floppy brim protected Laura's face and, along with her pale, float-skirted dress, made her look as if she had stepped out of a perfume advertisement. If not for the kid, and Tom Sorry less than a hundred yards away in the barn, and Mrs. Weatherbee puttering around in the house, he'd make love to her under the sun. For the time being he contented himself with his thigh resting alongside hers and the tips of his fingers laying a claim to her hand.

"Ryder?" She leaned her shoulder against his and lowered her eyelids. "What would you think about having a baby?"

He choked on his lemonade. He coughed to clear his burning throat while she thumped him on the back.

"Are you all right?" she asked.

In the back of his head, a little warning voice told him he'd never be all right again. He couldn't undo what they'd done, but if he had a trace of decency remaining he would stop compounding the problem. Until he had the proof he needed, that's what he ought to do.

He'd hired a private eye to investigate Teresa and see what evidence he could find; he was sorry as could be that he had done it. Every time the telephone rang, part of him died in apprehension. He knew if he was right in his suspicions, there would be hell to pay.

Especially if she was pregnant.

He wiped his mouth with the back of his hand. "Are you—" his voice dropped to a whisper "—expecting?"

She sighed heavily. "No. But I want to be." A smile wreathed her face and she dabbed at his chin with a napkin. "I didn't mean to startle you. Let's have a baby. Let's have ten."

Babies had never crossed his mind. When Abby had been born, Laura had her tubes tied so she'd never get pregnant again. Birth control had never been an issue.

She settled back on the blanket. Twisting the napkin in her fingers, she shrugged. "I talked to Dr. Millhouse and he doesn't think there is any reason I can't have a baby. He recommended an obstetrician. What do you think?"

Just how closely had Dr. Millhouse examined the woman in front of him? His thoughts drifted back to when Abby was a baby. Every day he'd bring her to the studio, and she'd lay in her car seat and watch him while he painted. For months she'd been like a little growth on his arm as he carried her around the way she liked to be held, draped belly-down over his forearm. She'd learned how to walk by holding on to the back of his legs. Her first word had been *Da-da*.

Babies, he'd decided, were as much fun as horses.

"Ryder?"

"Maybe we ought to wait, darlin'. Give you some more time to heal. Besides, the doc says you'll need another surgery on your face—"

"I don't think the nerve damage is getting worse. Mostly the surgery is cosmetic. I'd rather have a baby." She touched his cheek, her fingertip a flower kiss. "What's wrong?"

"Nothing." He pretended interest in the picnic basket. He picked up a cupcake.

"I'll be a good mother. I promise. If I have trouble, I'll hire a nanny. And Mrs. Weatherbee will help. Or I'll go to classes and counseling. I'll do anything."

He peeled the cupcake, not knowing what to say. A yearning ache formed low in his gut. He did want more children. An even dozen would suit him fine.

Her smile lost its sparkle. "I guess a baby will tie you down even more than you are now. You miss your friends, don't you?"

"What?"

She rested her chin on her fist. "I saw the letter and photographs your friends in Texas sent you. You're missing a lot because of me. Parties and art shows and camp outs."

He realized she was talking about the annual Cowboy Artists of America trail drive and get-together. He'd been boot printed into the CAA nine years ago, and this was the first year he'd missed the annual functions that went with the privilege of membership.

He wished it was that simple. "My friends understand. They're good old boys. They want you to get better just as much as I do."

"You don't... resent me?"

"No, darlin', not at all."

Dread closed his throat. Resentment didn't begin to describe what *she* was going to feel toward him if he found proof that she was actually Teresa Gallagher.

STOP IT, stop it, stop it, Laura admonished herself. What did she intend to do if she found proof of Ryder's infidelity, anyway? Divorce him? She loved the man so much, she'd probably forgive him if he kept a harem. Would she inform Becky Solerno? Ha! Considering her own past crimes, Laura might forgive Ryder for shooting her, too. It made not the slightest difference if he had had a girlfriend. Surely she was past history by now.

Still, every time she entered the office with the good intentions of helping Ryder with the paperwork he so obviously hated to do, nasty little suspicions popped up like weasels out of a stump. She had to know what kind of woman could lure Ryder outside his wedding vows. All she wanted was a name, a face. For her own satisfaction and peace of mind, she had to know.

So when she opened mail, she sought any personal notes for declarations of love written between the lines. She inspected telephone bills. Any number she couldn't match to galleries or printers or suppliers, she followed up on with a discreet call to see if a woman answered. She examined credit card bills for the purchases of gifts.

Today, on the pretext of updating the file cabinets, she sought old love letters or phone numbers.

Part of the nagging, chronic jealousy had to do with the book dream. The puzzle of the checkbook ledger wore on her like a dull knife sawing across her nerves.

For the first few nights after she and Ryder began sleeping together in the same bed, she'd slept blessedly free of dreams of any kind. But now it was back, more real and more terrifying than ever before. In it a woman—

herself—screamed her hatred and fury and wild demands for death. The word *blackmail* had become part of the dream, too. Twice the dream had awakened her, soaked in sweat and weeping in terror. Day by day her conviction grew that the dream wasn't a dream at all, but a memory of the day she was shot. Knowledge, she prayed, would kill the dream before she turned around and saw it was Ryder who pursued her.

She found a file containing birth certificates. Curious, she opened an envelope marked with Abby's name. It showed Abby had been born in Phoenix, Arizona, on December 12 to Laura and Donald Weis. December... Laura had been in the hospital for her daughter's sixth birthday. She started to slip the certificate back in the envelope when a prickling sensation of things remembered stopped her.

She stared at the printing on the cockle-textured certificate and rubbed her thumb over the raised seal of the vital records clerk. It meant something. In her mind's eye she clearly saw a sienna-toned certificate, and stuck to the paper was a sticky note. It said...it said...*bunny trail*.

Bunny trail?

Groaning in disgust, she shoved the certificate in its envelope. *Bunny trail!* She really was losing her mind.

"Mr. Hudson, I have the information you requested concerning Miss Teresa Gallagher. Would you care to meet at my office?"

The private investigator's voice sent chills of pure dread running up and down Ryder's spine. Suddenly cold, he passed a hand over his eyes. In the weeks since he'd hired the man to find what he could about his former assistant, Ryder had run the gamut of emotions from hoping for the truth to praying that no evidence existed one way or another so that all his fears that Laura wasn't Laura were so much smoke.

Guilt was killing him.

Laura—Teresa—wore on his brain the way a water drip wore on a rock. Because of her he was living his dream. He spent his days painting, blissfully content in knowing mother and daughter were doing fine without him running interference. Meals were family affairs, sometimes noisy with everyone talking at once, but always pleasant. Laura was resuming Teresa's assistant role, handling his calls, mail and the bills, leaving him free to worry only about his painting. He found himself as eager to leave his studio at day's end as he was eager to get to work in the mornings.

The best part of all was Abby. Laura was strict with her, insisting on good manners and safety, but never unkind. She encouraged Abby's interest in horses and other animals, never minding if the kid got dirty. Mother and daughter spent a lot of time together, reading, swimming and seeing to the redecorating of the house.

And the nights . . . about that he felt guiltiest of all. He didn't want to cheat on his wife, but Laura thought she was his wife, so it wasn't really cheating. A weak argument under the light of day, but at night, facing her as she stretched out silky as a cat on his bed while those big brown eyes teased him with come-hither glances and her lips were moist and ready to work magic . . . He couldn't stay away from her. She loved him. Around her he felt ten feet tall and mightier than Superman.

For the first time in his life he truly understood what it meant to love and be loved, simply and honestly.

But you're not being honest, are you? Ryder shoved aside the thought—and fear about what Laura might do if she found the truth—that he'd hidden his suspicions from her. If the private eye had no hard, irrefutable evidence proving Laura was Teresa, then Ryder intended to drop the matter completely. After all, Laura had spent most of her thirty-three years trying to be anybody except Laura. It made perfect sense for her to assume another identity—even the identity of sweet Teresa Gallagher.

If there was no proof, then he'd accept the bounty fate had dropped in his lap and be happy.

But if proof existed that Laura *was* Teresa...he'd rope that cow when it was flushed from the scrub.

Two hours after the phone call, he parked his old four-by-four in the big parking lot of the brick-and-glass building where the private eye had his office. Traffic noise from nearby I-25 made the air rumble. The building was as anonymous as a mail out from an insurance salesman, and about as personable. At this time of day the lot was full of cars, but not a person was in sight. Still, he kept his hat on his head and sunglasses on his face as he crossed the lot, entered the building and took the stairs to the second floor.

The private eye's office had only a number on the brass marker to distinguish it. Ryder steeled himself and walked inside.

Park Lewis was a former homicide detective. Once upon a time, Ryder's agent had hired Lewis to investigate Laura's background. Ryder hadn't appreciated it at the time—especially when handed evidence that Laura had not one but three former husbands—but Lewis had shown objective professionalism and discretion.

A receptionist greeted him politely. Ryder pulled off his hat and introduced himself. She showed Ryder directly to Lewis's inner office. The man sat behind a huge desk with a mirror-shiny surface. His broad homely face gave away nothing about his emotions. He rested a beefy hand atop a large Tyvek envelope.

"How are you doing, sir?" the private eye asked mildly. He smiled at the receptionist who brought coffee for Ryder. His smile said, go away, and she did, closing the door behind her.

Ryder looked hungrily at the envelope. He wanted to take it and go home.

Lewis said, "Mind if I smoke?"

Ryder didn't care if he set himself on fire, as long as he handed over that envelope.

Lewis lit up a Camel and dragged deeply before blowing the smoke toward an air-freshening machine. "You are aware that Teresa Gallagher is wanted by the police for questioning in connection to your wife's assault."

"I know that."

"You should also know that if I happen to locate Miss Gallagher, I have to tell the cops. Otherwise that makes me guilty of withholding information and interfering with the investigation of a felony."

Ryder's heart executed a painful flip-flop. If Lewis had located Teresa, then Laura was actually Laura. That meant he could go home and love her. He could love her the way she wanted. The way he was dying to love her.

"You found her."

"No. But I think I can. If you want me to pursue this."

"Let me see what you've got."

Lewis made no move to hand over the envelope. "I'm picking up some weird vibes, sir. I have to be honest with you. I don't feel good about this."

Ryder clenched his jaw. He doubted lunging across the shiny desk top and ripping the envelope out of the PI's hand would be the polite thing to do. "I don't understand."

"Do you know why the cops think Miss Gallagher might be involved in the assault?"

Ryder pulled off the glasses and rubbed the bridge of his nose. "They think Tess and I were having an affair. We weren't. She was my assistant, nothing more." He focused on his knees, afraid Lewis would see the lie in his eyes . . . *weren't* having an affair. What label fit his situation now?

"Uh-huh. I don't care if you were or not. None of my business. What is my business is that there are witnesses and circumstances that point to Miss Gallagher as being more than a mere material witness. She'd told a neighbor that your wife is a thief and a liar and that she'd been fired unfairly. In summation, she pretty much said she intended to get even. She also told her landlady that she was on her way to visit you. This happened to be the same day of your wife's accident."

"The police never told me about that."

Lewis chuckled and ground out his cigarette. "That's because the police think you fired the shot. If they'd found the assault weapon anywhere on your property, you'd be in jail now. But that's neither here nor there. I'm going to give you some advice. You can take it or not, it makes no difference to me, except my conscience says to speak up." He shoved the envelope across the tabletop. "This is yours. You paid for it. My advice is, don't open it. Burn it. Don't bother looking for this girl. Forget she ever existed."

"Why?"

"Because if you shot your wife, sir, and this girl is involved, then if she's found, she will implicate you. They always do. Trust me. Always."

Ryder bristled. "I didn't hurt my wife." He picked up the envelope.

Lewis lit another cigarette. "Do you think Miss Gallagher shot your wife? Is that why you're looking for her?"

Ryder kept a firm hold on the envelope and his emotions as he slid on his sunglasses. "Thank you for your time, Mr. Lewis." He rose.

"I work on my instincts, and they're dancing a jig right now. Something weird is going on. You just dumped five hundred bucks for a background check. That's unusual behavior, Mr. Hudson. Has this girl contacted you? Talk to me, maybe I can help."

Tempting, very tempting. Ryder was used to keeping his own counsel, but guilty secrets sat ill with him. "You were a cop, right?"

"Twenty-six years."

"So let me ask you a hypothetical question. What if Teresa did have something to do with...my wife. What if she was involved with the accident. Only she doesn't exactly know she had anything to do with it."

"I'm not following, sir. Your wife was shot, deliberately. Her car was wrecked, but the wreck didn't cause it to go over the cliff. It was pushed off. I can't imagine how anyone could remain unaware." He steepled his fingers and tucked them under his fleshy chin. "You're wearing the face of a man who has a lot on his mind. Do you know something?"

Not yet...

Ryder started to turn away. The envelope seemed to burn his hand, and the idea of opening it turned him raw and aching inside. "Mr. Lewis, you've been around. I imagine not much happening in this world surprises you."

"I've been caught flat-footed once or twice."

"What if somebody did something...criminal, only he doesn't remember doing it? Suppose a fellow robbed a bank then got himself conked on the head and didn't remember being a robber. Is he still a bank robber?''

"I imagine a good attorney could make some interesting arguments, but yes, he's still a bank robber. Does this pertain to your wife's amnesia?''

Knowing he'd said too much, Ryder laughed uneasily. "Just campfire talk, Mr. Lewis. Thank you much for your time." He strode out of the office.

He made it to the stairwell before the lure of the envelope snagged him. In the relative privacy behind the heavy steel door, he tore open the envelope and pulled out the top sheet, an invoice for services rendered. He upended the package and caught the falling contents in his left hand.

A name leaped off the page—Antoinette Gallagher. Deceased. Relationship to subject—mother.

Antoinette Gallagher née Artois had worked for the JCPenney company in their fine jewelry department for years before being stricken by breast cancer. And her grave, most likely, had a brass marker and a plastic holder for flowers.

Ryder staggered against the wall and bumped his back.

His Laura wasn't Laura.

With his throat so tight, he thought he might choke. But he made himself read. Teresa Marie Gallagher, age twenty-six, daughter of John, deceased, and Antoinette, deceased. Formerly of Pueblo, Colorado, she'd attended the University of Colorado in Colorado Springs. She owed sixteen thousand dollars in student loans, a debt that was now almost a year in arrears. She owed another twenty-some-odd thousand to Westworth Medical Corporation for bills her mother's illness had accrued. Her last known address was a second-floor apartment in a converted Victorian home in Monument, Colorado. She'd been a member of the Methodist church and she had sung in the choir. Her last known employer was Ryder Hudson.

Interviews with friends, neighbors and acquaintances all said the same thing. Teresa was a shy, sweet, unassuming girl whose biggest ambitions had been to pay off her debts and buy a little house in a pine forest. Other than the landlady, who had heard Teresa say she was going to get even with Laura Hudson, no one had ever heard her say a bad word about anybody.

She had no criminal record. No signs of mental instability. No strange or violent behavior. After losing her job with Ryder, she'd immediately found another job as a bookkeeper for an old family friend who owned a chain of convenience stores in Pueblo. She'd packed and moved from her apartment. All she owned, except for an old couch she'd given to her neighbor, had fit into her car. She'd never reported for her first day on the job. Her disappearance had distressed many people, not one of whom believed she could have had anything to do with the shooting of Laura Hudson.

The dozens of arguments he'd had with her about what she remembered replayed in Ryder's mind. All of it was right here in the report—and Laura Hudson would have known none of it. While he and the doctors had been convincing her she was making up a past to fill the void in her brain, she'd been telling them the truth.

She didn't look anything like Laura because she wasn't Laura. She didn't sound like Laura, or walk like Laura, or have Laura's tastes, or act like Laura, or love like Laura—because she wasn't Laura.

She didn't belong to him.

All the ugly what-ifs clambered to the forefront of his mind, jostling and shouting for attention.

What if the other Laura showed up and took Abby away? What if the real Laura was dead and Donny Weis took Abby away? What if the real Laura was dead and Teresa had killed her? What if the truth came out and the state swooped in and took Abby away? What if Teresa blamed him for robbing her of her identity and she walked out, never looking back?

All the what-ifs scared the pudding out of him. He couldn't see a way to set this right without destroying his life. And Abby's life, and Teresa's.

Lies were like bad ropes, tangling at the worst times, breaking at others. But truth was a persistent thing, always finding a way to pop out into the light.

He shoved the papers in the envelope. The Tyvek felt slimy in his hands.

Doing right meant just that, *doing*. The first thing that needed doing was finding Laura. With all the enthusiasm of a man climbing gallows steps, he pulled open the steel fire door. Lewis had found out this much about Teresa, he could surely provide similar information about Laura.

The private eye's door opened, and a tall woman stepped into the hallway. Her black hair gleamed under the diffused lighting. She looked at him, and hot color darkened her olive cheeks.

Ryder glanced between Investigator Becky Solerno and the envelope tucked under his arm. Solerno carried a thick case covered in black faux leather.

The woman recovered and raised a hand in greeting. "Mr. Hudson, fancy meeting you here. How is your lovely wife?"

His forehead tightened and the muscles in his back coiled. Park Lewis had set him up. Solerno had been in the office, probably eavesdropping on every word Ryder said.

Which meant the private eye, and the police, believed him a wife-killer still.

He pivoted on one foot and slammed through the stairwell door. His boots struck each metal stair like a cannonball.

Forget that low-down, dog-dirty, rattlesnake of a private eye. He'd figure this one out himself.

Somehow.

SOMEHOW SHE FINISHED ten laps. Panting, Laura clung to the side of the pool. Her arms and shoulders quivered, the muscles gelatinous. Each inhalation was a gulp, each exhalation a rasp. Patterns in the textured pool tile swam circles before her half-closed eyes. Still, she wanted to shout in victory. Ten laps, back and forth the entire eighty-foot length of the pool, had been her goal for what seemed like forever. Day by day, she grew stronger. She was able to walk a mile without collapsing in agony. She limped only when fatigued. Instead of two hour-long resting periods a day, she only needed a light afternoon nap.

She'd finally swum ten full laps.

Grunting with the effort, she hauled her trembling, tired body out of the water. She got as far as sitting up with her lower legs dangling in the pool.

Ten laps might have been a mistake. She could barely move and her towel looked a million miles away.

The door hinges squeaked and she lifted her head, smiling broadly. Ryder was home. Except the man silhouetted in the doorway was too short, too thin and dressed all wrong.

"Hello, Laura!"

She sagged, listening to her pulse beating a tom-tom against her eardrums. Donny Weis! With every ounce of strength she had remaining, she pushed onto her feet and limped heavily across the tiles. Without bothering to dry off, she pulled on her robe.

"Laura?"

"Hello, Donny. What are you doing here?" She kept her face down and hoped he didn't see her fear. Why he frightened her so, she hadn't a clue, but her instincts were screaming for her to run. "Abby isn't home. She's gone into town with Mrs. Weatherbee." The chronic ache in her back pulsed sharply in time with her racing heart. She didn't want to, but she had to sit. She eased onto a lounge chair.

Donny's bottle green eyes glinted, shimmering like the water. "Are you all right, Laura?"

The way he kept using her name grated on her nerves. He sounded as if he was making fun of her. "I'm sorry, this is a bad time. I asked you to call before you visited."

"It's an excellent time for visiting, Laura. Just you and me, just like the good old days."

Each step that brought him closer made her that much more aware of her helplessness. She was too weak to run. The only other person on the property was Tom Sorry, and he could be anywhere from the barn to the far pastures doing something with Ryder's longhorns. She hadn't asked Ryder why she divorced Donny Weis, and he hadn't offered to tell her. For all she knew, Donny had beaten her, or worse.

She clutched the robe closed at her throat. The pain in her back went *thump-thump-thud*. "I'm sorry, I don't feel like visiting. You must leave, right now."

He stopped five feet from her. His hair picked up blue lights from the pool water. His bright flower-print tie, natty trousers and shiny shoes made him look like a sleazy salesman. From his pocket he pulled out a slim cassette tape recorder.

Did he mean to kill her and record her screams? Her mouth went dry, and she worked her tongue against her palate.

"I need some money. I'm in a bit of a mess, so it's time for you to help me out."

She drew in her chin. It finally hit her that Donny had been the man who'd called and frightened her. Did this awful creature actually think she'd give him money? She wondered if she'd given him money in the past. "Go away," she said, "and don't come back unless I specifically invite you."

"I can't do that. You know how I am when I need money. Just pester, pester, pester." His teeth gleamed. "Whine and nag. It's my most annoying quality, but I hate being broke."

"I am not giving you any money." *Thump-thump-thud*. The pain built, radiating toward her hips and shoulders.

"Twenty-five thousand will do me okay for right now. Don't want to be greedy, you know."

"Go away!" She hadn't meant to scream, but pain and fear rushed the words out of her throat. She clenched her fists. "If you don't leave now, I am calling the police."

"Do that, Laura. I think they'll be interested in hearing what I have." He pressed a button on the tape recorder with his thumb then thrust the silver box toward her face.

A woman said, "I already gave you five thousand dollars, you little worm. Why isn't Ryder dead? Why?"

"Shh, shh," a man replied in a throaty whisper. "Want the neighbors to hear? We can't talk about this on the phone."

"I'll talk any place I want! You promised to do it, so you better do it now! Shoot him. Push him off a cliff. Drown him. I don't care how you do it, but you're not getting another penny until he's dead. Do you hear?"

Donny clicked off the recorder. He clucked his tongue. "Or better yet, how about if I let old Ryder listen. I bet that cowboy will just slap his knee and hoot and holler."

Thump-thump-thud.

"Twenty-five thousand cash, Laura darling."

"No," she whispered. In the far reaches of her mind she heard the woman from the book dream. *I want him dead, dead, dead!* "I never said those horrible things. Get off this ranch. Go away."

"Do you want proof, Laura? How about if good old Ryder has an accident? A break-his-dumb-cowboy-neck kind of accident. Then this tape shows up in the police station." He rubbed the little recorder against his cheek in a loving caress. "I bet the cops will figure out a way to prove this is you. That would make a juicy situation, wouldn't it? The old man dead, you in prison for life, and that just leaves me to take care of dear little Abby. And of course, all the money Ryder will leave her in his will. That lovely, lovely money. Boy, that makes twenty-five grand look like pocket change. Think about it. I'll get back to you."

Frozen in horror, she watched Donny Weis jauntily stroll out of the pool house. Long after the last echoes of the closing door faded, Laura lurched off the lounge and screamed, "No!"

Chapter Twelve

Ryder found Abby and Mrs. Weatherbee in the kitchen. Heavyhearted, he listened to the woman try to explain to the six-year-old how baking powder worked. Envisioning his life without Abby dug holes in his belly.

Envisioning Laura figuring out how to come out ahead in this caper and swooping back into his life made him physically ill. Laura had always been an enigma, but one thing remained constant—jealousy. If she ever learned he loved another—that he loved Tess—she'd find a way to use Abby to make him suffer.

"We're making cupcakes, Daddy." Abby hoisted a beater high. A fat drop of chocolate batter plopped onto her arm. She licked it off. "We're gonna decorate 'em. We got sprinkles."

"That's good, sugar bear. Where's your mama?"

Mrs. Weatherbee turned away from the stove. She gestured at him with a large wooden spoon. "Resting. I don't think she feels too good, sir. She won't let me fuss at her. No offense, but you're letting her push herself too hard."

Figuring she was taking an extended nap, he went upstairs. Come right out and tell her, he thought. No use delaying or beating around the bush. He had no right to withhold information.

He was going to lose her. The pain slashed across his chest and belly like a knife. Teresa had her own life. He was a married man. His wife, the other Laura, was out there somewhere.

He had to stop on the stairs and hold on to the railing until he found his equilibrium. If he found Laura, divorced her and convinced Teresa to stay with him, he would lose Abby. Even if Laura went to jail for trying to kill Teresa, she'd find a way to take Abby away from him. Out of spite and meanness, she'd throw her daughter into the bureaucratic maw for no other reason than not wanting Ryder to have her.

If he stayed married, he would lose Teresa.

The pain deepened in his chest, squeezing his heart.

He made himself lift one foot after the other to the top of the stairs and into his bedroom. No sign of her. He checked her suite. The draperies were drawn. The rooms had the feel of a silent tomb, echoing his despairing mood.

"Darlin'?"

A soft, heart-wrenching sob was his reply.

He hurried to the bed and found her huddled under the covers, curled in a tight little ball. Feverish heat rolled off her tear-dampened face.

"Darlin', what's the matter?" He stroked her back and shoulder. Guilt made him think she'd found out about herself and how he'd been lying.

She finally sat up, but drew in her legs and wrapped her arms around her knees. He left her in search of tissues. He found a box in the bathroom and returned to the bed. Even in the dim light, he saw the angry blotches on her face and her swollen, sore-looking eyes. She'd been crying a long time.

He used the house line to call Mrs. Weatherbee and ask her to bring up a pitcher of ice water. Then Laura asked him to fetch her pain medication. His alarm doubled. Ever since the cast had come off her left leg, she'd been downright perverse in refusing medication, even so much as an aspirin. Her asking for painkillers must mean she was in agony.

He returned to the bathroom and in the medicine chest found the codeine-laced painkiller. He shook two of the large white tablets into his palm.

Mrs. Weatherbee arrived with the water. Ryder gave her a pointed look. She closed the door behind her on the way out. Laura choked down the tablets and two glasses of water. She scrubbed her hot face dry with a mound of tissues.

"What happened, darlin'? Did you hurt yourself? Do you need a doctor?"

"Ryder, I . . . oh, God, I can't tell you. You're going to hate me forever!" She pressed the heels of her hands to her eyes.

"I'll never hate you, darlin'. Never." He sat on the bed and pulled her atop his lap. He held and comforted her as if she was a child, petting her shaking shoulders and murmuring soothing nonsense against her ear. "You mean the world to me. Nothing is ever going to make me hate you."

She finally calmed enough to look at him. Her breath came ragged and rough. "I want you to call your lawyer."

"What?" He almost flung her off his lap. Instead, he tightened his hold. She trembled in his arms.

"You'll hate me, despise me. But I can't fix this myself. I can't hope it'll go away. I want you to get your lawyer so we can make sure you have custody of Abby. You have to take care of her. Promise me that. No matter how much you hate me, you have to take care of her."

"I—"

"Promise me!"

"All right, all right, I promise."

He tried to ease her face around so he could see her eyes, but she resisted. Damp hair clung to her skin. Her bosom heaved.

"Laura—"

She slapped a hand against his shoulder. "Don't. Give me a moment. I have to...I have to tell you." Several deep breaths later, she stiffened her back and lifted her head. She looked across the room, giving him a view of her profile. "I know what happened the day I was shot."

His heart leaped into his throat. He slid a guilty glance at the Tyvek envelope he'd dropped on the bedside table.

"I figured it out." She licked her lips with nervous little darts of her tongue. "Please, let me go. I can't do this with you so close." She pushed against him.

Reluctantly, he turned her loose. An awful voice of doom told him he was never going to hold her again. He moved to a chair and sat stiffly.

She turned on the bedside lamp. "I love you," she said. "I don't know what was wrong with me before the accident that I couldn't love you, but I do now."

"You don't—"

She thrust out her hand. "Don't say anything! Please." Her voice, raw from weeping, cracked. She squeezed her eyelids shut, and her body rocked with a spasm. "I know who shot me. It was Donny Weis."

He got halfway out of the chair before realizing he had moved. His muscles trembled in protest as he made himself sit back down. "Weis? Are you sure?"

"I think so. You see...I gave Donny money to kill you."

His heart slithered from his throat and dropped into his belly, resting there like a lump of ice. In the back of his mind, he saw that glistening puddle underneath his Dodge and heard Tom Sorry saying, "Somebody cut the brake lines."

"Donny came by today while you were gone. He has a tape recording of me telling him I want you dead. He says if I don't give him twenty-five thousand dollars, he'll kill you and then give the tape to the police. I'll go to prison and he'll get Abby and all your money." She dropped her face into her hands. "Oh, Ryder! The book dream I keep having, it's a memory. It's the day I was shot. I was screaming about how I wanted you to die and then for some reason I was running away with the book—only it's not a book, it's a checkbook ledger. Donny and I must have argued. He must have wanted more money."

Donny must have thought clipping brake lines on an old truck was as good as killing Ryder at close range. That kind of failure would have driven Laura berserk.

None of this explained how in the world Teresa had gotten involved.

She snuffled loudly and snatched tissues out of the box with a sniffling sound. "This is what we have to do. Make your lawyer come here and we'll draw up custody papers. He has to come immediately. I already called Becky Solerno and told her that—"

He jumped to his feet. "You did what?"

She cringed. "I called Becky. I can't hide what I've done. Donny will hurt you. He'll hurt Abby. I can't let him blackmail us. I have no choice." She swabbed at her face. "Oh, Ryder, I don't care what they do to me, but what about Abby? How am I going to explain this to her?"

"You told the cops you tried to kill me?" He sank down on the chair. If ever he needed extra proof that this woman was not his wife, this was it. Laura would never, in a million years, confess to any kind of wrongdoing. "What did you tell Solerno?"

Snuffling, she shook her head. "I didn't actually speak to her. She wasn't in. I left a message telling her I remember what happened and I have to talk to her. I'm so sorry, but it's better this way. You and Abby will be safe."

"You can't talk to Solerno."

Her eyes were stricken, her mouth taut. "You are so good and kind and generous. Please, don't be stupid, as well. He meant what he said. He'll kill you and blame it on me."

"Donny Weis?" He shook his head. "Blackmail you, yep, I can see that. But, darlin', that man is as lazy as a twenty-year-old dog in August. Not to mention, he's a coward. He's not the kind to go around killing people."

"You don't—"

"No, *you* don't. You don't know him." He glanced at the envelope he'd dropped on the table. In a twisted way, her confession filled him with relief. Teresa must have stumbled into the middle of the plot—and what a plot it must have been if Laura had trusted her ex-husband with a murder scheme. There was no telling how long Donny had been able to string Laura along. No telling how long Laura would have believed in her powers over Donny and allowed him to string her along. The clipped brake lines must have been a gesture on his part to get more money out of her—Donny must have known Ryder wouldn't have been hurt.

"I don't remember him, true, but—"

"You don't know him. You never knew him. Donny Weis isn't your ex-husband."

"What?"

He pushed himself off the chair. "It's my turn to ask you not to hate me." He picked up the envelope. Better to lose her than have her go to prison for Laura's crimes. "I saw a private eye today. I hired him to investigate you."

She shook her head. "You knew I was trying to kill you?"

"You never hurt anybody in your life." He thrust the envelope at her. "You know how I and the doctors keep telling you you're crazy for those memories of yours? Well, looks like we have some crow to eat."

Hesitantly, she shook out the envelope contents.

"You're not Laura. You're not my wife." Emotion choked up in his throat and he couldn't say any more. He jammed his hands in his back pockets and lifted his face to study the ceiling.

For the longest time she shuffled through the private eye's report. Soft noises marked the diminishing tissue box as she absently wiped her face and throat, dabbed at her eyes and blew her nose.

Finally, she looked at him and whispered, "This is what I've been telling you. My mother, my apartment. I'm Teresa Gallagher?"

Taking her calmness as a good sign, he gingerly sat on the edge of the bed. "You're Teresa Gallagher."

"I'm not your wife? Abby's mother?"

"You were never married to Donny. You never tried to kill me." He dropped his face on his hand. "I wish you hadn't called Solerno."

"This is me. I'm Teresa. How long have you known?"

"I got proof today."

She blinked slowly, once, twice, three times. "How long have you *known?*"

He hung his head. "Since that night you first came to my bed. Laura never loved me the way you loved me." Heat climbed from his throat and spread over his face. "And I'm pretty certain you never loved another man, either."

She lifted a hand to her mouth.

"I'm not going into details, darlin', so trust me on this. If you need more proof than what's in that report, a blood test can prove you aren't Laura."

She kept looking at him as if his face was covered with polka dots.

"Say something."

She looked at the report again.

"I never meant any harm to you," he continued. "I had no cause to think you weren't my wife. By the time they let me see you, they'd shaved your head and you were so beat up no one could have recognized you. Not me...not the doctors."

"Until we made love." She frowned. "I was a virgin?"

He lifted his shoulders. "I think so."

"That was weeks ago, Ryder, why didn't you say something?"

"I wasn't sure and I didn't want to do a fool thing unless I had to. And—and—and I love you."

She raised the report so the lamp shone fully on the pages. "This is me. My life. I'm not your wife." All color drained from her face. "I'm not...what are we going to do about Abby?" she whispered. "What are we going to do?"

"More importantly, what are we going to do about Solerno? She suspects something anyway. She was there when I picked up the report. The private eye was trying to get me to say you hurt Laura or I did. She's not going to let this go."

She reached for him. She lifted her hand to his face, hesitated, then lowered it atop his hand. He turned his hand and entwined his fingers with hers.

"We have to tell the truth," she said. "I'm not Laura."

"We don't know what the truth is. Do you remember who shot you?"

"No."

"Do you remember why you came to the ranch?"

She lowered her face. "No."

"That tape Donny had. Did he leave a copy? Did anyone else see him?"

"No." Her chin quivered and her eyes teared up. "I was alone. You were gone and Mrs. Weatherbee was gone. It's just my word against his about him threatening you. I'm so scared."

Ryder envisioned the heyday the newspapers and television stations would have with this. Folks had pretty much forgotten the wrecked Mercedes and Laura's—Teresa's—horrendous injuries. But this would definitely renew interest.

The telephone rang. Teresa and Ryder swung their heads to face it. Neither made a move to answer.

"Outside line," she whispered. "It must be Becky."

"You better answer."

She did, bringing the handset to her ear as if it physically hurt her. "Oh, hello, Becky." She closed her eyes. A single tear coursed a silver path down her cheek. "Yes, sort of, it's very complicated. I think I better tell you in person." Her eyes flew wide. "No! I swear, I'm okay, but I just can't tell you over the phone. Tomorrow morning? Fine. I'll be here."

TERESA SAT on a lounge chair in the courtyard. All around her the terra-cotta pots were filled with geraniums, pinks and other bright flowers. She watched a hummingbird flit around a feeder hanging beneath a balcony. Masked by the drug, her aches and pains had faded to dull thrumming. Her body felt sluggish as a mud puddle, but her mind raced a million miles a minute.

Teresa Gallagher.

She kept rolling the name over her tongue. It wasn't quite familiar, yet it gave her a sense of belonging. Teresa Marie Gallagher, only daughter of Antoinette. She couldn't remember her father. Her mother was as clear and real as the clouds overhead and the white stucco walls. She had a past and it was real and it was hers.

She had no future.

A catch in her throat choked her for a moment. Ryder wasn't her husband, Abby wasn't her child. Because of her, they might both be in mortal danger. Where was Laura Hudson?

A door opened and Ryder stepped outside. He held the door as Abby marched with unusual care through the doorway. With both hands, she held a tray of cupcakes. With exaggerated motions, the little girl set down the tray on a table.

Teresa had barely made it through dinner without breaking down. Seeing Abby so proud of the cupcakes she'd helped bake and decorate made tears rise in Teresa's eyes. She rubbed her fist over the base of her throat.

Teresa took her time examining each frosted cupcake, bright with colored candy sprinkles and M&Ms. ''Those are the most beautiful cupcakes I have ever seen, honey.''

Abby shot her father a smug grin. ''Can I eat one now?''

Ryder took a seat. ''Sure. Pull yourself up a chair. We need to have a little family talk.''

A cold Teresa had never even imagined gripped her body, infusing her very bones. She couldn't bear to look at Ryder, knowing his handsome smile would never again be for her, knowing his beautiful midnight eyes would never again gaze upon her with heated love.

Abby plucked a cupcake off the tray and offered it to Teresa.

Don't cry, she repeated silently in her head. No more tears. This was no longer about her, or Ryder, it was about Abby. The grown-ups no longer mattered.

Abby scooted back on the chair seat and her boots wagged to an unheard rhythm. She greedily peeled paper off the cupcake.

"We have something to tell you, sugar bear. Something that might be hard to understand. So you need to listen real careful. Okay?"

The girl nodded, but looked more interested in licking off the frosting than in her father's somber words.

"Do you remember how your mama's car crashed into the quarry and she was all bandaged up and couldn't walk?"

"Uh-huh." Her tongue lapped the sprinkles off the frosting.

"And she couldn't remember anything. Not her name or you and me. Do you remember how Daddy went to the hospital every day."

"Sure."

Abby acted too casual. Her nonchalance worried Teresa. It had to be self-protection, for she was an unusually sensitive child.

Looking flustered, Ryder leaned forward. "Folks make mistakes. Even grown-ups. Sometimes those mistakes are doozies. Like for instance, the doctors and I and everybody else, even Mrs. Weatherbee, made a big old mistake. We have to fix it now and put it right. That's what we do about mistakes. For both grown-ups and little kids—if something is wrong, it's up to us to fix it. You understand this?"

"Uh-huh." Frosting gone, Abby nibbled the moist chocolate cake. A blue sprinkle clung to her upper lip.

Ryder laid a hand atop Teresa's. "Come to find out we've made a mistake about your mama. You know she loves you and she wouldn't ever do anything to hurt you. But she—we—have to fix the mistake."

Abby took a big bite out of the cupcake. She appeared engrossed in the sweet, except for a hot glitter of emotion in her eyes.

"I love you, Abby," Teresa said. "If I had my wish, I'd...oh, Ryder, I can't."

He squeezed her fingers. "What we're trying to say, sugar bear, is your mama isn't exactly your mama."

Abby popped the rest of the cupcake in her mouth. She chewed hard once, then mumbled, "I know." Her eyes darted warily, as if judging their reactions.

"You know what, baby?" Teresa asked.

"You're not my real mama." She swallowed. "But I like you better." Her face flushed bright red and she began kicking her boots against the chair. "You're Teesa."

Teresa could have fallen off the chair. A glance at Ryder showed him just as dumbfounded.

Tears shimmered on Abby's lower lids. She kicked the chair so hard her boots heels were putting dents in the redwood. "I'm sorry, Daddy. I didn't know it was a mistake. I'm sorry."

Teresa lunged from her chair and gathered the little girl in her arms. Abby wrapped her arms around Teresa's neck and let loose a wail. Horrified, Teresa looked to Ryder.

They finally calmed the child. Holding her on her lap, Teresa eased strands of hair off Abby's face. "You have nothing to be sorry about, baby. Nothing at all."

"I wished it," she mumbled, pressing her head firmly against Teresa's shoulder. "I wished real hard for Mama to go away and Teesa come be my mama. I wished and wished and wished. When you gave me butter rums, I got my wishes all true."

"Oh, my," Teresa breathed, remembering the funny urge to buy Lifesavers for Abby. When she went for her weekly medical appointments, she always bought a roll of candy. It had become a game between them for her to slip the candy to the child on the sly, always with the admonition, "Don't tell your mom, kiddo."

"Listen up, sugar bear. Wishing didn't make your mama go away. Wishing didn't turn her into Teresa. It just happened. It was a mistake. Now we're going to fix it."

Abby locked her chocolate-stained fingers in Teresa's blouse. Her little body trembled with wiry determination. "Teesa is my mama. She's *mine!* You can't take her away!"

IT HAD TAKEN hours for Teresa to settle Abby, but finally the poor child had fallen asleep. Teresa had not the slightest idea how to dislodge the child's notion that her wishing had caused the accident that switched Teresa for Laura. From a child's point of view, the logic was unassailable, and the only upsetting aspect was that fate or her father might undo her wish.

Now in Ryder's bedroom, she slumped on a chair and stared at the bed that was no longer her bed. Ryder emerged from the bathroom. He was barefoot, but still wore his shirt and jeans. He looked as awkward as Teresa felt.

"Why would Abby wish her own mother away?"

"Oh, darlin', I don't know where to begin." He flopped onto the bed. "Laura turned up on my doorstep when Abby was a few days old. The only reason she went through the pregnancy was to try to keep her marriage together with Weis, but he didn't want the kid. He dumped her." He rubbed his temples with the pads of his fingers. "She hated that baby."

"That isn't possible."

"I was living in my cabin where Tom Sorry lives now. Laura dropped Abby on the couch, then acted like she didn't exist. After about an hour of squalling, I picked up the baby. That's all she wanted, someone to hold her. Poor little scrawny thing. Laura never even looked at her. That's what I remember most. Laura never looked at her."

She rubbed her belly, unable to imagine how a woman could ignore her own baby.

"I've had mares do that. Drop a foal, then walk away. It's like a switch turned off or something. No mothering instinct. Old Mrs. Weatherbee laid one look on that baby and fell straight away in love." A sheepish grin pulled his lips. "Me, too."

"Did Laura abuse her?"

He nodded. "For the first three years or so, Laura acted like Abby didn't exist. Never touched her or talked to her. When Abby started talking, Laura got it in her head that a right proper little girl was a Shirley Temple doll."

"Did Laura physically abuse her?"

"There's other ways to hurt a baby, darlin'. Trust me. Do you remember Laura?"

Teresa thought hard, but finally conceded defeat. "I wish I could say, whoopee, I'm cured, but I don't think I am. I still don't quite remember being Teresa Gallagher."

"I don't know why I didn't see it before I married her. Or maybe I did, and it didn't matter. She can't stand not being the center of attention. She sure can't stand anyone telling her no. She used Abby against me. If I made her mad, she threatened to send Abby to boarding school. Or give Weis custody."

"That is so sick."

"The only way I could protect Abby was to take it on the chin myself. Trouble was, the more she treated me like dirt, the more she got to liking it. I wanted a divorce, but she wasn't about to give up my money or let another woman have me."

"She wanted you dead instead." She shuddered, feeling his shame and his pain.

He suddenly pushed upright. "I don't want to lose you, Tess. In spite of everything, this past year has been the happiest time of my life. I've done you wrong. I didn't mean to, I didn't know, but I did wrong, anyway. I want to make it up to you."

Her shattered heart throbbed in agony. "Don't blame yourself."

"I kept explaining everything away. Like when you took down the portrait, I told myself it was just your vanity not wanting reminders. When you were nice to Abby, I said it was personality changes from the accident. Even when you started working in the office, I pushed the suspicions aside." His expression skewed in a pained grimace. "The docs and I kept calling you crazy. I'm extra sorry about that."

"That no longer matters. What matters is getting this straightened out. Do you think it's true what Donny Weis said? That Laura tried to kill you?"

He chuckled. "A few days before your accident somebody cut the brake lines on my truck."

She gasped in horror. "Did you tell the police?"

The chuckle turned into a laugh. "I thought you did it."

"Me? Whatever for?"

"Because it was a dumb thing to do—more to make a point, maybe, than to actually kill me. I wouldn't have gotten out of the driveway before noticing I had no brakes. The worst that would have happened would be crunching the bumper, and probably not that. And you had a right to be mad as hell because of Laura firing you. Do you remember that?"

She thought hard. It was as if her brain was filled with potholes. "No."

"You ended up in her Mercedes somehow. I'm pretty sure she's the one who shot you and that's why she's hiding out. She must have taken your car and skipped the state."

"What happens if Donny finds out I'm not Laura and we can't convince the police he's trying to blackmail me? What then? What will stop him from taking Abby?"

"I'll stop him." Ryder clenched his fists. "I'll kill him if he tries. Truth is, I'm more afraid of the state. If the cops get wind of this, they'll take Abby out of the house just to be on the safe side. If she goes into foster care, I'll never get her back."

And she'd called the authorities herself. "I can't think anymore." Wearily, every joint aching, Teresa attempted to rise. When the first try failed, she tried again. Ryder was on his feet and at her side in a second. He caught her around the waist and steadied her.

Her eyes locked with his, and the physical pain was nothing compared to what was happening inside her heart.

"I never meant to hurt you, Tess," he whispered.

Tess, Tess, my darlin' Tess...

"Did we—I mean, you and me, before the accident—did we ever...you know?"

"If you're asking if we had an affair, no." His hand tightened ever so slightly on her hip. "You were—are—the best assistant I ever had. We were friends. You were always smiling and if there was a problem, you just went ahead and fixed it. You kept my life humming along, at least the artist part. I could count on you."

Now her very presence threatened his life.

"I used to wonder about us. What might have been if I'd met someone like you first."

"Laura is so beautiful. Would you have even noticed me?"

"Maybe not," he said honestly. "We're making this pretty hard on ourselves."

"I know." It had to be up to her. She gently pushed away. Just as reluctantly, he turned her loose. "Good night, Ryder." She limped out of the room, refusing to look at him, knowing if she did, she was lost.

Chapter Thirteen

Ryder's attorney arrived at eight o'clock sharp. Portly, garbed in a thousand-dollar suit, Gary Holstead had the smile of a clown and the soul of an IRS auditor. When Ryder and Teresa explained the situation to him, his only comment was, "You should have called me before you called the police."

Ryder sent Abby and Mrs. Weatherbee to Denver. First they'd go to Elitch's, an amusement park Abby had been begging to see all summer. Then Mrs. Weatherbee was to take the girl to visit Ryder's aunt, who lived in Westminster. If Becky Solerno decided to play bureaucrat and call in social services, Abby would be far out of their reach.

Becky Solerno arrived at nine o'clock sharp.

They gathered in the living room. Teresa and Ryder sat side by side on a love seat. Gary Holstead sat on a leather wing chair. A tape recorder rested on the table next to him. He held a notebook open on his lap. He and the investigator smiled at each other. Becky remained standing.

Teresa cleared her throat. She plucked at her skirt and smoothed it over her knees. "I suppose I should start. This is going to be a little difficult to believe, Becky."

The investigator held up a finger. She tracked a slow path through the air, pointing in turn at the attorney, Ryder and Teresa. "Let me guess. You're not Laura Hudson."

Teresa gasped. Ryder snapped backward as if punched on the chin. Gary Holstead kept smiling.

Becky slapped her knee. "I knew it! It has been driving me crazy trying to figure out how the woman I know is Laura Hudson. Sure, your looks changed, but your personality? The doctors say personality changes can happen, but this is too much. You don't match any of the comments people make about you. Are you Teresa Gallagher?"

Teresa nodded. Becky continued to smile pleasantly. There was no telling what she thought.

"And you," Becky said to Ryder. "You hired Park Lewis to figure out if she was Laura or Teresa."

"Why did he call you in?"

"He doesn't like wife-killers any better than I do. Laura has a long, detailed history of loving abusive men. Why shouldn't you be one of them?"

Gary cleared his throat. "Investigator Solerno, might I remind you this is a voluntary interview. We shall have no name-calling. My clients have committed no crimes."

"We don't know that. Teresa, is your memory back? Do you know who shot you?"

"This sounds crazy. I have a recurring dream. I think it might be from the day I was shot. I don't recognize any people, but I'm sure Donny Weis was there." Ryder's tough-skinned hand gave her confidence. She told the investigator about Donny's visit and extortion demand.

"Did he leave a copy of the tape?"

"No."

"Did he make arrangements for you to pay him?"

Teresa shook her head, her nervousness growing. Becky remained smiling, but something had shifted. She seemed colder, harder.

Becky focused her dark eyes on Ryder. "So where is your wife?"

"I don't know."

"Is she alive?"

"I don't know."

Teresa leaned forward, "Look, Becky, when I thought I was Laura and Donny Weis was going to kill Ryder, I called you right away. If I was trying to hide anything, I wouldn't have called. I wish I knew what happened and who shot me, but I don't. All I know is, Donny has a tape of Laura telling him to kill Ryder. Donny thinks I'm Laura and he's trying to blackmail me. Other than that, I don't know anything. Ryder doesn't know anything."

Gary Holstead rose from the chair. "Investigator Solerno, you have enjoyed full cooperation from my clients. This is a highly unusual situation, in which I'm positive my clients are the victims. Now, if you insist upon treating them as suspects, then I will make the recommendation that they refrain from making any statements to you."

"All right, I'm hearing you." Her dimples deepened. "You're right, too, in calling this unusual. I'm not exactly sure what kind of situation we have here. Would your clients be willing to take polygraphs?"

Teresa exchanged a look with Ryder.

"This is nutty enough it has to be true. But I'd like to make sure I'm getting the straight poop from you two."

"I'll take a polygraph," Teresa said. "I'll talk to anyone you want me to."

"Same here." Ryder looked at his attorney. "If that's all right with you, sir?"

"My clients have no objection," Holstead said with an air of magnanimity. He held up a hand in warning. "I demand a list of questions beforehand and strict adherence to a script. You will not, under any circumstances, turn this into a fishing expedition."

RYDER AND TERESA passed the polygraph examinations to Becky Solerno's satisfaction. She even managed to apologize to Ryder for suspecting he'd somehow figured out a way to switch wives for his own gain. Then the investigator, accompanied by a technician, returned to the ranch. The technician wired the telephones with recording equipment, setting the trap for Donny Weis.

The greatest victory was that no one mentioned Abby or the status of her custody.

The next morning, Teresa and Ryder went to the studio.

"The book dream," Teresa said. "That's the key to what happened." Arms crossed, one foot tapping, she stared at the desk in the office. Behind her, Ryder leaned a shoulder against the doorjamb.

"It's no dream, I'm sure of it now. I'm remembering the day I was shot. Where were you that day?"

He cocked back his hat with his thumb. "Colorado Springs. But first I stopped in Monument, looking for you. I left before Laura got out of bed. She always slept until at least noon."

"Where was everyone else?"

"Mrs. Weatherbee left around one or so to pick up Abby and then to go grocery shopping. Tom was repairing fences up in the north pasture. That's on the other side of the hill. Can't see the house from there. Mrs. Weatherbee was the first to notice the wreck. She spotted you on her way home from the store."

The blank holes in her memory made her crazy. Somewhere inside her scarred brain lay the answers. She hadn't a clue as to how to extract them. She rubbed the small of her aching back and pulled out the desk chair. Past Ryder she could see Abby standing before an easel with the legs shortened for her height. Wearing a white cowboy hat, holding a palette and brush, she looked like a miniature version of Ryder.

According to Mrs. Weatherbee, Abby had been a perfect angel at the amusement park and while visiting her great-aunt's house. She hadn't fussed or acted naughty all day. She'd been on such good behavior, it was almost painful to watch. Teresa guessed the girl feared making an error or angering somebody and having her precarious world destroyed.

She turned her attention to the desk. "Okay, let's go over this step by step. Laura fired me—" Catching Ryder's grin, she lost her train of thought. "What's so funny?"

"You. I don't know how I missed recognizing you. Welcome back, Tess."

"You're making jokes." His smile tugged at her heart, making her want to sigh. The melancholy had returned to his eyes, darkening them to midnight. She made herself look away. "We have serious work to do here."

He heaved a heavy breath. "Yes, ma'am."

"You said Laura said she fired me because she caught me stealing jewelry."

He shook his head. "Caught you trying on her clothes and *maybe* trying to steal. But I don't believe it. I was out of town so I think she saw her chance to get rid of you." He frowned, pulling on his jaw. "She was always jealous of you, but you and I weren't involved. It doesn't make any sense that you didn't talk to me. You knew where I was. You knew when I got back. You knew I'd listen to you."

She snapped her fingers. She sorted through the report Park Lewis had compiled. In the interview of Teresa's former landlady was the statement that Teresa had called Laura a liar and thief. "I bet Laura found a way to accuse me of being a thief. The checkbook ledger in my dream must contain the proof I needed to show you I wasn't stealing from you."

"I'm not following, darlin'."

"I've been through this office with a fine-tooth comb." Her cheeks warmed as she clamped down the urge to tell him why. "There's a ledger missing. I can account for some of the checks it contained, but not all of them." Even as she said it, the illogic caught up to her. "You never gave Laura any grief about money, did you?"

He shook his head. "She spent what she wanted."

"So why would I call her a thief?" She clicked her tongue and scowled. Realization rushed in like a gust of icy air. "Because she was trying to conceal where she got the money to pay Donny."

He glanced over his shoulder at Abby before moving to a chair in the office, out of hearing range. He straddled it, resting his forearms on the chair back and his chin on his arm.

"On the tape Donny played, Laura said she'd paid him five thousand dollars. Now that's a healthy chunk of money. If you had turned up murdered, the police might question it." She swiveled in her chair and turned on the computer. She opened up the accounting program and turned to the last entries she'd made before the accident.

She highlighted the out-of-sequence checks she'd noticed in the ranch account. "Look at the date. September, quarterly taxes are due. So I must have been pulling everything together for your accountant. I find two checks out of sequence, totaling five thousand dollars."

Ryder gazed solemnly at the computer screen. "And?"

"It seems suspicious to me that this is the only ledger book I can't find."

"Tom Sorry is the only person who uses that checking account. He buys feed, supplies, whatever."

"And when he needs a check, he comes into this office and writes it. Which means Laura could have done the same thing. I bet I caught her doing it. It should be easy to find out. We'll ask the bank for copies of the checks."

Teresa called the bank and asked for the accounts manager. She asked the manager to fax copies of the checks in question. The manager told her the fax would be forthcoming within twenty minutes.

"Laura spent money like a congressman," Ryder said. "Five thousand doesn't prove she bought a hit man."

"We'll let Becky figure out what's proof and what isn't."

When the fax finally arrived, Teresa was ready with invoices and receipts Tom Sorry had written. The checks in question had been written out for cash—something Teresa couldn't find noted on any other checks Tom had written on the ranch account. Neither Teresa nor Ryder could discern if the signatures were different, but Ryder pointed out that the rest of the writing on the checks didn't match Tom's.

"Do you have any samples of Laura's handwriting?" she asked.

"Laura wasn't much for reading and writing." He snapped his fingers. "Her address book. I'll fetch it."

Abby threw down her brush and palette to follow her father, but as soon as she saw Teresa was still in the office, she ran in there.

"Where's Daddy going?" she demanded.

"It's okay, baby. He just went to the house." Teresa petted the girl's shining hair. "Relax. We won't desert you. I promise."

Keeping an eye on Teresa, the girl went back to her painting. Teresa sighed, unable to squash the bad, bad feeling of impending doom.

While waiting for Ryder, she searched through the spreadsheet and compiled a report showing every cash withdrawal or check written for cash or cash advance Laura had made in the six months prior to the accident. Ryder walked in while Teresa was printing out the report.

"What did Laura do with herself?" she asked. She picked up the papers from the printer catch tray. The total—nearly thirty thousand dollars—astonished her.

Ryder shrugged. He dropped the address book on the desk in front of Teresa before resuming his backward seat on the chair. "She went to parties. She shopped."

"She spent a lot of money."

He shrugged again.

"I'm appalled." She handed him the report. "She pulled out enough cash to hire an army of hit men." She opened the address book and begin comparing the handwritten entries with the facsimiles of the checks. Laura had definitely written the checks. "I don't get it. It's obvious you didn't track how much she spent. Why steal money from the ranch account?"

"Donny probably told her to. Laura isn't all that smart, but Donny's got more than half a brain."

"Some smart guy," she said dryly. "It never occurred to either of them that Laura already used large amounts of cash. Do you think I found out she was trying to kill you?" She glanced at the door. "Wait a minute. Did I have a key to this office?"

"Sure did."

"Okay, so let's say I was doing the books, noticed the missing five thousand dollars and—" She laughed and swung her gaze to the fax machine. "I would have done the same thing, asked the bank for copies of the checks. I would have known they were forgeries." She grabbed the telephone and punched in the number of the bank. She asked the accounts manager to find out if Teresa Gallagher had made an inquiry into Ryder's ranch account back in September. Put on hold, Teresa said to Ryder, "They log everything into computers."

Unfortunately, her claim was overly optimistic. The accounts manager was unable to tell her if she'd inquired about the checks in question.

She hung up. "Even so, that's what I would have done."

"When you called Laura on it, she fired you. She threatened to say you stole the money."

"Right. Only I came back. I had the checkbook ledger." She closed her eyes and rubbed her temples, calling up images of her dream. "She's furious, scream- ing at someone about wanting . . . screaming about want- ing you dead. I caught her, Ryder."

"Who was she screaming at?"

"Donny?" Her gaze went distant. "It had to have been Donny, and she wasn't just angry about his failure to kill you. She used the word blackmail." She snapped her at- tention to Ryder. "Oh, my God, he knows I'm not Laura. He was here. He's probably the one who shot me."

Picking up on her thread of logic, Ryder nodded ea- gerly. "They try to kill you to cover up their scheme, but they mess up. So they panic and run. It was Laura using the ATM card."

"Now she and Donny are out of money. So Donny comes for a visit to find out how much I know. He's decided my amnesia is real, so they're blackmailing me." She leveled a hard gaze on him. "Becky is going to love this."

"What if she can't catch Donny? What happens to Abby?"

She slumped on the chair. Ryder might as well have a sign tattooed on his forehead—My Daughter Is My Achilles Heel. "You're the best father in the world. Nobody is going to take her away from you."

"Haven't you been watching the news? The courts don't care who's the best parent or what's good for the kids. All they care about is who's blood and who isn't. Biological parents can be the lowest belly-crawlers on earth, but they're blood and that's all that matters."

"Laura and Donny can't get Abby if they're in prison."

"No." He huffed a snort of disgust. "Then the social workers will take her. They'll put her in foster homes. They'll make her a ward of the state. If that happens, darlin', I'll never get her back."

"What does Mr. Holstead say?"

He lowered his face onto his arm. "He says the courts are hostile toward stepfathers. Especially stepfathers seeking custody of little girls."

Frustrated with his pessimism, she exclaimed, "Are you sure you aren't her father? Women lie about paternity all the time."

He pulled a face.

"Abby looks like you, she acts like you, she sounds like you. You said you and Laura had an affair. Haven't you ever done a paternity test?"

"When Laura showed up, Abby was only a week old. So Laura would have had to carry her for over ten months. Even a cowpoke like me can do the math."

"She lied."

"I've got Abby's birth certificate."

Having seen it herself, all she could say was, "Oh." She went to him and placed her hands upon his shoulders. "We have to draw Laura into the open. We have to convince her to sign over custody to you. She doesn't want Abby."

He laughed. It held a pained note. "You're right, she doesn't want Abby, she wants to kill me."

She lifted his hat off his head so she could see his eyes. The pain and worry she saw squeezed her heart as if with an iron fist. "I know how to bring her out in the open. I know how to catch her."

"How?"

She finger combed his thick, hat-flattened hair. "When Donny tries to take your money, I'll make him sign a paper giving you the right to adopt Abby."

His features skewed in puzzlement. "He'll never go for that."

"More importantly, Laura will never go for it. Abby is her only weapon."

"Then what?"

"Don't you see? If she had a plausible story to explain her role in my shooting, then she'd have come forward already. It must drive her crazy knowing I'm in her house, spending her money. Loving her man. This will push her into making a mistake. We'll catch her." She looked straight into his eyes. "I'll give her a choice. If she relinquishes all rights to Abby then I won't press charges about the shooting."

"You're nuts! Solerno will never go for it."

She caressed his cheek. "You used to pay me to solve your problems. That's what I'm good at. Trust me. I'll convince Becky this is the way it has to be. She can't catch Donny without me. She has to have my cooperation."

He stood abruptly and pulled the chair from between them. He gathered her against his broad chest and hugged her tightly. "I don't want to lose you, Tess. Not you, not Abby. We belong together. We're a family."

She melted in his arms, loving what he said, loving him. "We'll beat her at her own game, Ryder, I promise."

TRUST HER. That admonition played through his thoughts like a thread through canvas. Ever since he'd known Teresa, she'd proven herself capable, careful and smart. Besides, the more he thought about her plan, the more it seemed plausible.

Watching her now, as she argued with Solerno over the telephone, he admired her strength. Without being mean or strident, she held her ground, explaining patiently and logically why she believed Donny knew she wasn't Laura and how Donny and Laura were in cahoots.

After she hung up, she swiveled the chair to face him. "She'll get back to me."

"Abby's an issue now, isn't she?"

"I'm sorry."

"Get back to you," he mused aloud, feeling sick. "You know she'll be talking to child services and shrinks."

"Becky is a good person. She's always been straight up with me. We have to trust her now." She lowered her gaze, and her chin trembled. "She, uh, did make a passing comment about child endangerment. After all, Laura did try to have you killed."

His back prickled and he got the same case of dry mouth he'd felt when he learned about the cut brake lines.

Laura wanted him dead. Not merely out of her life, but six feet under. He'd loved her, tried everything he knew to make her happy, never asked anything except that she be kind to Abby, and she wanted him dead. As an added insult, she couldn't bother hiring a real hit man, but had asked her ex-husband to do the honors.

"I'm going to find Tom Sorry. I want to ask him about these checks."

"Does Tom know who I am?"

"He knows I suspect it. Should I tell him?"

"Might as well." She turned to the computer. He felt her reluctance to look too long at him. Yearning for what she didn't rightly own must hurt her as much as it hurt him. "I'll take the kid." He left the office.

Ryder thrust out his hand to Abby. She shrugged away from him and brandished her paintbrush like a sword. "I'm working." Her chin jutted and her eyes glittered, telling him she had no intention of leaving Teresa.

He planted his hands on his hips. Anger surged. Not anger with Abby, but with Laura, who was still creating strife and turmoil in the kid's life. He dropped to a crouch, putting himself almost eye level with her. "You know I love you more than anything in the whole wide world, right?"

Lips pushed into a tight little scowl, she nodded.

"I love your mama, too. We're going to work things out. Everything will be all right."

"I don't want Mama to go away. I don't want that other mama."

He glanced at the office, able only to see Teresa's back as she hunched over her work. He stopped himself before he made promises he might not be able to keep. "She's not going anywhere. Let's go find Mr. Tom."

They found the cowboy in the back corral. He'd rounded up and penned the year's crop of calves. Five longhorn weanlings with their big deer eyes and loppy ears watched Ryder's approach. In the distance, a mama cow peered at them from the safety of an oak thicket. Her spread of horns glinted in the sunshine. Even farther away, the rest of his longhorns grazed in a meadow. He kept his herd at fifteen adult animals, enough to make his ranch feel like a ranch and give him a good supply of models.

He climbed the fence and perched on the top rail. Tame as critters in a petting zoo, the young heifers and bulls ambled to the fence, their long tongues working in a search of treats. Abby used both hands to pet the calves.

Carrying a clipboard, Tom wandered across the corral. "What's up, boss?"

Ryder studied the biggest calf. The young bull had a dark roan coat, almost burgundy colored, with pure white socks and a handsome face. Ryder liked the look in his eyes, wise and a little bit wild. "I'm thinking we ought to keep this fella."

"Will you finally get rid of old Judy? She's too good a breeder for the likes of us. I know a rodeo stock man who'd pay top dollar for her."

Judy was the cow watching them from the brush. She had a mean streak that had set Tom to cussing more than once. With her long, sharp horns, she was capable of doing major damage to a man or horse if she ever set her mind to it.

"I'll leave that up to you." Ryder gestured for the man to come near. "Take a look at this." He handed the fax sheet to Tom. "What do you know about this?"

Tom studied the sheet for a moment. At first, his expression was carefully blank, but slowly his shaggy brows knit into a scowl and his lips tightened. He handed back the paper. "I don't know anything about it, boss. I don't write checks for cash. Never have."

Ryder turned to Abby. "Those babies are looking mighty thirsty, sugar bear. Run on over and grab the hose. Fill the trough over there."

She trotted away, and the calves followed her along the inside the fence.

Lowering his voice, Ryder said, "I know you didn't write these checks. I'm thinking Laura forged them. She needed cash to give Donny Weis."

"What are you saying, boss?"

Ryder watched Abby wrestle with the hundred-foot-long water hose. "Laura really isn't Laura, she's Teresa."

"She remembers?"

"Not exactly. I'll tell you later. More important right now is figuring out what happened to Laura. We figure she took off because she's the one who shot Teresa."

"Does your missus—Teresa remember being shot?"

He shook his head. "She remembers some things, but not everything. We think those checks are proof that Laura was trying to kill me. Donny Weis stopped by. He has a tape recording of Laura telling him to kill me. He's trying to blackmail her."

Tom slumped, his shoulders against the fence. Head down, his face hidden by his hat, he made a choked noise deep in his throat. "Where is he?"

"Don't know. Weis told her to cough up twenty-five grand or he'll kill me." Ryder passed off the threat with a wave of his hand. "He's all smoke, no fire." He glanced across the corral, then lowered his gaze to the fax sheet. "I won't ask you to get involved unless it's absolutely necessary."

"You don't know where Weis is?"

Ryder shook his head. As far as he knew, Weis had never lived anywhere for more than a few months. He thought only suckers actually paid the rent.

"Are you putting the cops on him?"

"Don't worry about the cops. Far as I can see, they've got no cause at all to bother you." Ryder hopped off the fence. "I'll let you know if I need your help."

Distracted by the animals, Abby appeared to forget her need to be clingy. Pointing the hose into the trough, she stood inside a knot of calves, the smallest of which outweighed her by a good two hundred pounds.

If he lost her, he'd die. "Come on, sugar bear. Let's go on in the house."

As Ryder walked away from the corral, he folded the fax and tucked it in his shirt pocket. Nothing to do now except wait and trust Tess to figure out the right thing to do.

The next few days were tense for all of them. Ryder couldn't paint, so he puttered around the ranch, never letting Abby out of his sight. Teresa spent a lot of time inside the office. He doubted if she'd discover any good evidence, but the busywork gave her something to do while they waited for Donny to contact her.

When he did, it was almost anticlimatic. He called on her private line and asked if Teresa had made up her mind. Cagey and sly, he didn't identify himself or make a direct reference to the money. When she mentioned money, he sidestepped. Finally, she told him he had to come to the ranch because she couldn't yet drive. Tomorrow, she said, Ryder would be gone.

After she hung up, she called Becky Solerno.

"Remember our deal," Teresa said. "You can't arrest him. He has to lead you to Laura."

She suddenly gasped and grabbed the telephone with both hands. "You can't do that! Abby is perfectly safe. She'll be with Mrs. Weatherbee. She won't be anywhere near the ranch when Donny shows up." She bounced on the edge of the bed and thrust the telephone at Ryder.

"Hudson, here, what's going on?"

"I was explaining to Teresa how Abby's safety is of prime concern," Solerno said. "I'm dispatching a deputy and a social worker to remove her from the premises."

"You can't do that!"

"I have no choice. I've talked to a judge, and explained how Abby isn't living with a custodial parent. Both her parents are involved in a criminal investigation. The judge issued the order. Please cooperate, Mr. Hudson. It's out of my hands."

Tears streamed down Teresa's cheeks. "I'm sorry," she whispered. "I'm so very, very sorry."

Chapter Fourteen

"Some bad people are doing bad things to Mama and Daddy," Teresa said. Abby, her eyes enormous and dark with distrust, stood before her. "So you need to go somewhere safe. Okay, baby?"

Abby shifted her suspicious glare to the brown-clad deputy and the social worker. "I'm gonna go see Aunt Gracie?"

"Not this time, sugar bear." Ryder ruffled her hair. "I want you to be extra good. I'll come get you just as soon as I can."

The social worker took Abby's hand. When the little girl struggled, the woman forced a grim smile. "Come along, Abby."

"No, Daddy! I don't want to go! Daddy!"

When Ryder moved in, so did the deputy. "Please don't interfere, sir."

Gary Holstead, who'd arrived only minutes ahead of the sheriff's department vehicle, put a restraining hand on Ryder's arm. "The paperwork is ironclad, Ryder," he said softly. "I'll get right on it. Don't worry."

"Daddy!"

The social worker picked up Abby and carried her, screaming and wriggling, to the patrol car. The deputy helped wrestle the child inside and shut the door.

Teresa shook with the effort it took to restrain her tears. She watched her baby leave until the patrol car was out of sight. She turned to Ryder. His face was gray, his eyes were stricken. His throat worked convulsively.

The attorney clapped a beefy hand on Ryder's shoulder. "You'll cooperate with the sheriff's department tomorrow. That'll go in your favor. You'll get her back. No sweat."

Ryder's gaze slipped unseeing past Teresa. She knew he blamed her. She blamed herself. When he trudged past her without a word, she suspected he hated her, too.

DONNY WEIS arrived right on time. Because of Ryder's suspicion that Donny had been surveilling the house, he sent Mrs. Weatherbee into town. He drove away from the ranch, too, heading toward Denver. He met with the deputies and showed them the back way onto the ranch so they could set up their recording equipment in the barn.

According to plan, Teresa refused to allow Donny inside the house. Becky Solerno wanted him in the open and vulnerable in case he was armed and decided to get stupid. Teresa made him follow her to the barn, where she sat on wooden bench. Sunshine made her squint.

Laura's ex-husband pushed his hands into his trouser pockets and rocked on his heels. He grinned, his gaze locked on the paper sack Teresa held on her lap. She hated him, loathed him, blamed him for her broken heart. If not for him and his greed, Abby wouldn't be lost inside the social services system. The judge wouldn't even allow Ryder to know the location of the foster home where she'd been taken, nor was he allowed the phone number so he could call her.

"It's hot out here," Donny said.

"Suffer. I don't want you contaminating my house."

He winced. "Touchy, touchy. Did I tell you you look like hell, baby? Didn't you get any sleep last night?"

"Why are you doing this to me, Donny?"

"Why not?" He looked over his shoulder at the log cabin where Tom Sorry lived. "Where's the old cowboy?"

"He went to Denver to sell some calves. We're alone."

"Good." He held out his hand. "You have something for me?"

She made herself look at him. "I want to know something first. How much money did you take from me? As payment for murdering Ryder?"

"What difference does it make?"

"Maybe I want to know what your limit is."

"Oh, baby, you've forgotten, old Donny boy knows no limits. Give me the cash."

"Where's the tape?"

He laughed. "I'm holding on to it." He cocked his head, smiling like a salesman. "Did I forget to mention, this is just the down payment? I figured, oh, let's say ten grand a month for the next year or so?"

"I can't believe you're blackmailing me."

He bent at the waist, leaning so close she could smell the sickly sweet scent of his cologne. "This is America, land of opportunity."

She clutched the sack with both hands. "There's only five thousand dollars here. If you want the other twenty, you have to do something first."

He snatched the sack off her lap. She grabbed for it, catching a corner. He easily dislodged her grip and strode a few steps away, hunched over like a coyote protecting a kill.

Teresa's breath caught in her throat. The muscles in her back went into a sharp spasm and her legs twitched. "Give me back the money, Donny. I haven't finished talking to you."

He grabbed the fat wad of cash and thumbed through it. "This isn't enough. I said twenty-five and I mean it."

"I have the rest of it, but you don't get a penny of it until you sign something first."

His face scrunched in a puzzled grimace. "Are you nuts?"

"No." She handed over a folder containing the termination of parental rights forms. "Sign these papers, then I'll give you the rest of the money."

He opened the manila folder and scanned the papers. "You are nuts. I'm not signing anything."

"I'll make it worth your while, Donny."

"Oh, yeah? How so?" He looked between her and the folder. "You care about the kid that much?"

"I love my husband and my child very much. I want Ryder to adopt Abby. If you make that possible, I'll give you anything you want."

A sharp report rang out and echoed off the surrounding rocks.

Teresa screamed and clapped her hands over her ears. Donny dived to the ground and locked his arms over his head.

Tom Sorry stepped from around the far side of the barn.

Wide-eyed, hand pressed to her mouth, Teresa whispered, "Tom? What are you doing here? What are you doing?"

He inhaled deeply and pointed the business end of the barrel at Donny Weis's head. "I saw his car, knew he was up to no good. This polecat's got to go." His finger tightened on the trigger.

Donny whimpered, only one eye showing. It was black with panic.

"Tom, no, you can't!"

He looked her straight in the eye. "He threatened you, ma'am. It'll be self-defense. I witnessed it, gave him fair warning. If we can get our stories straight right now, nothing needs come out of it."

"You don't understand—"

"Yeah," Donny said, "you don't understand!"

"No, ma'am, *you* don't understand." The rifle was unwavering. "See, you don't remember what happened. You don't know what kind of damage this boy can do to you and Ryder. He's a leech and a liar. Now, Ryder, he'll be wanting to do the right thing and all, so you and me, we have to work together. It's just like shooting a varmint. That's all he is, a no-account, egg-stealing varmint."

"Tom," she said, trying to stay calm. "Please put down the gun. We have this all taken care of. You don't need to get involved."

"Involved?" Donny taunted, his voice quavering. "This stupid stump-jumper is already involved up to his eyeballs. Tell her about you and Laura."

Tom snarled at Donny. "I made a mistake with Laura. She was so pretty and all, I thought she cared about me."

Beginning to suspect there was more to this than Tom coming home too soon, she asked, "You had an affair with Ryder's wife?"

"Everybody had an affair with her," Donny said. He looked at Tom. "She used you, cowboy, just like she tried to use me."

"She wouldn't let me alone. I never had a woman look at me like that." He gazed mournfully at Donny. "I guess, in the end, she's going to get what she wanted from me after all."

"Ah, no," Donny whispered and squeezed his eyes shut.

Teresa lurched off the bench and caught Tom's arm. "You can't shoot him. No, please, don't."

"Listen to her, man!" Donny cried. "I never hurt Ryder. I never hurt anybody. It was all Laura. She's the one." He turned his attention to Teresa. "Everything was Laura. She called me, she gave me the money, she laid out all the plans on how to kill Ryder. It was her. I just played along. I saved Ryder's life! Don't you see? If I told her no, she'd have hired a real hitter."

Teresa tightened her hold on Tom's arm. His muscles were like rocks, unyielding. The deadness in his eyes frightened her most of all.

She looked at Donny. "You know I'm not Laura. You've known all along. Where is she?"

"You know you're not Laura?" Donny recovered quickly and shifted his attention to Tom. "Ask the cowboy."

"She was trying to get Donny to kill Ryder," Tom said. "Then I was supposed to kill Donny for her. I don't know how it happened, but I got all tangled up before I knew it. I didn't want her killing Ryder. He's my friend. I thought I could handle her, but after she put a bullet in you, I knew there was no stopping her."

"What happened that day?" Teresa wanted to run, but fear paralyzed her. The barn at her back was full of cops listening to every word they said. So, where were they?

"Laura found out Donny was taping their phone calls," Tom continued. "So she lured him out here. I got him tied up in the barn and was supposed to kill him. Only he tells her he's got the tapes locked up in a bank box and a friend of his has instructions to turn them over to the cops if anything happens to him. She gets this plan. She gives her bank cards to Donny and tells him he has twenty-four hours before she reports the cards stolen. I'm supposed to follow him, find out who the friend is and kill him and Donny."

"Tell her the really good part, cowboy," Donny said. He flashed a grin at Teresa.

"You came back to the ranch to tell Ryder why Laura fired you."

"I heard everything?" Teresa asked.

He nodded. "You took off running. I didn't want nothing to do with it. None of it. Hell, I didn't even want to kill this worm here. She grabbed my gun and took off after you herself."

"Laura shot me?"

"She panicked. She got you in her car and took off. Wasn't twenty minutes later, she was back. She'd wrecked her car. So I went to the quarry and helped her push it off the side." His expression crumpled and his eyes turned red. "I didn't mean to hurt you. Honest to God, I didn't. I wasn't thinking. She was scared, I was scared. I knew she was going to blame it all on me. And I'd go back to prison. That's what I kept thinking. Then Weis here got away."

Donny actually looked proud of his exploits.

"Then Laura told me I had to kill Ryder now. We'd make it look like he'd killed you and then got killed himself. She was saying we could make it look like Donny was involved, but I know she was figuring a way to pin it all on me. And seeing her like that, I saw how ugly she was. I saw how she'd been using me. Ryder's my friend. I didn't want him dead."

"Tom?" she whispered. "Where is Laura?"

"Yeah, Tom," Donny said, "where is my lovely ex-wife? I saw you stuff her in the trunk of Teresa's car, but I didn't stick around to see what happened after that."

Tom winced, and pain rippled across his face.

"Where is she?"

"In the quarry. I didn't mean to kill her, but it was her or me. Self-defense. It was for Ryder, too. That woman was no good. You're good for him, Teresa. Always have been. It was pure luck, everyone thinking you're Laura. You can just keep on with it now. Donny's the only one who can blow it for you. With him dead, no one has to know anything. It'll be our secret."

"It's too late, Tom." Tears blurred her vision. She fumbled inside her bodice and found the miniature microphone affixed to her brassiere. "This is all a set-up. The police know I'm not Laura. They're listening."

His knuckles turned white where he held the rifle.

Donny relaxed and propped his chin on his fist. "You've been had."

"Oh, Tom, I'm so sorry."

"Drop the rifle, Sorry!" Becky Solerno yelled from the side of the barn. "Drop it and raise your hands."

Snake quick, the man jumped and turned. He shot out his left arm and swept Teresa off the bench. It happened so fast, she didn't have time to scream before he crushed her against his body, cutting off her air. He jammed the rifle bore against her throat.

"I can't go back to prison. Not because of Laura. She was evil, bad clear to the bone. I saved Ryder's life." He moved his back against the barn wall and held Teresa between himself and any threat.

"Don't do this, Sorry!" Becky yelled. "You're making it worse. Turn the lady loose."

"Tom?" Ryder said. He stepped into the open, holding his hands clear of his sides so Tom could see they were empty.

From concealment, Becky hissed at him to get out of rifle range.

"Come on, pardner," Ryder said, "this is no time for a showdown."

For a long, breath-stopping moment, Tom stood perfectly still.

"He's your best friend," Teresa whispered hoarsely. She could feel the bruises forming on her ribs where Tom held her so tightly her lungs hurt. The rifle bore was cold against her skin. "He's the best friend you'll ever have. Listen to him. Don't hurt him anymore."

"I killed Laura," Tom said dully.

"Don't hurt Tess," Ryder said. He walked slowly across the grass, placing each boot with care. "She's been hurt enough. Turn her loose."

"They'll give me life, boss. I can't go back to prison. I can't face lockup. You don't know what it's like. Saddle me a horse. I can make it into the mountains."

"There are four deputies inside the barn. They've got Jeeps parked over at Packerd Creek. They'll have mounted patrols and helicopters here in minutes. You'll never make it."

"They ain't taking me alive." He tightened his grip.

Teresa stiffened, straining away from the rifle.

Ryder stopped two feet away. He gazed steadily at the cowboy. "You're hurting her, Tom Sorry. Let her go." He held out a hand for the rifle. His fingertip hovered a fraction of an inch away from the barrel. "If you hurt her, you'll have to hurt me, too. Then they'll kill you, Tom. You want Laura to win?"

Tom pressed the rifle bore so hard Teresa thought it might pierce her skin. The pressure suddenly ceased. Tom turned her loose. She staggered and Ryder caught her, his strong arms preventing her fall.

"I'm sorry as can be, boss. Sorry as can be." He dropped the rifle and lifted his hands to his head.

Sheriff's deputies swarmed out of the barn. They handcuffed Tom Sorry and Donny Weis.

Donny cried, "Hey! He's the guy with the gun. Why are you arresting me?"

Becky Solerno's dimples deepened. "We'll start with extortion and work our way up to accessory to homicide."

Teresa groaned and buried her face against Ryder's chest. Ryder helped her into the silent house.

"I didn't know, I never suspected," she said, letting the tears flow. "I didn't mean for it to work out this way."

"I'm not blaming you." His face was pale, haggard.

Becky found them in the kitchen. "You did good, Teresa." She swung a wry gaze on Ryder. "And you, it'll be a while before I recover from the near heart attack you gave me. You want some advice, sir, don't walk up to nuts with guns. Okay?"

"I want my daughter back."

"That's out of my hands, sir." Her smile faded. "I'll put in a good word for you with the judge. Excuse me, I have a body to find."

Becky called in a huge truck equipped with a crane. If they found Teresa's car under the water, they intended to lift it out. Ryder had wanted to be there, but Becky requested that he remain away from the scene. He prowled the house, restless as a caged cougar.

Two hours later, Becky Solerno returned to the house. "We found a body inside the trunk of your car, Teresa. Mr. Hudson, I'd like the name of your wife's dentist so I can make a positive ID."

AFTER A DAY spent giving his deposition to an assistant district attorney, with his head stuffed full of legal talk, Ryder pushed through the front door of his house. The silence stopped him short and made him shiver. Abby had been gone a week. Social services refused to relinquish her until a judge ruled about Ryder's competency to parent the girl properly. He was only the stepfather, after all.

He noticed the pile of luggage sitting at the base of the steps. "Tess?"

No answer. He bounded up the stairs. Her room was empty. He hurried downstairs. He found Mrs. Weatherbee washing dishes in the kitchen.

"Whose luggage is that?" he demanded.

Mrs. Weatherbee turned around. Her face was blotchy with heat. Her eyes were red-rimmed and swollen. She'd been crying almost nonstop since losing Abby.

"It's Teresa's." She sniffed loudly. "She's leaving us, too."

He caught a counter edge with both hands. Between misery, haggling with attorneys, the police investigation, fighting social services and doing Tom Sorry's job, he'd barely spoken two words to Teresa. Looking back, he guessed she'd been avoiding him.

"Where is she?"

"In your studio. She's taking care of a few things before she leaves." The woman abruptly turned to the sink. Her broad shoulders shook with a sob.

He rushed out of the house and jogged across the grass to the studio. He could see the lights shining in the office. He burst through the door and shouted, "Tess!"

She stepped into the office doorway. She held a pen in one hand and a pad of sticky notes in the other. Her face was so pale and drawn, she looked ill. Huge circles looked like bruises under her eyes. He hurried to her, but stopped in the doorway, unable to go farther.

She shook her head and turned to the desk. The way she moved and winced let him know her back was hurting.

"It's been a bad week, but that's no excuse."

"Excuse for what?" She eased onto the chair and arched her back. Sweat glistened on her brow.

"Ignoring you. You're taking sick. The strain's been too much and Tom hurt you—"

"It's not your problem!" she snapped. "I'm not your problem anymore." She scribbled furiously on a sticky note. "I've got everything in order. I'll leave notes on the files so your accountant can see what I've done. Your taxes need doing, but I think everything is in order. I'll just—just leave these—"

"I'm sorry, Tess."

She lifted shining eyes. "I'm the one who's sorry. It's all my fault. I shouldn't have trusted Becky. I should've found another way."

"I'm not blaming you."

"It's all my fault! I keep hearing her screaming when they took her away. Seeing the look in her eyes." She hung her head. "I betrayed her and I miss her so much and I don't know how you can even stand looking at me. I'll never forgive myself."

He stepped woodenly into the office. "I admit, I was angry. But even I can see you had no choice. It's not your fault they took her away from me. From *us*. You can't leave me, Tess. I need you." He touched her shoulder. "I love you. We have to work together to get our baby back."

She slowly lifted her head. Her soft, anguished eyes melted him inside. He cupped her chin and pressed a kiss to her lips.

"I love you," he whispered. "I don't want to lose you."

"I don't belong here."

"Yes, you do!" He dropped to one knee and clasped her cold hands in his. "You turned our house into a home, full of warmth. You gave Abby a real mother for the first time in her life. You showed me what loving means and how good we can be."

"But Abby..."

"We'll get her back. We'll fight. We can do it, Tess, just don't leave me."

"I'm making things worse."

"None of what happened was your fault. When we get Abby back, she's going to need you." He glanced at a sticky note atop a file folder. He plucked it off and crumpled it. "You don't need to be leaving notes for anybody. You aren't going anywhere." He tossed the paper at a wastebasket. "Marry me, Tess. Stay with me. Keep loving me."

"Do you mean it?"

"Yes, ma'am. You're the finest wife a man could ever ask for. Let's make it official."

She burst into tears.

"Darn leaky woman," he muttered and stood so he could hold her in his arms. "You've cried enough." He held her tightly. "Everything will be all right, darlin'. I promise."

To his relief, the crying spell didn't last long. When she lifted her head, her face was streaked with tears and her eyes were hot and swollen, but she smiled.

"Will you marry me?"

"Yes."

"Okay, then let's get you to bed for some rest. I don't want you taking sick before we can find a justice of the peace. You need to be healthy for when our girl comes home."

She nodded. As she turned away, she froze, staring at the desk.

"What is it?"

She reached out with a trembling hand and touched a sticky note. "Ryder, there was a note. I saw it when— when—where did I see it?" She rubbed her temples and narrowed her eyes. "It's Laura, she was angry. She saw me looking at it and grabbed it away. When she picked up the paper, the note fell off. I picked it up. It said . . . you don't want Ryder hopping down this bunny trail."

"What are you talking about?"

"She had a—she had Abby's birth certificate!" She lunged at the file cabinet and fumbled open the drawer. "She was in a royal state."

"Whoa, now, you're getting all out of sorts, darlin'."

She pawed through the files and grabbed a folder. She pulled out the sienna-colored paper upon which Abby's certificate was printed. "She had a paper that looked just like this. It had a note on it. She tore it up. Little tiny pieces. I remember!" She slapped the certificate on the desk. "There's something wrong with this, something she didn't want you to know."

He'd seen the birth certificate dozens of times. He'd carried it to the administration office when he registered Abby for school. "There's nothing wrong with it."

"Did Laura give it to you?"

"Yes."

"Then get another. I bet you anything the real birth certificate says you're Abby's father."

"MR. AND MRS. HUDSON, please be seated."

So nervous her hands trembled, Teresa gingerly took her seat in Judge Moran's chamber. Ryder took the chair to her left. He laid his hand over hers and gave her a reassuring squeeze.

Also present were Ryder's attorney, the court-appointed attorney representing Abby's interests and Jean Patton from the department of child services. Judge Moran cleared her throat and tapped her knuckles on the table.

"I hope you don't mind me keeping this session informal, Ms. Patton. Mr. Hudson." The judge smiled blandly at the attorneys. "I don't see a need for representatives, but if I have everyone's promise that we can keep this short and sweet, I will allow the counselors to remain in the room."

Gary Holstead coughed into his hand. Other than that, no one made a move or noise.

"Very good. Well, I've reviewed this most interesting case. I can honestly say I've never dealt with anything so...odd in my entire career." The judge smiled at Teresa. "Do I understand correctly that you and Mr. Hudson were recently married?"

The ceremony had been short and informal, low-key to keep reporters away. Only Abby's presence could have made it better. "Yes, ma'am—your honor." She laced her fingers with Ryder's.

"That's nice." She picked up a sheet of paper. "So let me see if this is perfectly clear. Abigail Weis, the minor in question, was born November 1, but Ryder Hudson has always believed her birth date to be December 12. The late Laura Hudson doctored a birth certificate in order to conceal the child's actual age. This is correct, Mr. Hudson?"

"Yes, ma'am."

"She was able to do so because when you first met the child, you believed her only one week old, instead of six weeks old. Because her mother's neglect caused a failure to thrive, Abigail looked like a newborn."

"Yes, ma'am, that's also true. You have the doctor's statement saying that's possible."

"Apparently so, in light of the paternity test showing that you, not Donny Weis, are the child's biological father. What I don't understand is why your late wife would perpetuate such a lie?"

Ryder exchanged a glance with Teresa. Love for him welled like a rising spring inside, filling her veins. She wished into him all the strength and courage she could muster.

"I don't know, ma'am. I can only guess that she didn't know how I'd react if I thought Abby was mine. It was easier saying she was her husband's, free and clear."

"You strike me as a trusting soul."

Ryder hung his head. "To a fault, I reckon."

"I don't consider it a fault, sir. The world has enough cynics already." She held up a handful of papers. "I have here affidavits from schoolteachers and neighbors of yours. Oh, and your housekeeper, too. Everyone claims you're a very good father. I have not found a single reason to deny you custody of your child. Ms. Patton, I am hereby ruling that Abigail Weis, soon to be known as Abigail Hudson, is no longer a ward of the state. If you'd be so kind as to bring her in."

Ryder jumped to his feet and stared at the door. As soon as it opened, Abby's shriek rang throughout the chamber.

Teresa pressed a hand to her mouth.

Abby raced into Ryder's arms and he swung her high.

"Daddy!" She locked her arms around his neck and hugged him so tightly he choked.

Not quite daring to believe that it was all over, Teresa touched Abby's arm. "We're going home, baby. We're all going home."